BRING ON
THE BLESSINGS

Also by Beverly Jenkins

BRING ON THE BLESSINGS

Beverly Jenkins

AVON

An Imprint of HarperCollinsPublishers

FIRST AVON PAPERBACK EDITION PUBLISHED 2009

Designed by Rhea Braunstein

Library of Congress Cataloging-in-Publication Data
Jenkins, Beverly, 1951–
    Bring on the blessings / Beverly Jenkins. — 1st ed.
        p.   cm.
    ISBN 978-0-06-168840-9 (trade pbk. : acid-free paper)
    1. Kansas—Fiction. 2. City and town life—Fiction. 3. African Americans—Fiction. I. Title.
PS3560.E4795B75 2009
813'.54—dc22   2008036954

12 13 OV/RRD 10 9 8 7

*Blessings come in many forms, and the outstanding Avon editors
I have worked with during my career have been blessings indeed.
Ellen Edwards, Christine Zika, Cecilia Oh, Monique Patterson,
Erika Tsang, Esi Sogah—this one is for you.*

PROLOGUE

B ernadine Edwards grew up with her two sisters in the modest home of their loving parents on Detroit's west side. The college scholarship Bernadine won to USC gave her entrée into a world she still found a blessing, but more importantly introduced her to Leo Brown.

They married the day after graduation. He went to work as a quality control manager for one of the nation's big oil companies, while she commuted the ninety miles one way to her job as a social worker with the state's Child Welfare Department.

For a man of color, Leo moved up the ladder quickly. Inside of ten years he was an executive vice president making enough money for her to say good-bye to her commute and hello to the lifestyles of the rich and famous. She'd hated it. Oh, the money was good and all the material things Leo showered her with were appreciated, but the more he made, the less she saw of him. They became distant strangers, going to dinner parties and attending charity events, always wearing false smiles.

At the age of forty-five Bernadine looked up and realized she had nothing to show for her high-class life except jewelry, furs, houses, and cars. There'd been no children because according to Leo, they'd have plenty of time for that after he made his mark, but the time never came.

Two days after their thirtieth wedding anniversary, and the day before her fifty-second birthday, Bernadine walked into Leo's office and found him screwing his secretary on top of his desk. Bernadine was furious of course, hurt too, but not enough to cry, woe is me. Nope, she got herself a top-notch lawyer, hired a private detective, and took Leo to the cleaners. She got the house in the Hamptons, the condo in Atlanta, and the summer homes in Savannah, Miami, and Holland, Michigan. Thanks to California being a community property state, she also got half of his vast holdings in everything from computers to sex toys, along with half of the $350 million that her lawyer discovered Leo was really worth.

Once all the paperwork was signed and filed, Bernadine drove away from the courthouse on that sunny California afternoon with a cool $275 million and never looked back.

After the divorce she spent the next two years traveling the world; Paris, Spain, Egypt, South Africa. She ordered haute couture fashions from the shows in Milan and New York, went whale watching in Alaska, and toured Machu Picchu in Peru. She had as good a time as a woman could have with $275 million in the bank drawing interest every day, but having been raised in the church she knew that when much is given, much is expected, and so she got up every morning and asked God to send her a purpose.

Then, two things happened to change her life. She was going through some old boxes stored in the house in Miami, which she was putting on the market, when she ran across an article she'd clipped from a magazine a few years back. It was entitled, "A Place Called Hope," and it detailed a small town where older people, foster children, and potential foster parents lived together in an intergenerational community. The town was the brainchild of a professor of sociology from the University of Illinois and was set up on a closed-down U.S. Air Force base. Bernadine found the stories of the residents and their interactions so moving and inspiring that when she was done her eyes were misty. The children picked to live in Hope were the hardest to place: teens, sibling groups, children with special needs. Even though she'd spent most of her adult life as a pampered queen, the social worker she was inside had never died. As she put down the article, she felt as if her prayers had been answered. She now knew what God wanted her to do.

And then the second thing happened. That evening, while eating dinner and checking out the news, one of the reporters profiled a tiny Kansas town that had put itself up for sale on eBay. The place was going under financially, and with no money to pay a mountain of outstanding tax bills, the residents were hoping to find a buyer to rescue them. As the story went on to reveal that the area had been settled by Black folks in the 1880s and had a deep-rooted history, Bernadine was so excited she could barely sit still. When the TV story ended she put down her fork, looked up, yelled out, "Thank You, Lord!" and ran to her computer.

Hidden under the overpass of a Miami highway, seven-year-old Zoey Raymond pulled the big cardboard box over her head and closed herself inside. Night had rolled in, and in the darkness, she maneuvered herself so the box's flaps were firmly closed under her thin hips. She tried not to cry because it wouldn't change anything. Her mother, Bonnie, was dead. Zoey had covered the body with all the rags and newspapers she'd been able to scrounge while out looking for food, but the shroud wasn't enough to keep the rats from desecrating her corpse. This was the second night and they were on her again; squeaking and snarling and fighting each other. She'd tried to run them off the first time, but there'd been too many, so to protect herself, she scrambled under the box and sat quiet with her hands over her ears and the screams stuck in her throat until the sun came up and they went away.

But tonight they seemed to know she was inside. They were scratching at the cardboard and bumping the box, and she was shuddering with terror and fear. She tried to keep the box level so it wouldn't tip over, but seconds later light appeared from a hole made by teeth. It grew larger. The assault on the box became manic and then she and her box toppled. They swarmed over her like flies, and the last thing she remembered was the sounds of the rats and the night-piercing screams of a little girl.

CHAPTER
1

Trenton July, the mayor of Henry Adams, Kansas, called the emergency town meeting to order with a bang of his gavel. "All right. Let's get this started. Who wants to go first?"

Riley Curry, the former mayor, rose to his feet. He was wearing his favorite pinstriped suit with its ever-present fake red carnation pinned to the shiny worn lapel. As always, he looked around for a moment to make sure all eyes were on him before speaking. "I'll start by demanding we rescind the offer."

Murmurs of agreement rose from some of the thirty or so folks seated on the worn wooden folding chairs in the church's small sanctuary, but Trent saw disapproval on the faces of those who disagreed. "Offer's already been accepted, Riley. We signed the papers two weeks ago. Next person."

"I'm not done."

Trent sighed. "Go ahead."

Riley cleared his throat, nodded at his wife, Genevieve, who was smiling up at him as if he were the Second Coming, then declared, "The idea that you held this vote behind my back speaks to the underhandedness of the whole affair. I say we vote again."

Some people clapped loudly.

"We're not having another vote," Trent replied evenly. "And nothing was done behind your back. You knew what day we were holding the vote, just like everybody else."

"But I had to leave town. Which wouldn't have been necessary if we had a competent vet instead of that drunken—"

"Watch it," Trent warned coolly.

Riley puffed up and whined, "Okay, but if we'd had a real vet, I wouldn't've had to drive Cletus fifty miles downstate to get him treated."

Cletus was Riley's hog. Every three or four months, Cletus had to see a vet. It's a necessity when you feed a hog stuff like Doritos, Twinkies, and ice cream and cake because it doubles as the child you and your wife could never have.

Trent told him, "Sorry about Cletus, but there was no reason to change the date. Your one vote wouldn't have made a difference anyway. Proposal passed thirty-five to seventeen." There were only fifty-two registered voters on the town's rolls, and for once everybody turned out to have a say.

But Riley wasn't having any. "My constituents demand a revote. Who knows what this person's real agenda is? And a white woman too? Suppose she's just a front for people who want to build a casino or God forbid a strip club?"

More murmurs of agreement were heard.

Trent's jaw tightened.

"What do we know about her? Suppose she's one of those Aryan Nation folks wanting to turn Henry Adams into a terrorist training camp?"

Trent opened his mouth to argue but knew it wouldn't matter so he closed it.

Riley, on a roll, slowly took in the faces of those supporting him and those who didn't and asked, "Is the buyer even American?"

"Ms. Brown lives in Florida," Trent drawled. "Last I heard it was still part of the U.S."

"My constituents and I—"

Marie Jefferson snarled, "You don't have any constituents, Riley. That's why you're the *former* mayor."

"Ouch!" someone cringed loudly.

Snickers greeted that.

Marie, the town's retired school teacher stood up and glared at Riley from behind her signature cat's-eye glasses. "This is ridiculous. Henry Adams needs help now! Not tomorrow, not a year from now, but now, and Trent's found a way to make that happen." She looked around the sanctuary. "No, we don't know who this Ms. B. E. Brown person is, and we don't know what she plans to do, but she's agreed to keep the town intact and keep the Henry Adams name."

"What if it's a mistake?" Riley's wife, Genevieve, threw back.

"What if it's not?" Marie countered. "We don't know how this will play out. Before it's over we may regret selling, but the only idea Riley had was for us to be annexed by the city of Franklin. Annexed! The ancestors didn't build this town out of blood and sweat for it to be annexed and assimilated and forgotten."

Applause filled the church.

She added, "If this buyer, whoever she is, can come in here and save this place, I'm all for it. And all y'all who voted against the sale—get over yourselves." She sat.

More applause. Trent wanted to kiss her.

But Riley was still on his feet. "I will take this to the highest court in the land. Selling a town on cyberspace can't be legal anyway, no matter what Trent says!"

His side erupted in agreement. The other side yelled for Riley to sit his you know what down. Tempers flared. Verbal shots began to fly. Folks stormed to their feet in defense of themselves and their positions, and before Trent could tell everybody to sit down, all perdition broke loose.

"Order!" Trent yelled over the chaos. He banged the gavel against the table with so much force its head went flying across the room. "Order, dammit!"

But the shouting combatants, people who'd been friends and neighbors all their lives, weren't feeling him.

In the middle of the melee, Agnes Jefferson, who was Marie's mother, a Riley supporter, and a descendant of the town's first Black sheriff shook her cane in the face of her best friend, Tamar July. "You traitor! You voted to sell our town!"

Tamar, Trent's grandmother, snapped back. "Yes I did because I'm not stuck in the past, Agnes. And if you don't get that damn cane out of my face, it's going to be me and you!"

"You touch me and I'll take you down like Hulk Hogan!"

They were a nose a part.

Trent watched wearily. With his gavel dead and no one paying him a bit of attention, he threw up his hands and walked out.

The cool night air was a blessed relief to the heat and anger swirling around inside. Sighing, he pulled out his cigarettes. After lighting one, he drew the smoke deep down into his lungs and slowly exhaled.

"Thought you were quitting?"

The voice belonged to the town vet, Trent's father, Malachi. "Dealing with those folks in there, be glad I'm not shooting heroin."

Malachi chuckled.

Both men could hear the argument still raging inside.

"This buyer is our last hope, Dad."

"I know. They know it too. They just don't want to deal with it."

Surprised by the words, Trent turned to view his father's face. "I thought you were against the sale?"

"I am, but you said it, it's our last hope. I don't want to see this town disappear, and that's what's going to happen if we don't do something."

"Ms. Brown is going to give us 3.5 million to pay the overdue taxes. We can't turn down that kind of money."

"You're right, but—"

"But what?"

"Don't expect the folks against this to come around any time soon. You may have saved us, but no good deed goes unpunished."

Trent smiled. "Any pie left at the diner?"

"If there is, it's on the house for putting up with all this." Malachi patted his son on the shoulder. As they walked up the deserted street, they left their neighbors to the swearing and arguing.

Malachi could make the offer for free pie because he owned the diner. The dilapidated building with its tar-paper roof and sagging porch was short, squat, and narrow. It sat in the center of what used to be downtown and went by the name of the Dog and Cow, aka the D&C.

Inside, the D&C was empty, so Trent and his father took seats in one of the back booths. There were five booths in all, and their once fancy red leather seats now sported silver duct tape over the large cracks. Five equally taped-up backless stools were lined up around the well-worn wooden bar. The lone bathroom lacked any gender designation because everybody used it. Just make sure you knocked first.

The kitchen was housed in a room behind the bar. It was run with smooth efficiency by Rochelle "Rocky" Dancer, who was two years younger than Trent. Stacked and smart, she was in the words of the the Commodores, *a brick house*. She was also a Henry Adams native and one of the people who'd supported the decision to sell.

The listing jukebox played only old-school selections. At the moment, Martha and her Vandellas were imploring an old lover to "Come and Get These Memories." Usually, there were at least a few people sitting around inside talking, drinking coffee, or having the day's special, but this evening everybody was either at the meeting or at home with better things to do.

Rocky came out of the back with a pot of hot coffee in hand. She placed two mugs on the table and poured. "How'd the meeting go?"

Trent shook his head. "They're still over there arguing."

Rocky sighed. "Left up to Riley, this town would've blown away like tumbleweed ten years ago. You just keep the faith. You two hungry?"

"Any pie left?" Malachi asked hopefully.

"Yep. Figured you'd need something after the meeting. Saved a couple pieces. Be right back."

"When are you going to marry that girl?" Malachi asked his son.

Trent eyed him over his cup but remained silent.

"She's been sweet on you since elementary school."

"Rocky and I get along just fine the way we are. I don't want to get married, and far as I know, neither does she. Why marry and mess things up?"

"You need to make an honest woman out of her."

"This from the playa of Graham County; a man who had women fighting over him in *church*."

The two women, one local and one from out of town, had come to blows over which of them would sit beside Malachi in the pew that Sunday. When the dust settled, there were wigs, earrings, and pieces of clothing all over the church floor.

"A simple misunderstanding."

"*Uh-huh*. More like the Thrilla in Manila."

Rocky returned with two small plates holding pieces of her famous apple pie. She set both down and asked Trent, "Can I bring my car in for an oil change in the morning?"

He owned the town's only garage. "Sure."

She nodded. "If you all need anything else, just yell."

She left them alone.

Malachi watched her walk away. "Man, if I was ten years younger."

"She'd still hurt you, so put your eyes back in your head and eat your pie."

"Yes, Dad."

Grinning, Trent started in on his own.

"Bobby Lee asked me to marry him last night."

Rocky and Trent were lying in his bed in the dark. The revelation made his heart catch, not because he loved her, but because he didn't want her leaving his life. "What did you tell him?"

"Yes."

In the silence that followed, he could hear the sounds of the prairie through the open windows; the crickets, the dark rush of the breeze in the grass. "He's a good man."

"He is."

She turned over to face him. "You don't think I'm crazy?"

He studied her silently for a moment. "Do you?"

She shook her head. "No, but he loves me. Really loves me, and I'm tired of being alone. Tired of getting up every day and having nothing to look forward to but making more coffee and apple pies."

"You tell Malachi?"

"Not yet. Telling him in the morning. Wanted to tell you first."

"Appreciate that." And he did. He didn't want to think about her not being in his life anymore; at least not then. "Folks are going to miss your cooking."

"If Malachi finds somebody good, they'll forget about me the next day."

Trent knew Bob had two boys. "Get along with his kids?"

She lay back down and replied almost wistfully, "Yeah, I do. They're good boys. I could do worse."

"When's the wedding?"

"I told him to give me two weeks so Malachi could find a new cook, then we'll set a date."

The silence crept in again as they both mined their own thoughts. Finally, she said, "You've been a good friend, Trent."

"You too, Rock. Wish you had told me about Bob proposing before we did what we just did."

She laughed. "I know, but you can be so honorable sometimes, and I wanted one last go for old times' sake."

"You're gonna make us both burn in hell."

She chuckled in the darkness. "I know. Selfish I guess."

"You're Bob's lady now, Rocky. No more knocking boots with me."

"I know. It's been mighty good though."

He grinned. "Go on to sleep."

"Good night, Trenton July."

"Night, Rock."

CHAPTER
2

Naked and lying on the bed in the dark, Lily Fontaine stared unseeingly up at the ceiling. Her lover, Winston, was in the bathroom with the faucets running, but the sound of the water was not loud enough to drown out his off-key singing. The song, an old-school hit by Rick James, was begging a woman to *give it to me, baby*. Winston sang the chorus as if he'd written the lyrics personally. She supposed the tune was appropriate—she had just *given it to him*, but she didn't know why he sounded so pleased? Winston was terrible in bed.

Lily sighed. Professor Winston Seymour had been after her for over two years to marry him, but Lily kept putting him off. Why, she wasn't sure. They'd dated, gone on trips, seen plays; hell, even her godmother, Marie, wanted to know what the problem was? Everybody knew Winston was a catch; he wasn't gay, didn't live with his mama, and was a highly respected professor at the local community college. Winston had it going on. Except in bed.

Lily sat up and tried to figure out how she was going to fix her face to lie when he asked her how *it* had been for her. She couldn't tell him the truth. A woman wasn't supposed to tell a man he had no sex skills, especially not one determined to put a ring on her finger. She sighed again. Was she so hard up that she'd marry a man who didn't seem to know the first thing about knocking boots, as the kids used to call it? Lily had been divorced at the age of nineteen, and although she'd been without a steady man since then, needs were still important. Just because she was forty didn't mean she was dead—or maybe she was: Winston's version of lovemaking certainly hadn't made her feel alive.

She picked up her robe and slipped it on.

Winston stuck his head around the door. He had a thin towel wrapped around his paunchy fifty-five-year-old waist. "Hey, baby doll. You want to get in here?"

She gave him a small smile. "After you're done, is fine."

He started singing the chorus again, "Give it to me baby," complete with gleaming eyes and waggling eyebrows.

She grinned.

"How about another round?"

The grin faded. "I—need to get home, Winston."

He studied her for a moment. "You sure?"

She nodded.

Their eyes met. He said, finally, "Okay. No problem. Let me get through in here, then it'll be your turn."

"Thanks."

An hour later, Lily was showered, dressed, and ready

to head back to her small townhouse on the other side of Atlanta. She was slipping on her raincoat when Winston asked, "So, what's wrong?"

Lily shook her head and lied, "Nothing. Why'd you ask?"

"Because you're not acting like a woman who just had her world rocked," he boasted proudly.

Lord. "I'm just tired. Been a long day."

"You sure, baby?"

She fussed with the belt on her coat. "I'm sure."

His face said he didn't believe her, but she looked past it. "I'll call you tomorrow. Okay?" She walked over, gave him a quick kiss on the lips. "Stop worrying, you were fine."

After telling that lie, she left and closed the door softly behind her. On the drive home, she wondered why she didn't just give in and tell Winston she'd marry him. No, he wasn't any good in bed; rabbits took more time, but he was steady, dependable. He even got along with her twenty two-year old son, Davis. Could she live life without fire? Every now and then she saw flashes of his sense of humor, but the times were so few and far between she could count them on one hand. So why was he even in the running? *Because I think I am getting desperate,* she admitted to herself.

She turned onto her street. Her place was in the middle of the block nestled amongst the other townhouses and condos in the upscale subdivision. She eased the car up her driveway and into the matching brick garage, then turned off the car's engine. For a few moments, she sat there in the dark trying to empty her mind of all the jumbled thoughts, but it was hard. *So what is it that you want, girl?* her inner sister asked. Lily answered truthfully: *Not to be alone.*

She thought back on her life. After her unplanned pregnancy, her quick marriage, and even quicker divorce, she'd had no choice but to pick herself up and keep stepping; she had her degree in business management to finish and a baby to feed. There'd been no time to feel sorry for herself. The phone company didn't care that her husband, Randy, had broken her heart by sleeping with half the women on campus. They just wanted their money. The electric company didn't care about her troubles, and neither did her landlord. In order to make it through those early years, she'd had had to transform herself. Life made it clear that she could no longer be the wide-eyed small town girl she'd grown up as. What she needed to do to get over was to become a walking, talking urban Black woman. Once she figured that out she embraced the role and her new self. When life shouted at her, she stuck her hand on her hip and shouted right back. She didn't take no mess, not in school, not on the job, not in the line at the unemployment office. Lily's late mama, Cassandra, had raised Lily to be a lady, and those parts of herself were always out front, but she'd learned to stand up for herself and for her son.

But now, twenty-one odd years later, she was tired of being strong, tired of carrying the load alone. Davis would be graduating from college in a few weeks, then off to Silicone Valley for a good-paying job at a high-profile tech company. With him gone, she'd be able to kick back and chill, especially now that she'd taken her company's cash buyout and didn't have to take on another job unless she wanted to, but she had no special person in her life to chill with, and hadn't for a very long time.

She opened the car door and stepped out into a dimly lit, cluttered garage. As she stuck her key in the door, she told herself maybe the melancholy feelings were a result of empty nest syndrome creeping in. She didn't believe that for a minute, but went with the assessment anyway because it was much easier to deal with.

The message light on the phone was flashing when she entered the kitchen, so she took a moment to listen. It was her godmother, Marie Jefferson, and the sound of the familiar voice put a smile on Lily's face. Marie had called to tell Lily about the party she was throwing to celebrate her sixtieth birthday party and wanted to know if Lily could attend. Lily decided then and there that she would. Going back to Henry Adams where she'd grown up came with its own unique issues, but hey, maybe returning to her past would help her figure out her future, so she picked up the phone to give Marie a call back.

At Detroit's 13th Precinct, Sgt. Greg Fisher looked up from his paperwork at the perp being brought in by two uniformed officers. "You again?" he asked in a voice filled with disbelief. The kid grinned. "Yep. How ya doin', Sarge?"

Fisher questioned the female officer, "Where was he this time?"

"Freeway. I-94. Doing ninety."

"Anybody hurt?"

"Nope. Car was stolen though."

"Of course. His last name is Steele. What was he driving?"

"Escalade."

Fisher was outdone. "How can you even see over the wheel? What are you, ten?"

"Eleven last week, and I roll with my own pillow and blocks."

The male officer raised a dirty black chair pillow for the Sarge to see, then showed him the short stiltlike block of wood Amari "Flash" Steele had made so he could reach the car's pedals.

Fisher leaned down and looked the kid in the eyes. "You know, if you'd use that sharp mind of yours for good instead of this, you could be something one day. How many times have you been arrested?"

"Recently? Or all together?"

Fisher knew that if he looked it up the number it would just inflame his ulcer, so he said, "Never mind. What's your foster mother's number, Amari?"

"All you're going to get is cussed out. She said if I got picked up again, don't call her—call CPS."

Fisher studied the bright, engaging kid and said resignedly to one of the officers, "Call Child Protective Services. Tell them we got the ghetto's version of Jeff Gordon in here again."

"Yes, sir."

Amari flashed a grin, made himself comfortable on one of the benches, and settled in for the wait.

CHAPTER
3

Vhen Trent awakened at dawn, Rocky was already gone, and he thought that was as it should be. They'd been two lonely souls seeking solace and warmth and now he would go on alone. That was as it should be too, he supposed, since every relationship in his life had left him in the same place. He and Rock had never loved each other; he'd used her and she him in a symbiotic relationship that satisfied both of their needs, but it hadn't been just about sex and lust though: they'd traveled together, watched DVDs together, drove to Kansas City to shows and ball games. For ten years, they'd been a couple, but not in the real sense because she'd seen others and he had too, but they'd always drifted back to the familiar when things inevitably fell apart.

He didn't think her relationship with Bob would fall apart. Rocky wanted this marriage, and he knew she'd wade through fire to make it work. She'd been looking for someone to love her the way she deserved to be loved for a long time. Sadly, it hadn't been him. After two failed marriages he was real gun shy about committing himself. His first wife, Felicia, a high-powered lawyer, had picked making partner over the kids he'd wanted. He hadn't held her ambition against her, in fact he'd done everything possible to support her dream, but upon finding out that she'd had a secret tubal ligation in order to not conceive had crushed his heart. Two years later, his second walk to the altar with bookstore owner Mia ended after only six months. She and his business partner had been conducting an affair right under his nose, and the sense of anger and betrayal made him chuck life in the fast lane and move back to the place where he'd been born, a place where he could go to ground and lick his wounds. A place he'd sold.

He sat up and looked out of the window at the sun coming up. The decision still weighed on him. Intellectually he knew selling had been the only option, but it didn't salve the guilt he felt inside from being unable to keep the town going. Henry Adams had been handed down for five generations, and no matter what life or the country threw at it, it had survived. Until now. Now there was no tax base, no population, no schools. Farms had gone under, elders had died. The young people who'd left in search of real lives and never returned. Except for him, of course, but this wasn't about him. It was about legacy and family and a way of life that would be no more. Back in the day, his great great-great-grandmother Olivia Sterling July had been Henry Adams's mayor. She'd loved her town and her people. Now, because of him, she was probably spinning in her grave.

Trent sat in the half dawn for a few moments longer,

then got up to start the day. He was due to pick up Ms. Brown at the airport that afternoon, and frankly he wasn't looking forward to it.

After her flight from Kansas City to Hays, Bernadine walked into the terminal and followed the other passengers from the small jet to baggage claim. While waiting for her luggage to show, she glanced around for Trent July. Although she had no idea what he looked like because her lawyers had handled everything so far, she assumed he'd be Black but saw no one fitting that description.

Once the bags arrived she grabbed her two sand-colored suitcases off the belt and followed the exit sign to the doors leading outside. After being cooped up in airports and planes since early that morning, the fresh air felt good; it was hot though. From the discreet stares she received from people walking by, she assumed they didn't get too many folks at the airport who looked like her, but she didn't let it bother her and continued her visual search for the man she was supposed to meet. As time passed and no July, she wondered if he'd forgotten about picking her up or just running late.

She was digging around in her handbag for her phone just as a big black pickup eased up to the curb. A tall dark-skinned Black man wearing shades, jeans, a worn green plaid shirt, and a straw cowboy hat stepped out and went inside the terminal.

A few moments later he returned. He glanced at his watch and then at the faces of the few people milling about as if searching for someone in particular.

"Mr. July?" Bernadine asked, hope in her voice.

He hesitated, looking her over. "Yes. I'm July."

She stuck out her perfectly manicured hand. "B. E. Brown. Pleased to meet you."

His jaw dropped. "You're Brown? Nobody told me you were—"

"Black?"

"Well, yeah."

"Does it matter?"

He sized her up. She sized him up.

"No. No it doesn't. Just surprised I guess. How about I pull my foot out of my mouth and we start over?"

She decided she liked him. In this day and age, some people would rather lose a limb than own up to an apology—for anything. "I'd like that. I'm Bernadine Edwards Brown."

"And I'm Trenton July. Most folks call me Trent. Welcome to Kansas, Ms. Brown."

"Thank you."

"Let me take those bags and we'll head out."

Bernadine let out a sigh of relief. First hurdle passed.

"Watch your step."

He opened the door and she stepped up as gracefully as she could in her dark green Italian suit and matching pumps and settled into the seat.

"Buckle up."

She reached for the seat belt and he closed her in.

Bernadine had never ridden in a pickup. The interior was soft gray leather and the space was clean. It was a stereotype, of course, but she'd always associated pickups with empty beer cans, discarded jerky wrappers, and pork rind bags. This truck was nothing like that. The air-conditioning felt good too.

The door to the driver's side opened and Trent got in. "I put your bags in the bed."

With a smooth turn of the steering wheel, he guided the truck back into the traffic and drove away from the terminal.

Although Trent didn't express it aloud, to say that he was surprised by her race was an understatement. He naturally assumed she'd be White, and so did everyone else in town. It never occurred to anyone that B. E. Brown would turn out to be someone who looked like them, but here she was, dressed in a fancy designer suit and shoes, and sporting tasteful diamonds in her lobes and around her neck as if she were on her way to Paris or L.A. instead of a dusty little town in north-central Kansas. He just hoped she was ready.

"How far are we going?" she asked.

"About forty miles. Should be there in under an hour if we don't get stuck behind a combine."

Bernadine knew what a combine was. She'd seen the huge farm machines on the Discovery Channel. It never occurred to her that one would be out on a road though. The TV always showed them working in some field. Not wanting to expose her ignorance she nodded her thanks and turned her attention to the countryside.

They rode along in silence, and to her it seemed as if they'd left civilization behind. She couldn't believe the sparseness of the land. Pancake-flat plains of green and gold shimmered unchecked to the horizon. The number of trees could be counted on one hand—the number of houses on the other. For the hundredth time that day, she wondered if maybe she had been crazy to take this all on. How in the world was she supposed to grow a community out here in the middle of nowhere? She had enough confidence in herself and her mission to know that everything would work out in the end, but getting there was going to be the problem. "Not many trees out here."

"Nope. Not enough rain."

"Must make it hard to farm."

"Sometimes. Some years are drier than others."

They left the interstate and were now on a bumpy dirt road traveling past fenced-in rolling fields that could only be described as amber waves of grain. "What's that growing?"

"Winter wheat."

"Is there spring wheat?"

"Yeah," he said smiling as he looked her way. "Winter type grows better around here. Mennonite immigrants brought it to this part of the country when they came from Europe."

She waited for him to say more, but when he didn't it made her wonder if he was just not much of a talker or if he still felt guilty about his small faux pas at the airport. She hadn't been offended. Out here on the plains of Kansas, she was sure the local population had never met a woman with her spending power, and especially not a Black women, but rather than press him, she sat back and watched the wheat.

Now Bernadine appreciated silence and introspection, but after ten miles of it, she was ready to talk—about anything. "You must have some questions about why I'm doing this."

"I do, but thought I'd let my neighbors do all the asking. I've embarrassed myself enough for one day, I think."

Yep, she liked him a lot. "I bought Henry Adams for two reasons. One, it's not often we Black folks get the opportunity to save *our* history. When I saw the piece on TV about the town going up for sale, I knew what I had to do."

"Not many people in the country know how famous Henry Adams was once upon a time."

"I didn't either until I Googled it." And she was astounded by what she found. "I'd never heard of the Dusters or the Great Exodus of 1879." Tens of thousands of Black people fled the south after the Civil War and settled in places like Kansas, Nebraska, and Colorado in order to escape the violence perpetrated by the Redemptionist Democrats against the newly freed slaves and their families. It was the largest mass exodus of the race of its time. "I was surprised to read that Frederick Douglass was against our people leaving the South."

"Douglass was a politician losing his constituents just like the White planters were losing their cheap labor."

"And Congress held hearings about the Exodus?"

"Yep. The country thought so-called agitators were behind all those Black folks pulling up stakes, like maybe the race couldn't think for themselves and enjoyed all the killing and murdering the Klan and the Democrats were doing."

She shook her head. One of the articles she'd read on the subject told of an army general writing to President Hayes to inform him that in an effort to keep the Blacks from leaving the South, planters were lined up along the Mississippi armed as if the country was still at war.

He went on, "Entire church congregations from places as far east as Tennessee and Kentucky packed up everything and everybody and lit out for Kansas, looking for peace and opportunity. During the first winter, many of the colonies didn't have housing, so folks lived underground and in places carved out of hillsides; called them dugouts."

Bernadine found that amazing. As much as she loved her creature comforts she couldn't imagine having to live that way, but she supposed if she had been one of the dusters dealing with all the violence and hate, underground might not have looked too bad.

"We called our high school sports teams the Henry Adams Dusters."

"I saw in the report that the town no longer has a high school."

"No. Tornado came through about ten-twelve years ago and took it to Oz."

"And you never rebuilt?"

He shook his head. "The state told us if we did, we'd have to pay x amount for new insurance, new site developments, new environmental assessments. We didn't have that kind of money, so we shut down. The few high school kids left were bused over to Franklin, about fifteen miles west. Been no Henry Adams Dusters since."

Bernadine sensed his disappointment. She thought how

hard it must have been for him to watch his hometown slowly disappear like sand through fingers. In its prime, Henry Adams and the surrounding valley had been home to nearly six hundred people. Presently there were fifty-two.

"You said you had two reasons for wanting to buy. What's the second?"

She told him.

When she finished he whistled. "That's pretty ambitious."

"It is, but when much is given, much is expected, and I have a *lot*."

"Then if I were you, I'd wait to drop that dime. Let folks get to know you first."

"You don't think they'll like the idea?"

"Can't really say. I've no problem with it, but there's a small group who didn't want to sell. They'll scream long and loud when they hear this."

She didn't like the sound of that. "They have any clout?"

"Only if you call making me crazy clout, but I'll let you judge them for yourself. Wouldn't be fair of me."

"You always this noble?"

He grinned but kept his eyes on his driving.

They turned off onto another dirt road so filled with holes and ruts the truck bounced and bucked like a rodeo rider. Bernadine swore her behind was cracked in at least six places. "How much would it cost to put in a paved road?"

Humor flashed across his dark brown face. "You'll have to ask the state."

The next turn was onto another road barely wide enough for the big truck to negotiate. Door-high grass slapped against the windows like a bizarre car wash. The bucking and bouncing continued. She supposed if she planned on living there she'd get used to the rocking and rolling, but for the moment all she could do was hang on and hope she didn't hit her head on the ceiling of the truck.

When they came out into a clearing and the road evened out, her rattled bones gave up a weary and grateful hallelujah. Off in the distance she spotted weathered old wooden homes standing against the horizon like abandoned sentinels. "Is this it?"

"It's just around the next turn."

Bernadine could feel her excitement rising. She'd owned a lot of things in her life, but a town? Never.

"This is what's left of the neighborhood closest to town. Back in the day a good two hundred families lived here."

Viewing the scene through her window, she noted that now there was nothing to mark their existence but occasional piles of bricks hidden within stands of tall grass that made the homesteads look like the deserted nests of some strange bird. The truck rolled past the remains of fences, and sad-looking barns with caved-in roofs perched on walls too tired and too old to care. The area could have passed for the movie set of a ghost town.

And it got worse. He turned into what had once been the main business district. "This used to be downtown. There was a hotel over there, a livery, a general store. Had a couple of barber shops, tailors, and a seamstress shop. At the end of the block was the local gambling joint called the Liberian Lady, and next to it was the post office."

As with the area they'd driven through earlier, now there was nothing left standing but a handful of boarded-up and abandoned storefronts interspersed with tumble-down piles of stone, wood, and brick. It was easy to see that at one time buildings had lined both sides of the street. If she closed her eyes, she could almost imagine Henry Adams in its nineteenth-century prime; its streets filled with wagons, the wooden walks filled with men and women going in and out of the shops as they went about their daily errands. July was driving slowly, enabling Bernadine to get a good look at the old town she'd purchased, and the emptiness of it saddened her, mainly because the Dusters had had such dreams.

"Can we get out?" she asked him. She wanted to walk a bit, feel the historic ground beneath her feet.

He seemed to view her and her attire skeptically for a moment then said, "Sure."

They were standing in front of the old Henry Adams Hotel. Like the rest of the buildings that had once stood so proudly, there wasn't much left to proclaim it as the vibrant and classy hotel it must have been once upon a time.

"Lady named Sophie Reynolds originally built the place," he explained. "Had four floors, indoor plumbing, a ballroom, and a fancy dining room. My grandmother said folks for miles around came here just to see the big winding staircase that led to the rooms upstairs. After Miss Sophie died, the Jeffersons ran it; then sometime during the 1930s it was converted into a movie theater. It closed for good back in the seventies."

Standing in the heat, Bernadine took in the carved detail on the brick above the plywood covering the doors and wondered if it like the town could be brought back to life. She looked up and down the street and envisioned what downtown might look like with a brand-new library, businesses, and a new post office. The more she saw the more she seemed to envision.

They continued the tour and walked across the cracked paved street to the empty field where the general store once stood.

"Rich woman named Virginia Sutton built it in the 1870s, and it sold everything from penny candy to rifles. Its biggest claim to fame was that it had the tallest flagpole in the county. Legend has it that my great-great-grandfather Neil tied a man named Malloy to it for insulting my great-great-grandmother Olivia."

"Really?"

"Yeah, he and his brothers were something else. All outlaws."

Bernadine stared.

He nodded. "Have my grandmother show you the old picture albums. Neil and the rest of the Julys, including their baby sister, Teresa, were wanted from Mississippi to the Mexican border for train robbing."

Bernadine knew there'd been Black outlaws in the Wild West days but had never imagined actually meeting one of their descendants. "I'm impressed."

"This was quite the town back in the day. Some Black

people may not know their family history, but around here
we do. Our elders were smart enough to write everything
down. Wait until you see all the scrapbooks and old newspaper articles. Some of the state's colleges and museums
have been after us for years to turn our archives over to
them so they can preserve them, supposedly, but no. We're
holding onto it all."

She could only agree. "What else is in the scrapbooks?"

"Elder meeting minutes from the end of the nineteenth
century. Menus from Miss Sophie's dining room—stuff
like that. There's even the original drawings of the town's
layout from the 1870s. You can barely make out the plots
now because the maps are so old, but we have them. Not
many towns can say that."

"You're very proud of your ancestors, aren't you? I can
hear it in your voice."

"Real proud of the town and that my people were originally Black Seminole."

She stopped. "Really?"

He grinned. "More history here than you can shake a
stick at, as the old folks used to say."

"I guess. Going to be a lot of pressure on me when I
start to rebuild, I take it."

"Oh yeah."

They continued their walk and she continued to be
marveled by his tales and descriptions of buildings that had
come and gone. The more she saw of how little remained of
the Dusters' dreams, the more she felt the call to resurrect
the place. It didn't matter that she would have to start from

scratch—she had the money—what mattered most was to put life back into the place so that the history could continue to be handed down. "Have you lived here your whole life?"

He nodded. "Lived ten years in California, but after two divorces and a bellyful of corporate life, I came back. Only one of the few people who has. Everyone else who's left here never looked back."

"What would make people return and stay?"

"Jobs and being able to farm and make a decent living."

She mulled that over and filed it away for later.

He changed the subject. "Folks are having a reception for you. Be a good chance for you to meet everybody. That okay?"

"That's fine," she said, fighting off the nervousness kicking in. She wasn't sure she was ready but she knew she was in this to stay.

CHAPTER 4

They got back into the truck and drove a short distance down Main Street. Trenton slowed down and parked in front of a short, ramshackle one-story building that appeared ready to fall down. Edges of its tar-paper roof fluttered in the hot breeze. The structure itself was a hodgepodge mixture of old gray wood, which was scorched black in some places, and bricks; many of which were missing. The listing sign above the screen door read in faded painted letters: the Dog and Cow. "That's not a name you see every day."

He chuckled. "This is our diner."

Bernadine wondered what kind of food a place that looked as bad as this served.

"You ready?"

"Yep."

He came around and helped her down. Even though the walk had let her stretch her legs, lingering aftereffects of the roller-coaster ride from the airport still had her behind feeling like cement. Looking down at her dark green suit, she noted that she wasn't real wrinkled though. Thank God for money.

"Looks like everybody's here too."

His nod directed her to the field next to the diner. It was filled with cars and pickup trucks. All but a few had seen better days and all were covered with dust. The sight of so many vehicles made her wonder what kind of reception she'd receive. "Any advice?"

"Just be ready for anything."

That didn't help her nerves, but then she heard the distinctive voice of Aretha Franklin singing "Chain of Fools" floating out of the diner's open windows. Because ReeRee, as Franklin was affectionately known back in Detroit, was a homegirl, Bernadine took it as a good sign. Straightening her jacket, she set her purse strap and followed him inside.

It took her eyes a few moments to adjust to the dimness, but once they did she saw that the place was indeed packed. If there were twenty vehicles parked outside there had to be forty people inside. All of them, men and women, were staring at her curiously. As Aretha sang the last note you could hear a pin drop.

"Everybody," Trent announced in the silence, "this is Ms. Bernadine Edwards Brown, our buyer."

Gasps of surprise met openmouthed stares. Stunned faces looked her up and down. "I thought she was supposed to be White?" someone called.

"Well—"

"A Black woman?"

Then suddenly someone in the dimly lit place began to clap. Others joined in, and soon applause and cheers filled the air. A few of the older men even waved their canes.

The surprise must have been evident on her face because as she turned to Trent he nodded and said, "Welcome to Henry Adams, Ms. Brown," and joined in the applause.

Bernadine could see that most of the people were seniors. All were wearing their Sunday best and they were beaming, clapping, and hooting. Overwhelmed, she gracefully wiped away the moisture forming in the corner of her eyes. She didn't know what she had been expecting, but it certainly hadn't been this outpouring of welcome. In a few more seconds she was going to bawl.

"Thank you," she said trying to keep it together. "Thank you very much."

An elderly lady who introduced herself as Agnes Jefferson stood and asked Bernadine, "Do you know the history of this place, young woman?"

Bernadine was in her midfifties. No one had called her young in years but she'd been raised well, so she said, "Yes, ma'am. I do. That's why I wanted to help."

There were more whispers of excitement.

"Are you going to rebuild the town?"

Agnes reminded Bernadine of the little old blue-haired ladies at the church she grew up in. "That is my plan. Most of the paperwork for the deed transfer has already cleared. My lawyers—"

"You have lawyers—as in more than one?" another woman, tall with dark skin and flowing silver hair, asked before introducing herself. "I'm Tamar July by the way. Trent's gram."

"Pleased to meet you, ma'am." And she was. "To answer your question—yes, more than one."

As she watched Tamar and Agnes exchange an impressed glance, she added, "I hope to start building right away, but first I want to talk to you and get your take on what you might want the new town to look like. Second, I need to find a place to stay until I can get a house built."

A short light-skinned man with thinning straight hair and who looked to be sixtyish or so rose to his feet and stuck up his hand.

"Yes?"

He stepped out in order to be seen. His black pinstriped suit was shiny with age. "Ms. Brown, I'm Riley Curry, former mayor of Henry Adams."

A few people let out load groans.

Bernadine pretended not to hear. "Nice to meet you, Mr. Curry."

"You mentioned having a house built. For what purpose?"

"Residency." Bernadine gave Trent a sideways look but he kept his face void of any response.

"You're going to live here?"

"As much as possible, yes."

"Why?"

Not sure where this was going, she told the truth, "I figure when you buy a town, the least you can do is live in it." She glanced out at the other people in the room. "That make sense?"

There were answering nods and murmurs of agreement.

But it seemed he wasn't convinced. "I don't know if Mr.
July has told you, but there are those of us here who question whether selling was a good idea."

A male voice in the back of the room, shouted, "Oh, sit
down, Riley. You can bore her some other time. We want
to eat!"

Laughter erupted. Bernadine wanted to kiss the owner
of the voice, whoever he was, but knew she should address
Curry's concerns. She also decided now was the time to
reveal her full plan, despite Trent's advice to the contrary.
She respected his take on the subject. After all, he knew
his neighbors and she didn't, but she didn't want to be accused of having a hidden agenda. She'd need their help to
pull this off, and the sooner she figured out who was with
her and who wasn't, the better off she'd be. "I know better
than to hold up a good meal but I want to tell you the other
reason I bought the town."

"Splendid," he said tightly, but his face said something
else entirely "Are you going to disband the council?"

Caught off guard, she asked, "What council?"

"The duly elected Council of Elders that runs this
town."

"I didn't even know there was a council, Mr. Curry."

Someone shouted, "Sit down, Riley. The council hasn't
had a meeting since the town went broke. Let her finish so
we can eat!"

Bernadine could see the displeasure on Riley's face, so
she said in as polite as voice as could be managed. "As the

construction progresses, we will be needing some type of board to keep an eye on things. How about we talk about the council later? Is that okay with you for now?"

His expression said that it wasn't, but she hadn't come here to go back and forth with him all day, so she moved on by telling them about the tour of the town Trent had given her and some of the things she'd envisioned like a neighborhood center, a library, and a health center. "In addition there'll also be a small subdivision of new homes built in the old neighborhood behind Main Street."

There was silence for a moment as folks looked at each other with what appeared to be mild confusion.

Marie Jefferson wearing her cat's-eye glasses with the rhinestone frames introduced herself and asked, "Who're you building the new houses for?"

"Any of you residents who want one and the new people I'm planning to bring in."

"What new people?"

"Foster parents and foster children."

Every eye in the room widened and shot her way. To say they looked stunned was an understatement.

"Foster children?" a tall thin elderly man asked.

"Yes."

Riley snapped, "I knew she had something up her sleeve. Her buying us out was too good to be true. I knew it! Foster children?! What are we going to do with a bunch of ghettofied hoodlums?"

"Raise them and love them, I'm hoping," she replied simply.

The room quieted. She had their full attention now

and took a moment to tell them the story of a place called Hope.

When she finished, Agnes asked in a wonder-softened voice, "And you want to do that here? In Henry Adams?"

Bernadine nodded and then continued quietly, "Listen. What better place to raise children than in a historic environment like this where there is stability, elders they can call on, and is safe? And they aren't hoodlums," she added giving Riley a cold glance. "Children in the foster care system are not there by choice. Most are there because of tragedies in a life they had no control over. I'd like to bring a few here and give them a new start. With your help."

Agnes Jefferson, who'd been siding with Riley on the town sale issue appeared so moved by Bernadine's plea that Tamar had to hand her a tissue so she could wipe her eyes. When the Jefferson matriarch pulled it together her voice wavered with emotion. "Young woman, I've been prepared not to like you, but this? This is why our ancestors founded our town—to get a new start. For you to bring that forward, I think it's a marvelous idea."

Riley snapped hotly, "No, it isn't. I've seen these kids on television and they are trouble with a capital *T*!"

Ignoring Riley, Trent asked, "How many children are you going to start with? Will they be local?"

"I want to start small, so it will just be four or five at first. And no, they won't be local. The foster parents probably won't be either. Good stable people are hard to find."

Riley's wife, Genevieve, asked, "What makes you think you're qualified to do something like this."

"My MSW."

Some people looked confused.

"Masters in social work," Bernadine explained. "I worked in foster care for over ten years, and I'm hoping my experience will help me choose the right kids and the right foster parents."

There was more silence. She wasn't sure if she had them on board or not so she added sincerely, "I understand your skepticism and that you may have concerns, but I know all of you here have something valuable you can teach these children. All of you. They'll need tutors and mentors and just plain family. We can give them that."

Someone else asked, "Will they be Black?"

"I'm sure some will be, but if you think about it, a needy child is a needy child no matter the color."

Folks nodded, apparently seeing the rightness in her words.

"The construction will begin ASAP, as I said, because I want to get as much done as we can before winter, and I'll really need your support if this is to work. I know you all don't know me from Adam at this point, but I'm hoping the longer I live here the more trust we can build."

Another man spoke up. "Ms. Brown, I'm Clayton Dobbs, a Vietnam vet, and back in the sixties we Black folks were all about community. What you're proposing reminds me of that. I'm in."

Many people added their support. Others, like Riley, just looked disgusted, but she didn't care. She was glad to have Agnes Jefferson on her side though. Agnes and Tamar July appeared to be the oldest people in the room. With their support, she hoped the mountain looming ahead would be easier to climb. "Are there any more questions before we eat?"

Tamar asked, "Suppose we don't want new houses, but want our old places fixed up?"

"I'm sure we can work out something."

Tamar seemed satisfied with that.

Riley wasn't and asked angrily, "Isn't anyone concerned that we don't know where all this money she's supposed to have comes from? What if it's drug money or laundered money from some illegal offshore operation?"

People began to boo.

Bernadine looked him in the eye. He was tap dancing on her last nerve. "Mr. Curry, I got my money the old-fashioned way—I earned it in a divorce settlement."

Soft chuckles followed that.

"How much I'm worth, which is what I really think you want to know, is none of your business, but to put you at ease take the three and a half million I paid to buy Henry Adams, multiply that by say, eighty and you'll be in the ballpark."

Jaws dropped all over the room. Even Riley looked rocked.

She asked him coolly, "Anything else?"

He gave her a hasty shake of his head and sat down.

"Good. If there are any other questions before we eat, shoot."

They wanted to know things like when did she anticipate bringing in the children, would the neighborhood center have a lap pool, would the farmers in the area be able to secure low-interest loans?

Bernadine answered as best she could, and she promised to get back to them on the ones she could not. Riley Curry didn't have anything else to say apparently, and as a result the rest of the discussion went smoothly.

Tamar stood and said, "Okay, let's let Ms. Brown eat."

Bernadine smiled and asked Trent, "Where can I wash my hands?"

He directed her to the restroom. "It's unisex, so make sure you knock."

"Got it."

The small restroom was a clean, sparkling contrast to the D&C's drab hangdog interior. As she was leaving, a sign on the door caught her eye. In big bold letters someone had written this reminder: If You Are a Man—Go Back and Put Down the Seat!

Smiling, she walked out and rejoined the festivities.

The food was spread out buffet-style, and as guest of honor Bernadine led the line. Some of the best-looking barbecued chicken she'd seen in a long time filled a platter in the center of the long table. As she added baked beans and coleslaw to the other offerings on her plate, she saw nothing but kindness on most of the faces of the people around her.

Agnes Jefferson took one look at Bernadine's plate and declared, "I like a woman who's not afraid to let folks know she eats. Those little toothpick girls on the television make me sick."

Bernadine was five-eight and a healthy size 18. She loved her curves because she loved herself. "Good food is good for the soul."

"Amen!" Tamar said.

Over the course of the meal, she was interrupted by people who came over and introduced themselves again, men like WWII veteran Bingham Shepard and Clayton

Dobbs, who wanted her to take a look at their ideas for irrigation improvements. Then came some of the women, including Genevieve Curry, who after introducing herself boldly asked if the diamonds in Bernadine's ears were real?

"Yes," Bernadine replied coolly.

The residents of Henry Adams were farmers and truck drivers, day workers and retirees. They showed her pictures of their adult children now living in big cites like Kansas City and Topeka. Others proudly whipped out pictures of their grandchildren, and she was moved by the love she saw in their eyes. All in all she found her new neighbors to be decent folks. Of course, it was her first time meeting them, and they could all turn out to be spawns of the Corn God or some other crazy demon from one of those slasher movies her nephews were always going to see, but for now she was content.

As people took seats and conversations began to flow around the space, she asked Trent, "So how'd I do?"

"Considering you didn't take my advice and are still alive and eating, I'd say you did just fine. Got people thinking if nothing else." He looked up from his piled-high plate, "You don't do things by half do you?"

She shook her head. "I'd rather be up front, that way there's no confusion later."

"There's certainly none of that here."

"Do you think they'll be good for the kids?"

He nodded. "I do."

"Do you have any children?"

"No."

Bernadine detected a sense of sadness in his one-word reply, and it made her wonder about its root, but she didn't know him well enough to be in his business so she went back to her plate and changed the subject. "Who owns this place?" She could see people going in and out of what she guessed might be the kitchen but no one looked to be in charge—except maybe Agnes and Tamar, who were overseeing the replenishment of the bowls and platters on the buffet tables and seemed to be giving all the orders. Someone had punched up the old jukebox again, and this time Eddie Kendricks and the Temptations were urging folks to "Get Ready."

"My father, Malachi. He's also the town vet."

"Is he in the kitchen cooking?"

He laughed. "Malachi? Oh no. Last time he got near the grill he almost burned the place to the ground. He's not allowed to even look in there. Right now he's over at Lake's farm. One of their mare's having trouble foaling. You'll meet him later."

She wondered if the father was as good-looking as the son. Not that she was looking for a man, but truth be told, he was dark chocolate and fine. "So who does all the cooking here?"

"Officially, no one. It used to be Rocky, but she got married last week. Malachi's supposed to be looking for a replacement, but so far nothing. You wouldn't happen to cook, would you?"

"Yeah right," she said, grinning. She spotted Riley Curry and his wife observing her from where they sat close by. She'd decided she didn't like either of them, but she set the thoughts aside. All she wanted to do was enjoy the fabulous meal and continue basking in the wonderful welcome she'd received. "Are there any other places to eat close by?"

"Nope. There's a couple fast food places in Franklin but all the real restaurants are down in Hays."

While the music and the gathering continued, she glanced around at the taped-up booths and the dangling bare bulbs with an eye toward making improvements. "Do you think your father would be interested in renovating his place?"

He shrugged. "After he gets through hitting on you, you can ask him."

"Hitting on me?"

"Yep, so be ready."

Tamar set a plate in front of Bernadine that held a wedge of chocolate cake and ice cream, then set a duplicate in front of her grandson. Apparently she'd heard her grandson's remarks because she said, "Trent's right, Ms. Brown. I love my son as much as I love my name, but Malachi's full of snake oil when it comes to women. Watch yourself."

Bernadine was too stunned to say anything except, "Yes, ma'am."

Folks nearby laughed.

Bernadine saw the smile on Trent's face. "You all are just messing with me, right?"

"Wish we were. People around here called him the Gigolo of Graham County when he was young; some still do."

Bernadine tasted the ice cream. It was homemade and her taste buds died and went to heaven. "You won't have to worry about me. Been there, done that, which is why I'm divorced. I don't do players very well, which is why he has a new wife now, complete with fake nails and weave."

"*Ouch.*"

"I'm just saying."

After dessert, the leftover food was divided up and distributed among the attendees, and the welcome reception began breaking up. Nearly everyone stopped by to tell Bernadine good-bye and to thank her for rescuing the town. Their praises and pledges to help in any way they could with the kids humbled her. The Currys offered nothing. They just walked out.

As the numbers of people dwindled, she asked Trent, "Is there a place nearby where I can spend the night. Hotel, motel, Holiday Inn?"

He smiled hearing her spout the lyrics from the old Sugar Hill Gang tune. "Nope, but Tamar will put you up."

"I don't want to impose."

"You won't be and she'd enjoy the company."

Sure enough, when Tamar was ready to leave, Trent asked her and she told Bernadine the same thing. "I'd love to have you stay with me."

"Are you sure you don't mind?"

"Positive."

"Then okay. I'll make some calls in the morning and see if I can't get a trailer or a modular home delivered ASAP. I don't want to wear out my welcome."

"Don't worry about it."

Outside, while Bernadine looked on, Trent transferred

her luggage to his grandmother's old beat-up green truck. "Thanks for everything," she told him. "They're some nice people here."

"They are. Some are old and set in their ways, but they were on their best behavior with you."

"You still think I'm going to be butting heads?"

He shrugged. "I don't know. You laid out plans for a pretty powerful mission, but Riley's going to hassle you mission or no mission. It's seems to be his reason for living."

"How long was he mayor?"

"About thirty years."

She found that surprising. "How long have you been in office?"

"Two, and he's been a thorn in my butt the whole time. Swears I don't know what I'm doing. He's planning on running against me in the November election."

"Does he have the votes to win?"

"Right now, no. Come election time, who knows."

Bernadine sensed she'd get more cooperation for her project from July than she would from the sour-faced Curry, and so she planned to change her voting address as soon as possible. "You've been very kind and you're a great tour guide."

"You're welcome. I'll probably see you tomorrow."

"Take care."

He touched his hat, got into his truck, and drove away.

Tamar was a short distance away talking to Agnes and her daughter Marie. When she was done they drove off and she walked over and asked Bernadine "You ready?"

"Yes, ma'am."

They got in. Tamar turned the key in the ignition and the old truck roared to life. Bernadine had to admit she had a few misgivings about riding with Tamar, based on how old she guessed Tamar to be, but as they peeled out of the parking lot, they proved to be true for a different reason. The old lady drove like a bat out of hell. Praying, Bernadine bit her lip and held on as Tamar tore through turns and switchbacks at speeds nearing her eighty-four years of age.

Luckily, they didn't have to go far. Her home was less than fifteen minutes away, but still, Bernadine stepped out of the truck on shaking legs. "You ever thought about driving at Daytona?"

"Like my driving?"

"I'm not sure. Kinda scary."

"The shortest distance between two points is speed."

"I'll write that down."

They sat on the porch and rehashed the meeting. Bernadine asked Tamar to give her a thumbnail sketch of some of the people she'd met so far. "Tell me about Mr. Shepard and Mr. Dobbs."

"Bing was Clay's dad's best friend. When Bing's wife died, we thought he was going to die of a broken heart, wouldn't eat, wouldn't leave the house, we really worried about him, so Clay convinced him to move in."

"Does Mr. Dobbs have a wife?"

"No. The girl he loved and probably still loves married somebody else."

Bernadine thought that was sad.

"Mr. Shepard said he was a World War Two vet?"

"Yep. Left with Clay's dad to go fight Hitler together, but they wound up helping the Black troops build a highway up in Alaska."

"Alaska?" It was yet another little-known fact of Black history associated with the town that Bernadine had no clue about.

"Yep. Have him tell you the story sometime. Be good for the kids to learn about it too, I'll bet."

Bernadine bet she was right. "Do they farm?"

"They used to when they were younger. Clay raised hogs until last year and had the best bacon around now he's living on Social Security like the rest of us."

"What about Marie Jefferson?"

"Agnes's only child. College graduate. Taught school here until the tornado tore the place up. Never married."

"Okay, so tell me about Riley and Genevieve. How long have they been married?"

"Almost forty years. She grew up over in Franklin. Her father owned the funeral home over there. She came from money, which everybody thinks attracted Riley to her in the first place."

"How'd he make his living?"

"Helped out at the funeral home after they got married, then when her father passed, the place went to one of her cousins instead of him. Made him pretty mad. He moved back here and opened up a barber shop. Was pretty successful until the town started to die. He still cuts hair though. Menfolk say he's pretty good. Of course, they have to listen to him preach the Gospel According to Riley, but they're used to it by now."

"Is he on Social Security too?"

"Yep. Growing up, he told anybody who'd listen that he'd be a millionaire by the time he turned thirty."

"Never made it."

"Nope. Kinda hard to do living out here on the plains with only a high school education. The world wasn't as open for us back then as it is these days."

"But people did make it."

"Oh, of course. Look at that man that started *Ebony* magazine. John Johnson. Started out picking rags. Riley never had that much ambition though. He's always been looking for somebody to hand him the money."

"Like with the annexation deal?"

"You got it."

The info gave Bernadine a somewhat clearer picture of the former mayor. "But why was he mayor for so long?"

"Nobody else wanted the job."

"*Ah.*"

Later, as she snuggled beneath the soft bedding in Tamar's spare bedroom, she thought back on the remarkable day and the equally remarkable welcome she'd received. Smiling, she offered a whispered thank you to the Big Sister up above for all the blessings, then closed her eyes and slept.

Trent moved around his silent studio apartment above the town's garage and prepared for bed. It had been an interesting day. He still couldn't get over the fact that Bernadine Brown was Black and that he liked her. She seemed to be no-nonsense. She also didn't put on any airs, which he found surprising considering how big her bank account must be. He didn't know anyone capable of putting their hands on 3.5 mil to buy a whole town let alone a Black woman.

Yet her debut had gone fine, practically had people eating out her hand by the time she was done. He shook his head and sat in the old rocker Tamar had donated to his furnishings and took off his boots. Her plans were ambitious ones and only time would tell if she'd bitten off more than she could chew, but he'd help in any way he could if it meant the town would be reborn.

He wondered about the children and how they'd react to being here in the proverbial middle of nowhere. Would they think of it as a haven or try and leave as soon as possible? Although his neighbors had pledged their support of the plan, how would they really react to children who weren't their own? Ms. Brown was right about the people in the area being able to teach the kids things, but would they want to learn about farming or how to build houses or how to plant crops?

On a more personal level, he'd always wanted to be a father. Would mentoring the foster children be an outlet for that unfulfilled dream? Trent had no clue and rather than make himself crazy with questions he had no answers to, he turned off the lights and went to bed.

That night In Milwaukee, twelve-year-old Preston Mays was being driven home from the ER by his foster mother. He'd had a bad asthma attack a few hours ago, but because she wouldn't buy him an inhaler, he'd had to flop around on his bed, gulping like a fish

out of water and wait until she got home from having her nails
done so she could drive him to the doctor. He hated hospitals, but
he hated her even more. "The doctor said you need to get me an
inhaler," he told her.

"If you'd lose some weight and stop trying to tell me what to do
all the time, you wouldn't be having these problems."

Looking out at the night and the lights of the buildings, Pres-
ton rolled his eyes. "I need an inhaler."

"You need to shut the hell up. The money the state's paying me
ain't worth all this drama."

He sighed and wondered where the state got these people. He'd
been in seven different homes in the past year. All of them worth-
less, but rather than argue further, he took matters into his own
hands.

Later, after she went to bed, he set fire to the house. He started
at the back to ensure they both got out safely. He wasn't trying to
murder anybody; he just wanted to be out of her life, and to have
an inhaler, of course.

When he confessed to the firemen that he'd done it on purpose,
they called CPS.

CHAPTER
6

Driving north on Highway 183, Lily Fontaine couldn't believe she was actually back in Kansas, but all she had to do was look out the window of the rental car at the flat rolling plains of green and gold to know the truth. She'd been born and raised in Kansas, Topeka to be exact, but had spent her teenage years living in Henry Adams under the watchful eye of her mother's college roommate Marie Jefferson while Lily's mom, Cassandra, did a three-year stint with the Peace Corps over in southern Africa. Marie was also Lily's godmother, and when Cass lost her battle with cancer during Lily's junior year at the University of Kansas, Marie had been with her at the grave site.

Lily's son, Davis, had never known his grandmother and that fact always saddened her, but she felt blessed to have been Cassandra Fontaine's daughter and to have had her dynamic personality in her life.

After Cass's death, the bond between Lily and Marie cemented. As a youngster, Davis had spent many summer vacations out here on the plains running barefoot and free, and as far as he was concerned, Marie was his gram. Most times Lily had stayed home to get a break from raising such a rambunctious boy child and because of her workload as the executive secretary to the president of one of the nation's biggest pharmaceutical companies. Her last visit to Henry Adams had been ten years ago, when she'd flown in to help the town celebrate Marie's fiftieth birthday.

In reality, Lily was looking forward to spending ten days doing absolutely nothing in a place that offered absolutely nothing to do. Now that her company had been purchased and swallowed up by one of its major competitors, she had time to smell the roses and enjoy the simple things in life, like visiting her godmother.

She was also looking forward to the news about Henry Adams's new owner. It had broken her heart to hear about the town's financial difficulties. When she last talked to Marie the buyer was supposed to be flying in to check out the place, and Lily was anxious to find out how the meeting had gone.

This trip back did have a potential bad side though. One of the things she wasn't looking forward to was Trent July. When she last visited, he'd been living in California, but she knew through Marie that he'd since returned and was now the mayor. Lily had no idea what would happen when they met face-to-face after all these years, but the guilt was rising.

Setting that aside for now, she fiddled with the radio. The rental car had no CD player, so for the last thirty-five miles, she'd been forced to listen to static, farm reports, and what passed for talk radio out on the plains. She knew it was useless to search for real music, but she was hoping to hear something a bit more conducive to an urban woman like herself, but she got nothing. Strike that. When smoke began streaming out from under the hood like a house on fire, she got plenty.

By the grace of God she was only a few miles outside of Henry Adams and she and the sputtering car managed to make it into the local garage. Back in high school, Rocky's dad had owned the place, but she had no idea whether he still did. The gray smoke billowing from under the hood was making it nearly impossible to see, and she prayed not to hit anybody or anything.

"Stop!" A man yelled.

She stomped down on the brake.

"You almost hit me!"

He came striding out of the smoke. He was dressed in a pair of oil-stained denim overalls and wiping his hands on a dirty rag, and his face—the grim but familiar face—hit her with such force she went instantly still. Memories washed back, hot and strong, bringing with them a decade's-old shame.

His eyes met hers through the open window, and he stopped, whispered, "Well, I'll be damned."

She swallowed and managed a fake little smile. "Hey, Trent."

"Lily."

His one-word response held about as much warmth as his eyes, but it was no more than she deserved, she supposed. "You, *um*, work here?"

He nodded.

She could tell by the set of his jaw that he was remembering too. She forced herself to keep her gaze steady. "You think you could see what's going on with all this smoke?"

"Pop the hood."

She reached down and pulled the lever. Straightening again, she realized her hands were shaking. Drawing in a deep breath to settle her nerves, she wondered why he'd come back. He'd gotten his engineering degree from Stanford and had worked for one of the big multinational construction firms. In high school he'd been captain of the football team, and wherever he went it was wet panties all around. Women young and old adored him. Lily had adored him too. He'd adored her as well, but after she went off to college things became complicated. During one of his visits to see her freshman year, she'd hurt him so badly they broke apart like a dropped piece of china, and she hadn't set eyes on him since.

"There's oil all over the engine," he told her. "Whoever worked on it last didn't replace the cap."

"So that's what making all the smoke?"

He nodded.

"Can you clean it up? This is all I have to drive while I'm here."

"Glad to hear you won't be staying."

She supposed she'd earned that but she hadn't come to town to start anything. "How much?"

"Won't know until I'm done."

"Okay." Lily knew there was no way she was going to hang around the garage while he did whatever he had to do to the car, and she was pretty sure he didn't want her there, so she reached for her phone lying on the passenger seat and punched up Marie . . . or at least tried to. The phone didn't respond. No bars. "There's no cell service out here?"

"Nope. Land line only. The one tower we had was blown down two years ago."

"And the phone company didn't put it back up?"

"No. Said the small population wouldn't justify the expense."

"Then do you have a phone I can use?"

"In the office."

She got out and followed him back.

He stood in the door while she dialed. His silent scrutiny made her turn away. When Marie answered, Lily explained about the car. "Will you come get me?"

"I have a pie in the oven. Have Trent run you out."

Not a chance. She ignored his chilly stare. "He's working. I don't think his boss will just let him up and leave." There weren't any other workers inside the small cramped building, but she had seen three beat-up old cars waiting like patients at an Auto Urgent Care.

Marie's response brought Lily up short. *"He* is the boss?" She caught the ghost of a smile that crossed his dark face just before he said, "Leave the keys and take your valuables."

He walked away.

Marie told her to go over to the Dog and Cow and wait there. She'd pick her up after the pie was done.

When Lily came back out to the garage, he was nowhere to be seen. Not that it mattered. The less they saw of each other the better. She beat down the gnawing guilt that came with the knowledge that she alone was responsible for the gulf between them and turned her attention to how she was going to get to the Dog and Cow without a ride.

Out in back of the garage, the tight-jawed Trent stood and waited for his emotions to slow. Lily. He wished Marie had warned him she was coming so he could have been prepared. As it stood, seeing her again brought back memories he thought he'd buried, but the old anger rose again, reminding him of that humiliating day when she and her big city college friends had broken him down and sent him slinking home like a dog with its tail tucked between its legs. Willing himself not to remember that at one time he'd loved Lily Fontaine as much as he'd loved breathing, he reined himself in and went back out front but found her gone. Looking up the road he saw her walking away. He let her go.

Lily decided she didn't want to wait at the Dog and Cow. It was a good five miles to Marie's place and she hadn't walked five miles in, well, years, but it was either that or face Trent again and beg a ride, so she chose to hoof it. One encounter with him had been more than enough. In her haste to get away, she'd left her water on the seat and the late morning sun was kicking her behind. The rolling suitcase being pulled behind her was a problem too. The wheels were designed for the smooth polished floors of airports, not the dusty pock-filled dirt that passed for roads in north-central Kansas. Every few feet the damn thing went off track or hit a rock and she had to stop, untangle the wheels, and start up again. It was like pulling a balky mule.

She pressed on however, alternately cursing and begging the angels for mercy.

They must have been listening because a half a mile out, an old red truck rolled up on her. It stopped, the passenger-side door opened, and inside sat the smiling Malachi July under the wheel.

Looking all the world like his son would in fifteen years he called out in a surprised voice, "Lily Fontaine? Is that you?"

She grinned back. "Sure is, Mr. July. How are you?"

"Get in and I'll tell you."

Needing no more of an invitation than that, she tossed her suitcase in the bed and he drove them away.

He handed her a canteen, and she drank down the ice-cold water gratefully. Handing it back, she wiped her mouth, as ladylike as she could and sat back against the seat, content.

"Since you were lugging that suitcase I'm assuming you just got in? Why're you walking?"

"Rental car had issues so I left it with Trent."

He looked over. "How'd it go?"

She shrugged. "He was polite."

"Good. He never told me why you two broke up and I don't expect you to either, but you'd've made a great daughter-in-law, Lily."

For all of his womanizing ways Malachi Trent had always been kind to her and she appreciated that kindness now. "It was my fault." The memory of the anger and hurt on Trent's face that day in her dormitory was as fresh in her mind as if it had happened yesterday. The harsh demeaning laughter directed his way by her so-called college friends rose to taunt her as well. Looking back she was appalled at how she'd treated him. She was surprised he hadn't tossed her out of his garage headfirst.

"You staying with Marie?"

She nodded. Thinking about the rift with Trent cast a shadow over her mood.

"Lily?"

She looked his way.

"It'll work out."

She didn't know if she agreed but she said softly, "We'll see."

They drove along in silence and the familiar lay of the land touched her. When she graduated from high school and moved downstate to attend college, you couldn't have paid her to come back. The big city with all its glitter and glitz filled her in ways Henry Adams had not. She'd gotten to see plays, attend concerts, lectures, and make friends with people from all over the world. In spite of the drama surrounding her marriage and the subsequent divorce, re-settling here held no draw whatsoever, but now after decades of raising Davis and running from pillar to post with her job, the slow life had an odd appeal she found surprising.

Malachi's voice broke into her thoughts. "I promised Tamar I'd bring her some eggs. You mind if we stop a minute?"

"No. Be nice to see her. Marie says she's still going strong."

"Eighty-four and counting. Still driving too."

"She's an amazing woman."

"It's that July blood. Great-aunt Teresa lived to be a hundred and five."

As the drive continued and she listened to him tell her about his wild outlaw ancestors, Lily's mood lightened.

Bernadine finished breakfast with a smile. The eggs, bacon, and toast had been just enough. She'd turned down the waffles Tamar first suggested. Waffles were a little too heavy for the summertime. She looked across the table at her hostess. "Thank you for breakfast and for taking me in."

"My pleasure. Glad to have somebody to cook for besides myself."

Bernadine got up and began clearing the table.

"And what do you think you're doing, missy?"

"Cleaning up."

"Sit."

Bernadine ignored her. The least she could do was earn her keep. "Tell me where everything goes, let me do these dishes, and then I'll sit."

Tamar's unwavering gaze made Bernadine think of a hawk. In a way she did resemble an exotic bird with her dark skin, sharp features, and brilliant black eyes. Gray hair gleaming with the high sheen of silver ran down her back like an undulating river. "You defying me?"

"Yes, ma'am."

Tamar finally smiled. "Then go on. I like a woman with backbone."

Once the chores were done, Bernadine grabbed a second glass of ice tea and joined Tamar on her porch. It was one of those old-fashioned wraparound porches that was sheltered from the Kansas sun by an overhanging roof. Although the day promised to be hot the porch was shady and the surrounding landscape was still. Bernadine felt as if she'd stepped back in time.

"So, what are your dreams?" Tamar asked once Bernadine got herself settled on the old sofa.

"To do something worthwhile with all I've been given."

Tamar studied her. "Got a good relationship with the Great Spirit, do you?"

"Yes, ma'am."

"Glad to hear it."

Bernadine like her. Trent's grandmother was a spry old thing and her mind was as sharp as her eyesight. Last night, they'd discussed everything from politics to the economy to Tamar's love of Mos Def.

"That boy's got talent," she'd said, much to Bernadine's delight.

So with all that in mind, Bernadine told Tamar, "My dreams are the ones I told you all about yesterday. This town. The children."

Tamar didn't say anything for a long while and Bernadine wondered if maybe Tamar didn't support her plans, but then Tamar looked her way with those hawk-bright eyes and said, "Not going to be easy."

"I know that too. Do you think Riley and his people will come around?"

"If they don't, will it stop you?"

"Nope"

"Then why worry about it? This is your town now. If you want to turn it into Amos 'n' Andy Land, who's going to tell you no?"

Bernadine burst out laughing. "You are very wise, Tamar July."

"Amen. Anything that can make this town rise again I'm all for. My grandmother was the mayor here back in the 1880s and she did a lot of good things. She'd like the idea of what you're going to do." And she added, "If I didn't say so at the meeting, I'll help any way I can."

That made Bernadine smile. "Let me get my laptop. I want to show you some of the drawings from the architect."

Bernadine returned and opened the top of her machine, but when she turned it on, nothing happened. She went through the boot-up ritual again. Still nothing. Picking up her BlackBerry, she tried that. Nothing. And just like Lily, a surprised Bernadine asked, "There's no cell service here?"

"Nope. No cell service, no cable TV, no nothing."

"Well that's not going to work. How am I supposed to stay in touch with the world?"

"Dial-up. We have a land line."

"I need wireless. Lord." She sat back against the old sofa, her mind racing with the hows of getting this fixed. "How was Trenton able to e-mail my lawyers then?"

"Dial-up."

Bernadine was too through. "There's no cell service, anywhere?"

"Not out here. Lots of small towns are the same way."

"That's crazy."

"No, that's economics."

Further conversation was put on hold when a red pickup truck stopped in front of the house.

"*Ah*, my son," Tamar said, smiling and getting to her feet. She moved with the aid of a cane but walked straight as a beam of steel. She turned to Bernadine. "Remember now. Snake oil."

The twinkle in Tamar's eyes made Bernadine let go of the tech dilemma for now and smile in reply. "Yes ma'am."

Tamar called out. "Who's that with you, Mal?"

The passenger door opened and a woman wearing nice jeans and a red blouse stepped out.

Tamar's brown face lit up. "Lily Fontaine?"

"Yes, ma'am," the woman answered as she walked to the porch. She gave Bernadine a friendly nod, before asking Tamar, "How are you, Ms. July?"

"Get over here and give an old lady a hug. You come to help Marie celebrate her birthday?"

"Yes I have," Lily responded.

The demanded hug was given while Bernadine looked on with a smile.

Tamar then made the introductions.

"Pleased to meet you, Lily," Bernadine said genuinely.

"Same here."

But Tamar said to her son. "I already told Ms. Brown here you were full of snake oil, so no hitting on her. You hear me?"

Bernadine thought Malachi looked like an older version of his son. He too was tall dark and handsome. She stuck out her hand. "Pleased to meet you, Mr. July."

"Apparently my reputation proceeds me, but good to meet you, too, Ms. Brown."

Lily seemed shocked, "You're the new owner?"

"Yep."

Bernadine could see Malachi studying her but she politely ignored him and kept her attention focused on Lily's smile.

"Nobody told me you were Black."

Bernadine laughed. "Nobody knew."

Lily looked to be barely forty. With her angular face, smooth brown skin, and sherry brown hair, she made Bernadine think of Tyra Banks. Lily lacked the model's height and drop-dead curves, but something about the hair and the sparkle in the eyes made Bernadine envision an older Tyra.

"This is amazing. Folks here treating you okay?" Lily asked.

"Yes, they are."

"Then welcome again."

"Thanks." Bernadine got the sense that Lily was a nice person. She wondered how long she'd be visiting.

But Tamar changed the subject by asking about Davis, and as Lily responded, Bernadine could see Malachi checking her out, but she kept ignoring him.

"Well, it's good to have you home, Lily," Tamar said genuinely. "Have you seen Trent?"

"Yes."

The short reply made Bernadine think maybe there was

some kind of drama going on between Lily and Trenton July but knew it wasn't her place to ask.

Malachi added, "I told her she would've made a fine daughter-in-law."

Lily laughed, "Now, that's enough, Mr. July."

"I'm sorry, but the truth will set you free."

Tamar cracked, "Set yourself free and go get me those eggs. You did bring them, didn't you?"

He leaned over and kissed his mother's smooth cheek. "For you, Lady Macbeth, the world."

She cut him a look. "Me and this cane got your Lady Macbeth." She glanced Bernadine's way. "See what I'm talking about? Snake oil."

It was obvious to Bernadine that mother and son loved each other. Malachi's eyes swept Bernadine's and she smoothly looked him off.

"I'll get your eggs and then I'll run Lily on over to Marie's. You need a ride anywhere, Ms. Brown?"

"No, but thanks for offering."

He nodded and stepped off the porch to retrieve the eggs. Returning, he gave the carton to his mother, then he and Lily said their good-byes.

As they drove away, Bernadine asked, "How old is your son?"

"Be sixty in October. Pretty handsome, isn't he?"

He was—extremely, with his dark good looks, graying hair and mustache, and mischief-filled eyes, but Bernadine wasn't going there, so she shrugged. "I suppose."

"Just remember what I said. Snake oil."

"I won't forget."

*   *   *

That night, in a small backwoods town on the Georgia-Alabama border, eight-year-old Devon Watkins took off his tie, then his suit, and hung them on the lone hanger in his tiny closet. He'd buried his grandmother today. She was the only family he'd ever known, and now he had no one else in the world related to him by blood. In spite of his grief, he felt good about the sermon he'd preached and the going-home service he'd led.

The future was cloudy though. With no relatives to claim him and no one in the poor rural community able to take him in, CPS would be coming for him in the morning. This would be his last night in the house he'd been born in. Being eight years old, he knew nothing about what would happen to his grandmother's land or how to access her Social Security benefits, nor did he even think about those things; all Devon knew was the Lord, and because he did, he said his prayers, crawled into bed, and put tomorrow in His hands.

For the next few days, Trent avoided Lily and Lily avoided Trent. Malachi doctored animals all over the county with Bernadine Brown on his mind while Riley sat in the Dog and Cow trying to figure out a way to get the town's sale reversed. For her part, Bernadine spent her time talking on Tamar's land line phone to the agencies in charge of the kids, checking in on the potential foster parents she'd chosen, and orchestrating efforts to bring Henry Adams into the twenty-first century.

The phone companies were not cooperative. They gave her a hundred and one reasons why they wouldn't replace the tower, all based on their bottom line. She understood that. Capitalism and the pursuit of profit had made her who she was, but there was still no high-tech anything in her town and she was determined to fix that.

In the end, it came down to lawyers. She sicced her legal beagles on the phone companies with a threat to file a class-action suit on behalf of small-town Americans everywhere if they didn't get it together. And since she was a *major* contributor to both the Democratic and Republican Parties, she threw a few senator friends into the mix. When they began making noises about hearings on the companies' discriminatory policies, all of a sudden the sellers of cellular and wireless services wanted to be her friends.

The Henry Adams residents monitored all of this with amazement. Riley kept telling anyone who'd listen that she'd never be successful and it didn't matter how much money she had, the phone companies weren't going to budge, but that evening as they gathered in chairs outside in the shade behind the church, for her first town meeting, he had to eat his words.

Bernadine looked around and said, "The phone company is going to replace the tower. It should be up and running by the weekend."

Applause rang out followed by whistles and cheers.

"And," she added, stretching out the word for emphasis, "Everybody who wants a cell phone will get one."

Gasps filled the air.

"It seems they want to do a research study on seniors' cell phone usage, or at least that's what they're calling it, so you'll be getting the first year of service free."

Eyes widened. Jaws dropped. Even Riley's.

In reality the company's offer was nothing more than a bribe to make Bernadine and her minions go away, but she didn't care. She'd gotten what she'd wanted and her residents would benefit as well.

That next evening while she and Tamar sat on the

porch watching the sunset, Tamar pointed out, "You've been pretty busy the past few days."

Bernadine had just finished yet another phone call. This one to a dealership. She needed wheels. Her double-wide trailer would be arriving in the next few days, or so the salesman had promised. "I know and I feel like a dead woman walking."

"Pace yourself, okay?"

"Yes, ma'am," Bernadine replied, even though she had no idea how she could in the face of the thousand and one things she needed to get done. She had the kids picked out and hoped to have them in town by the end of the week, providing the foster parents signed on. The foster agencies were so desperate for placements they'd bent all kinds of rules for her in order to make her dream a reality, but if she didn't have one parent for each child, there'd be no deal. That rule was in set in cement. The state also required that each child have his or her own bedroom, which meant she'd have to come up with some type of temporary housing by the time they arrived, because the contractors were nowhere near done with the construction of the new subdivision.

As if reading her mind, Tamar reached over and patted her on the knee. "Everything will work out. Don't worry."

Later, after night rolled in and Tamar took off to the solitude of her room, Bernadine sat on the porch and watched the stars come out. Because they had no big city lights to compete with, they shone like brilliant diamonds on a bed of black velvet. She had seen stars from five continents over her lifetime, and no matter where she was the beauty of them always made her go, "Wow . . ."

Like now. Maybe one day when things calmed down she could take a class in astronomy so she'd know the names of the star shimmering to the right of the moon and that big six-carat one glowing on the other side. She had to make sure all of the kids she recruited received telescopes. Filling them up with the wonders of the world had to be a good thing. She made a mental note to ask if anyone in the community was a sky watcher because the kids would need help.

Her reverie was broken by the sounds and sights of a truck pulling up to the house. Out of it stepped Malachi July. He left the engine running and the headlights lit the night.

"Tamar gone to bed?" he asked, looking up at her from where he stood on the bottom step.

"I think so." A look over her shoulder showed the lights out in the back of the house. "You'd know better about whether to wake her up or not."

"I'll talk to her in the morning. So how are things?"

"Just fine."

"Enjoying the night?"

"I am."

"Have dinner with me?"

Even though he was fine as the night itself, she said, "No."

"Because?"

"Because your mama says you're full of snake oil."

He dropped his head. Even he had to smile on that one. "Look—"

"No," she said softly, and she hoped kindly. "The only reason I'm here is to help this town. I know you have a reputation with the women, but I think a man in his sixties still trying to be a player is pitiful."

He stared and stammered. "Excuse me? I'll have you know there are twenty-year-olds who can't get enough of this funky stuff."

Unimpressed by him or his sampling of Kool & the Gang's lyrics, she stood and warned in a humorous voice. "You need to cut back on that Viagra. Good night, Mr. July."

"Hey, you're just going to walk away?"

"Yes, I am. Good night."

"You're a cold sister, Bernadine Brown."

Amused, she tossed back, "You ain't seen nothing yet," and went into the house, closing the door.

Malachi smiled and shook his head. He couldn't remember the last time he'd been so dismissed. By anyone's standards she was a fine woman and not one of those skinny model types usually associated with money. Ms. Bernadine Edwards Brown was a big girl, and he liked size on his women. Classy too, with her well-done hair and makeup and thin gold bracelets on her wrist. The fact that she claimed to be disinterested didn't matter. Big girls needed love just like everybody else, and so, brightened by the notion, he whistled as he got back into the truck and drove home.

He lived in the small apartment behind the Dog and Cow, and had since buying the place back in the eighties. The one-room efficiency was smaller than a gopher's hole, but he didn't need anything more than that.

The D&C was dark when he drove up. Usually the last person to leave for the night knew to turn off the coffee pot and the lights. He still hadn't had time to get a replacement for Rocky, what with him driving all over the county dealing with sick stock and the like. If Trent had married Rocky like he was supposed to, he wouldn't need a new cook.

As if on cue, Trent drove up, and Malachi got out of his truck and walked over to greet him. "Hey son."

Trent powered down his window. "Dad. What's up? Came by earlier and you weren't here."

"Checking on me?"

Their eyes met.

When Trent didn't respond. Malachi said, "I've been sober eight years, son."

"I know and we're all real proud, but—habit, I guess."

Malachi mulled that over for a minute. "I suppose I should be grateful anybody's looking after my ass."

"That too, so in the future how about I check on you just because you're my father and you're old?"

Malachi shot him a look. "Did you get Lily's car fixed?"

"Yeah. Called over to Marie's and told her she could pick it up in the morning. How'd your day go?" he asked changing the subject.

"I think I'm in love."

"What?"

"You heard me. I think I'm in love."

"You'd be in love with a Greyhound bus if it had on a halter top."

"I'm serious."

"So am I. Who is it this time?"

"Bernadine Brown."

Trent shook his head. "Dad, leave that lady alone. She's not here for that."

"That's what she said."

"Then problem solved."

"Called me pitiful."

Trent hid his laughter with a faked cough.

"Said she thought a sixty-year-old man calling himself a player was pitiful."

"You have to admit, she does have a point."

Malachi glared. "Told her I have pretty young things all over me when I go to Kansas City."

"That's because you lie to them about owning hotels in Las Vegas."

"Don't hate."

"So what did she say when you told her about these pretty young things in Kansas City?"

"Said I should cut back on my Viagra, like maybe it was making me crazy."

"Could be she's on to something."

"You laugh now but just wait. When your hammer stops being strong enough to break through the pearly gates, you'll be looking for little blue pills too."

Trent grinned. "I don't think I'm old enough to hear this, so tell you what . . . I'm going home. Just wanted to check on you. I'll see you tomorrow."

He turned the wheel and backed up only to have Malachi call out, "What're you going to do about Lily?"

Trent didn't stop as he yelled his response, "None of your damn business."

"Coward."

"That's my name, don't wear it out!"

Grinning, Malachi walked to the door and went inside.

At the garage the next morning, Trent cleared off a spot on his desk so he could put down the foil-wrapped plate holding his breakfast. The only thing he missed about living in LA was being able to drive up to a fast food joint and get fed. Here, because his father still hadn't found a replacement for Rocky, he had to either cook for himself in his small apartment up above the garage or go begging from people like his grandmother. Luckily for him she loved him and would feed him until the Second Coming. Beneath the foil lay waffles, grits, eggs, and four slices of Clayton Dobbs's prize-winning bacon. Trent wasn't as trim as he'd been twenty years ago, but what man was. He was still in good shape though and active enough to handle a hearty breakfast, especially one that came out of Tamar's kitchen.

Taking a seat he undid the foil and pulled out the silverware. Lily claimed she'd be coming by the garage early to pick up her rental car, but he hoped she'd hold off long enough for him to eat. He dug in and as he did his mind floated back to the woman he used to call *Lily Flower*. Last night Malachi had asked him what he planned to do. Truthfully, Trent didn't think there was anything to do. After their breakup, she'd gone on with her life and he'd done the same. Time passes, and it wasn't like they were going to pick up where they left off. Yes, she was still a good-looking woman, even pissed at her he'd noticed that, but she'd kicked him in the heart so hard he still had the bruises to prove it, and he wasn't looking to get sucker punched again. So, no . . . He'd be polite, hoped she'd enjoy herself while she was in town, and then she could take her trifling little behind back to Atlanta.

He heard a car pull up. Being the area's only mechanic, he knew the sound of every vehicle in town. Marie's old Pontiac was idling out front. She'd probably given Lily a ride over and his bad mood was all over his face when he turned around and found her standing in the doorway.

Her face was no happier than his. "Sorry for the interruption. How much do I owe you?"

"Nothing."

Irritation flashed in her eyes. "Right, Trent. How much?"

"Just take the car. Keys are inside."

"Fine. Thanks." She disappeared.

A few moments later, he heard the rental car's engine start up and the car drive away. Cursing teenage love, he went back to his plate.

Lily's jaws were tight as she drove the five miles back to Marie's. All she could think about was his angry face. Granted she'd hurt him, but good Lord, they were teenagers then. Would she have to pay for her sins every time she ran into him from now on? If so, it was going to be a long two weeks. *He's going to mess around and get cussed out*, the angry sister voice inside warned, but it was just like him to fix the car for free just to show her how generous he could be in the face of how badly she'd treated him. She slammed her fist against the wheel and set off the horn, scaring herself half to death.

Pulling it together, she stared at the road ahead. And

this was the reason she had dull old Winston in her life, at least for now. With him there was no drama—at all. Of course, there wasn't much of anything else either.

When she got back to the house, Marie had her keys in her hand. "I need to do some grocery shopping, you want to ride?"

Lily nodded. "Is Ms. Agnes going?"

"And miss Regis and then *The View*? Nope."

Agnes called from the living room. "You got that right. See you when you get back."

Minutes later they were on the way. Lily knew her godmother didn't like a whole lot of talking when she was driving, so while Marie drove, she contented herself with watching the wheat fields roll by.

For the first time in months felt relaxed. Unlike Atlanta, on the plains there was no stress causing traffic, no hip-hop bass rumbling from cars, no breaking news of man's inhumanity to man every time you turned around. She was enjoying the peace so much she was toying with the idea of extending her stay. Winston on the other hand hadn't been happy when she talked to him about it on the phone last night, but she had no intentions of letting him have the final say.

Something else was in the mix too. Bernadine Brown's plans for Henry Adams seemed to have infected everyone with its purpose and hope and Lily was no exception. Ms. Brown and her revival campaign were the topic of conversation all over town. Lily wanted to help too, and who wouldn't want to be in on something so exciting and so real? Bernadine not only wanted to revitalize the community, she wanted to impact lives; children's lives. She blew Lily away.

They passed a road sign noting the remaining distance to Hayes, and Lily cracked, "Do you think Bernadine can build us a mall so we don't have to drive to east west hell every time we need something?"

"I don't see why she can't. The woman's going to build everything else. She is something, isn't she?"

"Yes, she is."

"And the beautiful thing is that she's doing this out of the goodness of her heart. She's going to be blessed for the rest of her life for wanting to take care of a bunch of old people and children."

"I know."

Marie turned her cat's-eye framed gaze toward Lily, "You've been awfully pensive this morning. Something going on you want to talk about?"

"I'm thinking about staying an extra week or two."

"You know I'd love that."

"I would too, but—"

"But, what?"

"I feel like I'm going nowhere. Not professionally but personally and spiritually. Like I should be doing something different with my life." She thought back on all the angst she'd been dealing with for the past few months, how she felt about her Davis moving on with his life now that he'd graduated and had a real job, and about living the rest of her life with comfortable old Winston. In her heart of hearts she knew she didn't want to marry him, but finding the inner strength to chuck everything and go in a new direction was hard for a woman who liked the universe drama free and well ordered.

Still, she felt constricted, as if her life and the future were conspiring to choke her to death when all she wanted to do was breathe. "Can you stand having me around for another two weeks or so?"

"Sure, and if you want to stay for good, I can do that too."

"Quit reading my mind."

"Was I doing that? Sorry. It's an old fairy godmother habit."

They shared a grin, and afterward Marie said in a more serious tone, "If you are thinking about moving back, you and Trent are going to have to settle up."

"I know." Squaring things with him was one of the larger items on her to-do list, but at least she'd admitted out loud that she wanted to change her life. It was a first step and it would have to do for now. Like the old gospel hymn, she'd figure out the rest by and by.

CHAPTER
8

Bernadine was swamped with faxes, contracts, e-mails, and tons of all kinds of paperwork associated with the Henry Adams project. Now that her laptop and BlackBerry were back online again, info was coming so fast and furious she felt like Noah in the flood. It was scattered all over her small bedroom at Tamar's, and because of the volume she was having trouble putting her hands on what she needed when she needed it.

In truth, she would be the first one to admit that she didn't know a thing about managing something as big as this undertaking was going to be. Sure, she'd worked in offices during her social worker days, but she'd only been in charge of her small cubicle and her file cabinet. The daily logistical operations had been handled by somebody else, and it was that faceless somebody else that she needed.

Tamar appeared in the doorway and looked around. "Every day I come in here, you got more and more paper."

Guilt stung Bernadine. "I'm so sorry. You offer me a place to stay and I turn it into a landfill."

"That is a good description," Tamar offered while taking in the papers covering the old wing-back chair, the dresser top, the window seat, and the floor. "Not a good organizer, huh?"

"No, ma'am. To tell you the truth, I've never done anything like this before in my life. Pulling this all together is more than a notion."

"Simple solution. Since you have plenty of money, just hire somebody, save yourself the aggravation. We can't have you dropping dead from stress before we get the kids here and the first building up. Speaking of which, Trent just called and said the construction crews are downtown. He needs you there to sign something."

Bernadine sighed. She needed to clone herself into four or five individuals in order to keep up with all the plates she was juggling. "Okay. Let me grab my keys." Her new vehicle had arrived yesterday, a Ford F-150 pickup. A big truck for a big girl. Cobalt blue. Silver trim. Sweet.

When she got to the site, the first thing the construction crew chief did after introducing himself as Warren Kelly was to ask her, "Where's your architect?"

"Miami."

Kelly was middle-aged, with blue eyes, his tanned face leathery from years in the sun. "When's he or she coming?"

Bernadine shrugged. She knew she was going to sound clueless, but she told him the truth, "I didn't know he needed to be here. I hired him to do the blueprints. He did them. I paid him."

Kelly looked annoyed.

She got on the phone and talked with the secretary at the architectural firm and was told that the architect, Martin Baird was in Peru. "Peru?" He was working on the reconstruction of an ancient temple found recently by archaeologists. He'd be gone most of the summer. She closed the phone. "He's in Peru."

"Then who's going to oversee the project on your end? You?" he asked as if he knew that couldn't be the answer.

Trent surprised her by saying. "I have an engineering degree. I'll do it until you can hire somebody."

Bernadine was speechless. Why didn't she know this? It made her wonder how many other residents had hidden talents she knew nothing about.

Kelly asked skeptically, "You done construction before?"

"All over the world."

Smiling now, Kelly stuck out his hand. Trent did the same.

Glad the problem was solved, at least temporarily, Bernadine thanked Trent, signed a slew of papers, told him to call her so they could talk later, then climbed back into the truck she'd named Baby and drove back the way she'd come.

She'd been gone a little under an hour, and when she returned to Tamar's, Lily Fontaine was in Bernadine's bedroom sitting in the middle of the floor sorting paper. Caught off guard, Bernadine entered the room slowly. "Can I ask what you're doing?"

Lily looked up. "Tamar called and asked if I'd wade through some of this for you. I was an executive secretary back in Atlanta and she thought I could help. Hope that was okay?"

Bernadine wasn't sure.

Lily continued, "I didn't know how you wanted everything broken down, but in the pile on the dresser are all the financial papers I found. On the chair, things related to the subdivision, and here—"

Bernadine held up a hand. She looked around the room. In the relatively short time she'd been away, Lily had brought order where there'd been none. Papers were neatly stacked and labeled with sticky notes on the top of each pile. Talk about hidden talents. "How much do you make a year where you're working now?"

Lily was the one caught off guard now. She started to explain about the buyout and all but decided to just ask, "Why?"

"Because I want to hire you and I'll pay you thirty grand more than whatever you're making now." Bernadine firmly believed that God put certain people in your life for a reason and the Lord knew Bernadine needed help.

Lily smiled and shook her head.

"What's wrong?"

"Nothing. This morning, I was telling Marie that maybe I wanted to move back here."

"And?" Bernadine answered with a smile of her own.

"I guess I am."

"Wonderful." Bernadine wanted to shout *hallelujah!*
Bernadine guessed she should probably be asking for ref-
erences and other documentation, but she didn't feel the
need. It was as if an occult hand had dropped Lily in her
lap, and she wasn't about to look a gift horse in the mouth.
"Welcome aboard, Ms. Chief Operating Officer."

Lily stared.

"You think I'm playing? You get a title and all the benefits that will go with the job description just as soon as I
have the lawyers draw it up."

"Okay," Lily laughed.

"First thing I want you to do. I ordered a trailer to live
in. Find out when it's coming." Bernice read Lily the phone
number of the dealer stored in her BlackBerry. Lily found a
pen and wrote it down.

"Next. Get yourself a round-trip plane ticket to Atlanta
so you can get packed up and make arrangements to ship
your things back here."

"Shipping is expensive. How about I rent a U-Haul,
and—"

Bernadine interrupted, "How about you listen to your
Got Rocks boss?"

Lily chuckled, "Yes, ma'am."

"Thank you."

They spent the next few minutes firming up Lily's
move.

Bernadine confessed. "Lily, I have no idea how to set
this up. I'm going to be relying on you big-time for just
about everything office wise."

"That's okay. I've done it all from mail room to executive secretary. My bosses know that I'm detail oriented and meticulous."

"Good. Do you have a laptop?"

She nodded. "It's at Marie's. Wireless. Thanks to the new router, it's actually working."

"Then start ordering whatever you think we'll need to do an office from the ground up. Everything. If you can find some good deals that's okay, but nothing cheap. Here's a credit card."

Lily took the offered square of black plastic.

"Get furniture, printers, paper, desks. The works."

"No problem."

Bernadine thought for a few more minutes. "We're also going to need either trailers or modular homes for the foster parents and kids to live in until the new houses are done. The parents are supposed to be visiting the day after tomorrow and I'll be bringing in the kids by Friday, hopefully."

Lily stared. "So soon?"

"Yep. The sooner we get them here, the sooner they can start adjusting, but I've only got two couples and they're both shaky."

"How shaky?"

"To the point that I'm real worried, but we'll talk about that later. Go ahead and order the trailers, add one more because we're going to need an office until we can get one built."

"You want to lease them for now?"

She nodded. "See if we can have them for sixty days. Mr. Kelly says, weather willing, we should be in the houses and the new rec center by then."

"I hear they're working faster than beavers."

"Hope they build them as well as beavers."

"Anything else?" Lily asked, grinning on the heels of that last remark.

"Yes." And in a soft voice laden with sincerity, Bernadine said, "Thank you so very much for taking the job."

Lily acknowledged her with a quiet, "You're welcome."

They were about to further separate the piles of paperwork Lily had begun when they heard Tamar call out, "Bernadine and Lily we have visitors."

They shared a confused look and went to see who'd come to call.

There was a big black SUV parking out front. The logo on the side indicated it was from one of the cable news giants. Trent's black truck was parked beside it.

As they watched from the porch, two men, one carrying a TV camera, got out of the SUV.

"Wonder what they want?" Lily asked in a low voice.

"My guess is Bernadine."

Bernadine hoped she was wrong.

Trent walked up to the porch. The man beside him looked vaguely familiar to Bernadine, and after Trent made the introductions, she knew why. His name was Greer Parker, and he'd done the news story that had inspired her to buy Henry Adams.

"I contacted Trent a few days ago," Parker said, "and told him I was in the area working on a story down in Hays and wanted to talk to him about doing a follow-up on what happened after he posted the eBay notice, and he told me about you, Ms. Brown."

Bernadine wished somebody would have let a sister know. Not that she didn't look good, she always did, but she could've freshened her lips gloss and checked her hair.

Trent seemed to read her mind. "Been so busy I forgot to tell you, sorry."

"It's okay."

"Do you have a minute or two to talk to me?" Parker asked.

"Sure."

Tamar and the others went inside while Bernadine and Parker took a seat on the porch's old sofa. Once the camera man was set the interview began.

It didn't take long, but Parker was very interested in her foster care plan. "If I may, I'd like to come back after you get the kids here."

"Let me get them settled in first. I don't think a whole lot of hoopla will be good right off the bat."

"How about you call me when you think it's appropriate. Trent has my card."

"That I can do."

He seemed okay with the compromise. "Once this runs I think you're going to draw a lot of interest, maybe more foster parents or just new residents who want to live in a place with so much history."

"We'll take both. The more foster parents we get the more kids we can help."

"I'll do my part. This will probably begin running in the morning. Want me to send you a copy?"

"Please."

He stood. "Been nice talking to you, Ms. Brown."

"Same here."

"Can you let Trent know I'd like to see him a minute before I go?"

She stood to comply but stopped at the sight of a battered white pickup truck rumbling onto the property. She sighed. Riley.

Bernadine called through the screen door. "The Currys are here, Tamar."

Before she could get a response, Parker yelled with surprise, "What the heck is that?"

Bernadine turned and stared with wide eyes. Riley was walking toward the porch holding a leash on—a hog?

Tamar stepped out on the porch and answered drolly, "That, ladies and gentlemen is Cletus."

The cameraman turned, focused, and jumped in reaction.

Lily looked equally floored.

The animal was as big as a VW and it was wearing clothes. A blue and white sailor suit to be exact, complete with tie and a little tiny hat perched between his pale gray ears. His coloring made him resemble a gigantic rat.

As Riley got within hailing distance he called out, "Hello, Mr. Parker. I heard you were doing a story. My name is Riley Curry, former mayor of Henry Adams. That's my beautiful wife Genevieve sitting in the truck, and this," he gestured proudly, "is Cletus Curry."

"It has a last name?" Bernadine whispered amazed.

"You don't know the half of it."

Bernadine didn't know whether to laugh or be appalled. She had never seen anything so bizarre before in her life.

Lily cracked, "I'm scared that somebody made it clothes to wear."

Tamar groused, "Parker's going to think we're a bunch of country lunatics."

"Well, yeah." Bernadine replied in agreement.

Riley continued by declaring, "Cletus is the most intelligent hog in Kansas. As his agent I have an idea for a reality show that I know the networks will all be wanting."

Stunned, Bernadine looked at Tamar who replied, "I warned you." And added, "He's been trying to get that hog on TV for years."

Only then did Bernadine notice Trent's granite set face. She hoped Parker wasn't about to film a murder.

Apparently, Parker knew crazy when he saw it. "Nice meeting you, Mr. Curry." He turned to Trent. "I'll be in touch."

And before anyone could say another word, he and his cameraman were hurrying to their SUV. Seconds later they drove out to the road and disappeared in a cloud of dust.

If Riley was disappointed he didn't show it. Instead he shot everyone a snarling look before escorting Cletus back to the truck. Once the smartest hog in Kansas was secured in the bed, Riley and Genevieve drove away.

"Good lord," Bernadine whispered.

"You got that right," Tamar replied.

That night as Bernadine sat on the porch watching the moon rise and the stars come out, she finally relaxed from what had been a whirlwind day. She could still see that hog and wondered wildly, *Who puts clothes on a hog?* Apparently, the Currys. *Too bizarre.*

She turned her mind from that craziness to the ongoing construction. Everything was proceeding well. According to Tamar, Trent was more than qualified to handle the job of foreman. With his schooling and hands-on experience she felt he was wasting his talents in Henry Adams and was glad Bernadine had put him in charge, if only temporarily.

But Bernadine planned on appointing him permanently, whether he wanted the job or not. One, because she trusted him to do the right thing and two, she didn't know the first thing about hiring someone to replace him or what qualifications the person needed to have. She didn't know certifications, housing codes, or anything even remotely related, but with Trent driving, she could sit back and stay out of the way.

Hiring Lily would also lighten the load. Bernadine didn't know a thing about her either, but she had decided to just *trust*. If it didn't work out, she'd know soon enough.

The breeze picked up, temporarily blowing away the heat. Tamar's nineteenth-century home had no AC, so for the first time since leaving her parents' home, Bernadine was forced to endure summer the way God had intended— without air-conditioning. It was killing her, but rather than whine and complain like she wanted to, she just dealt with it. Her trailer was supposed to arrive soon, Lord willing and the creek didn't rise, and even if she had to buy a generator big as a 747, that sucker was going to have air.

All in all though, she was surviving. The stars were shining. The moon came up again tonight. *God is good*, she thought to herself. Smiling like a woman with many blessings, she stood and went inside.

It was pouring rain in Dallas, and Yvette Carr was driving home after a long, tiring day. Between darkness and the rain, visibility was bad. When she saw what looked to be a woman hitchhiking up ahead she stopped, powered down the passenger-side window, and yelled over the elements, "Get in!"

The woman yanked open the door and slid into the seat. Yvette took one look at the young but heavily made-up face and knew this was somebody's child. The girl settled in, Yvette raised the window, hit the locks, and eased back out into the traffic. "Where you going?" she asked.

"New Orleans."

"In this weather?"

The girl looked out of the window. "Sometimes a woman's gotta do what a woman's gotta do."

"Your family know where you are?"

"Oh yeah," she said dismissively. "They sent me bus fare, but some crackhead jumped me a little while ago and took my purse."

"I see." But Yvette saw much more. Her trained eye said the girl was fourteen, fifteen tops.

"Mind if I take off this wet jacket?"

"No. How about I turn on some heat too."

"That'd be great," she replied, running her hands up and down her thin shivering arms. She had tattoos on both biceps, but because of the gloom, Yvette couldn't make out what they were.

"My name is Yvette, by the way."

"I'm Crystal."

"Glad to meet you, Crystal."

"Same here."

"Pretty dangerous hitchhiking at night."

"I know, but I only get in a car if a woman's driving. I ain't crazy."

"That's smart."

The girl looked around. "You got a nice car. I like this."

"Thanks."

"What do you do?"

Yvette turned into a parking lot and parked by the door. "I'm a social worker, honey, and I specialize in runaways."

The girl's eyes widened, then when she realized they were parked in front of a police precinct, panic filled her face and she grabbed frantically at the door, but Yvette had put the locks on lockdown the moment Crystal entered the car.

"Bitch! Let me out!"

When the door didn't budge she turned to swing on Yvette, but the determined Yvette grabbed her thin wrist and held it tight. Her tone was even. "Crystal, look at me and look at you." Yvette out-weighed the teenager by a good 100 pounds. "If this gets physical I could whip your ass all over this parking lot, but that's not me. You're a runaway and somebody somewhere is worried about you, so let's go inside and take care of this."

The girl's mutinous face didn't change as she snatched her arm away and sulked in the seat.

"And sweetheart, if it turns out that you do have family in New Orleans, I will drive you there personally, free of charge. Okay?"

"Just open the damn door! Bitch!"

Yvette undid the lock on the driver-side door. "Come out this way." She didn't want to have to chase her if she took off.

The furious Crystal scooted across the seat and joined Yvette in the rain.

Yvette used her clicker to reset the lock and escorted the girl inside.

CHAPTER
9

Trent stopped by Tamar's to see Bernadine. She and Lily were outside on the porch going over paperwork when he arrived. Tamar was off somewhere tearing up the roads with her buddy Agnes.

"Morning, Bernadine." He gave Lily a quick look. "Lily."

Bernadine noted Lily's frostiness but she kept her attention focused on Trent, who seemed to be doing his best not to focus on Lily. She sighed. "What's up?"

"Brought you the blueprint changes for the rec center."

"Okay, thanks. I'll drive out in a little while and you can tell me what I'm looking at."

He nodded. "Have you found a construction boss?"

"Nope. Stopped looking."

"Why?"

"Because I already have one. Why in the world would I pay some stranger good money when I can pay you?"

"But I don't want the job."

"I know, but your grandmother said hire you anyway, so I did."

"I don't want the job," he repeated, taking off his shades.

"Too busy over at the garage?" she asked innocently.

He couldn't lie and say he was and they both knew it. There weren't enough vehicles in the area to make the place viable, and the only thing he was really doing over there was restoring old cars and trucks.

"Trent, you're a July," she told him. "Your family has lived in this place for generations. Who do you think your great-great-grandmother Olivia would want to be in charge of rebuilding her town, a family member or a stranger?"

"That's pretty low, Bernadine," he replied, unable to hold back his smile.

"Tamar called it the guilt card. Told me to play it if I needed to."

"You'd think such an old lady wouldn't fight so dirty."

Bernadine waited.

"Okay. You're right, but I don't want a salary. I've plenty coming in from my patent royalties."

"On what?"

"Made improvements to some machinery while I was interning at college. The company I was working for helped me get them patented."

Bernadine was impressed with him all over again. If Lily didn't hurry up and get it together, she just might make a play for him herself. Not really, but what was a gorgeous, talented man like him doing working on old cars in the middle of nowhere? More mysteries, she said to herself before turning her mind back to the conversation. "Okay, but I have to pay you something, so if you want to stash it in the bank or give it to charity, fine."

She turned to Lily, "Would you please do whatever we need to do to get him on the payroll?"

She nodded.

"Now that that's settled, I think I'm ready to go check out my town. See how things are going. Lily, you ready to ride?"

"Whenever you are."

"Trent, meet you there?"

"Yes, ma'am." He stepped off the porch.

Bernadine called to him, "Trent?"

He looked back.

"Thank you."

He touched his straw hat respectfully and was gone. Bernadine saw Lily watching him drive away. Her questions about them rose again, but she kept them to herself. "Are you two going to be able to work together?"

"Sense the tension, do you?" Lily asked.

"A little bit, yeah."

"We've got issues, but I can work with anybody. Even him."

Bernadine noted the determination in Lily's gaze. "Okay then, but you're my right hand and he's my left. Can't have the hands fighting."

"I understand."

Lily proved it when she sought Trent out at the garage later that evening. "Here's the payroll paperwork. I need to you to fill it out and get it back to me soon as you can."

He took the papers from her hand. "Sure."

An awkward silence followed and Lily wondered how to convince him to take down the wall between them. "Do you ever hear from any of the old crew? Kenny? Sherman?"

"Every now and then. Sherman's in San Diego. Kenny's in Topeka."

"Be nice to see them again."

"Yeah. I'll bring this back in the morning. Anything else?"

His dismissive tone stung. "No. I'll see you later."

He went back inside without saying another word.

Lily climbed into Marie's old Pontiac and drove off.

Bernadine had no idea how Lily had done it, but by noon the next day, the brand-new double-wide trailer homes the families would be using arrived. Trent and construction-boss Kelly pulled all the crews off the various work sites to help with the installation. The locals helped too. Bing Shepard, a certified plumber, worked with the hookup of the water lines. Tamar and her friends rode over to Hays armed with Bernadine's credit cards and purchased everything from beds to food to new appliances.

Bernadine knew the foster parents would probably have furniture of their own, but until they could ship their own things, they'd at least have decently furnished places to live. If they all agreed to become a part of her plans.

She talked about the dilemma later that evening at the D&C over dinner with Tamar, Lily, and the rest of what she now called her main crew. Clay Dobbs was the designated chef that evening, and as Bernadine tasted his roasted chicken, she didn't understand why Malachi, who was sitting right across from her at one of the tables, hadn't already hired Clay to replace his former employee, Rocky, because the man could cook!

Agnes asked, "So what's going on with the foster parents?"

Bernadine shook her head. "The two couples e-mailed me earlier. They've changed their minds."

"Oh no," Marie said. Bernadine felt the same way; their backing out was a blow to her plans and her heart. "So unless I can find replacements soon, I'll have to delay everything. I have my people doing background checks on a few other couples, but I'm not holding my breath."

Tamar and the others looked as sad as Bernadine felt. Three of the applicants in the new batch of foster parents had been dismissed out of hand. One was a registered sex offender, another had been convicted of welfare fraud, and the third was in the country illegally.

Lily added, "But what about the two who e-mailed you last night?"

As a result of Parkers' news story, two new couples had expressed an interest. "One's very surprising—a Mr. and Mrs. Reginald Garland. You may know Mrs. Garland as Roni Moore."

Malachi's jaw dropped as did Clay's. "Roni Moore?" they asked in unison. "The singer?"

"Yep."

Tamar appeared confused: "Why in the world would somebody that famous want to work with foster kids in nowhere Kansas?"

"I've no idea." Bernadine couldn't answer, but like most lovers of great R&B music, she knew all about superstar vocalist Roni Moore.

"She hasn't performed in years," Marie said. "And after that terrible shooting who can blame her?"

Malachi nodded, adding seriously, "Having a crazy man gun down your back-up singers onstage during a concert would have sent me into seclusion too. I didn't think she was going to step back forever, though."

"Me either," Lily said, "Loved her voice."

Bernadine had as well, along with millions of fans worldwide. "When she e-mailed me, I thought maybe she'd fostered or adopted before, but my people couldn't find anything in the public record, and believe me, they looked."

Marie said, "I don't remember anything about her being married though."

Clay said, "Seems like I read about that in *Jet* magazine. Husband was one of the doctors who took care of her after the shooting."

Bernadine wasn't sure what to make of the Garlands' desire to be foster parents, but she hoped their commitment was real.

Bing asked, "So what about the other couple? Who are they?"

"The Paynes. He's a career marine. Retired."

Malachi shrugged. "Might be a nice addition. Some of those military types are crazy, though."

"Yeah," Clay added. "We already have Riley. We don't need any more escapees from the asylum."

Bernadine smiled. "He and his wife have no children,

and they've been stationed all over the world. The background check didn't find anything scary in their backgrounds. Having a marine in the mix might help with the discipline the kids'll probably need."

Trent walked in. He'd been dealing with the electric company hooking into the power grid, and they'd just finished. "What did I miss?"

"Go get a plate first and we'll catch you up," his grandmother said.

When he returned from the kitchen he took a seat in the booth next to his father. Bernadine gave him a thumbnail sketch of what they'd been discussing and then said, "Now, the kids."

She was worried about this portion of the meeting. On paper a couple of the children looked problematic. She looked down at her notes. "Up first, Amari Steele—aka Flash."

"Why Flash?" Bing asked.

"Apparently because he steals cars really, really fast."

"What?" they all shouted.

"Am I stuttering?" she asked amused, "The child is a car thief named Steele, of all things. Busted five times in the last six months."

"How old is he?" Tamar asked.

She looked up from the sheet. "Eleven."

"You're kidding?" Agnes said.

"Nope. Our first candidate is a convicted carjacker. I expect you all want to spit me like a chicken after hearing this."

The elders simply shook their heads.

"Who's next?" Malachi asked.

She read silently for a moment. "Zoey Raymond. Seven. Doesn't speak."

"Doesn't speak as in mute?" Marie asked, her confused face accented by her black cat's-eye glasses.

"No. Says here, physically fine, but doesn't speak. Suffered some type of trauma. Mother was a crack addict. Father unknown."

"That's sad." Bernadine agreed and went on to the three other kids the agencies wanted to place. "We have next, Preston Mays. Twelve. Eight foster homes in the past year." She found that shocking. More than a placement every two months. The sadness in that fact tugged at her heart. "Asthmatic. Tests in the upper second percentile of his class at school."

"A smart young man," Tamar said, impressed.

"Known to be a fire starter."

"Get out!" Clay exclaimed.

Dismay flashed on every face in the place.

"Next, Crystal Chambers. Fourteen."

"Her issues?"

"Chronic runaway." She shook her head. "The social workers aren't making this easy for us, are they?"

"No, they aren't," Agnes replied as if miffed. "Who's the last one?"

"Devon Walker. Eight years old. Been in the system less than two months. Grandmother raising him died of cancer. No other known relatives."

"Poor baby. If his grandmother loved him, he's probably still hurting."

"Yep. Says here he's an ordained deacon."

Malachi cracked, "Does that mean we'll all have to go to church on a regular basis?"

"Hush," his mother told him.

Lily said, "An eight-year-old deacon, a carjacker, and a runaway. That's quite a mix we have here. You sure you still want to do this?" Lily asked.

Bernadine knew that if she could walk into Leo's office and find him screwing his secretary on top of his desk and not have a heart attack or kill them both—she had this! "Yes," she said to Lily. "Yes, I do."

Lily raised her glass of sweet tea. "Then I'm with you."

Glasses all over the room went up and tears stung Bernadine's eyes. Even though none of the children could be viewed as normal, these wonderful people were pledging to jump into the deep end of the pool right along with her.

"We're all in this together," Marie said as if reading her mind. "The ancestors demand it, carjackers or not."

Her heart full, Bernadine looked around the faces in the D&C. A month ago, she hadn't known any of them. God is good.

Trent brought the discussion back by asking, "You have five children and potentially only two families. What will happen to the other three kids?"

Bernadine shrugged. "Since I've always wanted a child, I'm going to take one."

She saw the speculative interest on Malachi's face but continued, "Not sure about the rest. I'm supposed to be picking them up on Friday, and not having enough parents makes me have to choose from two bad choices. I either fly all five kids out here and disappoint some of them when I say they have no families, or call them now and disappoint them and say, they have no families."

Bing said quietly, "The older ones have probably been through that a lot."

"I know."

Lily tried to lighten the air by saying, "You could leave the fire starter and the carjacker off the list and I'd be fine."

"But would they, is the question?" Trent asked her coolly.

Lily shot him a hot look. "I was just kidding, Trent. Goodness."

For a moment there was silence as they eyed each other, and again Bernadine wondered what was up with the two of them.

"So, what are the alternatives?" Malachi asked. "Could we take them all and maybe double them up or have them stay with Tamar or Ms. Agnes temporarily until we find more parents?"

"State regs say they can't be doubled up unless they are siblings. And sadly, Tamar and Agnes wouldn't be approved because of their—wisdom."

Tamar smiled. "I like her."

Agnes grinned. "I like her more."

"If push came to shove, I could take the little preacher, temporarily," Lily offered. "Give the carjacker to Trent. Maybe he could show the boy how to fix cars instead of stealing them."

The room went silent.

Trent eyed Lily again. "Sure. I'll take him."

Jaws dropped.

Bernadine stared. "You're kidding, right?"

He swung his gaze her way. "Nope. I'm dead serious. What do you think, Tamar? You want a great-grandson?"

She studied him and shrugged, "If you want to take him, I suppose I can support you, but if he steals Olivia, he'll never steal anything again. Bet you that."

Grins showed on everyone's faces.

Trent looked to his father next: "Dad? You up to helping me raise a carjacker?"

Malachi's answering shrug mirrored Tamar's. "Why not? This town could use some excitement. Besides, how many cars can the little brother steal way out here? I say we take him."

Bernadine was stunned. "Trent, are you sure?"

"Nope, but the boy needs a home."

"This will be a commitment for the long haul."

"I know."

The seriousness of his tone was mirrored in the eyes now holding hers. "Okay. I'll get you and Lily paperwork and see if we can't push it through quickly. I guess we now have our five parents."

Applause sounded.

Tamar added. "I've always believed the Spirit puts people in our lives for a reason. I'm not sure if that applies to eleven-year-old carjackers, but we'll work with what the Spirit sends."

"Amen," they said in unison, and began to discuss what needed to be done next.

*   *   *

Dr. Reginald Garland studied his wife, Roni, as she looked out the window of their Upper West Side apartment, and finally asked her quietly, "So why do you want to do this?"

"Because you've always wanted children."

He held her eyes. He had wanted kids, a long time ago. "This shouldn't be about me. We're a team, remember?"

She turned away and focused her attention back on the twinkling lights of Manhattan at night. "We are a team, and I'm grateful for you every day. If you hadn't been on rotation in the ER that awful night of the shooting, I never would've made it. But you're a pediatrician for a reason and I know all this solitude has to be hard on you."

He nodded as much to himself as to her. "It is, but I love you. Goes with the territory."

He smiled. She did too before saying softly, "I just think it's time for me to do something else. Time to move on. Deep down inside, I've always wanted kids too. Couldn't see where to fit them in back then, but now, I'm ready."

She turned to him knowing he could see through her, but it was okay.

He walked over, fit himself against her back, and wrapped his arms loosely around her waist. "Roni, your life is on the stage."

"Not any more."

"You're running away again."

"I know," she replied, gazing up at him. "But you love me, and I love you, so let's go to Kansas."

*   *   *

Sheila Payne had spent the day packing the suitcases that would be needed and mentally preparing her counters to her husband's arguments because she knew he'd have many. No way he'd want to move to Kansas and open his heart to a needy child, but she had her mind made up. So at dinner that evening, she announced, "I've decided where we're going to live."

The newspaper he habitually read during meals was raised like a shield between them. In response to her declaration it didn't move, but he asked from behind it, in an almost disinterested way, "Where?"

"Kansas. Graham County to be exact."

The paper came down. "Where?"

"Graham County, Kansas. We're going to be foster parents."

He snapped the paper back up. "We're not moving to Kansas, Sheila."

"Yes, we are, Barrett. I've already talked to the lady in charge. She's asked us to fly out tomorrow so she can meet us."

"Tomorrow? No. We are not."

"Barrett Montgomery Payne, you promised me that when you retired I could pick the place where we'd live, and I pick Graham County, Kansas."

"That's ridiculous."

"Are you saying your promise was a lie?"

Silence.

A long beat later the paper lowered. They'd been married twenty-five years, and during each of those years she'd packed up and followed him all over the world. Not once had she complained or demanded he give her permanence or a real home. He held the stern brown eyes of his lady and saw the face of the woman who'd deferred to him on every decision, while she played second fiddle to his love for country and the Marine Corps. "No, the promise was not a lie, baby, but this doesn't make sense."

He hadn't called her baby in years.

"It doesn't matter. This is what I want, Barrett. Me. For us."

The paper went back up. "Let me know what I need to do then."

"Thank you."

"You're welcome."

CHAPTER

10

Because of the chasm between them, Trent didn't like being around Lily on a day-to-day basis, but they both worked for Bernadine and it couldn't be helped.

"For heaven's sake, can you smile?" Lily asked from behind the video cam. In addition to her other duties she'd been appointed videographer for the project. Bernadine thought it might be nice to videotape the before and after of the construction.

Trent didn't smile. "I have work to do here, Lily."

"Yeah, yeah," she replied filming him and the crews putting up drywall at the new rec center.

"Go away."

"You're not the boss of me, Mr. Billy Goat Gruff."

The words were out of her mouth before she realized what she'd said, and they both froze. The workers looked on curiously, they too had sensed the tension between Ms. Bernadine's two trusted employees from day one, but what they didn't know was that Mr. Billy Goat Gruff was what

Lily used to teasingly call Trent back in the day when he was being a grump.

For Trent her words brought back all kinds of memories, none of which he wanted to deal with, so he asked her, "Are you done now?"

Caught off guard by how easily the phrase had slipped from her lips and the memories that flooded her as well, she studied him for a moment. His eyes were so hard and distant, she nodded and walked away.

He watched her go, torn between calling her back and cussing himself out for wanting to do so. The men in his crew watched him curiously. He looked them off, saying "Let's get back to work."

For the rest of the morning, Trent was plagued by two issues: memories of Lily Fontaine, and whether he'd made the right decision agreeing to take on a foster son. On the one hand he'd always wanted to be a father, but on the other hand a voice inside wanted to know if he'd lost his mind? Trent was forty years old, and if this Amari was only eleven, Trent was looking at a good ten years of hands-on child rearing. He still wasn't sure why he'd volunteered. At first, he thought it grew out wanting to get back at Lily for that crack, but it was deeper than that. For one, agreeing to raise the boy felt right. The kid obviously needed a real home, and he and his family could give him that, but on the other hand who could resist Bernadine and her dream? She'd infected everyone with a boundless purpose that hit you in the heart and refused to let go. And it wasn't as if he'd been doing much with his life up to that point, so why not step up? Before her arrival, he'd been content to get up every morning, go to the garage, tinker with his old cars, then eat and head to bed at the end of the day. He'd been simply existing; but now he could feel the man inside stirring again, like a hermit coming out of his cave stepping into the light, and it didn't feel too bad.

So he made his peace with being a foster parent, and with half the town to help, how bad could it be? He'd figure out what to do about Lily when he got around to it.

The following morning, Bernadine sent a car service to the airport to fetch the Garlands and Paynes, and while waiting for them to arrive she couldn't believe how nervous she'd become. Add to the fact that she was going to be in the same room with one of her favorite singers, and you had Bernadine Brown, aka Verging on Basket Case. She drew in a deep breath and reminded herself that she'd met presidents and numerous heads of state, and the last thing she needed was to lose sight of why these people were coming. It had nothing to do with fame and being starstruck, but everything to do with the kids in need of fostering.

"They're here," Lily announced, standing in the doorway of Bernadine's trailer looking out as the big black car pulled up. "You ready?"

"Ready as I'll ever be."

"Then let's do this."

Outside, Bernadine greeted each of her guests warmly but professionally. "I'm Bernadine Brown and this is my assistant, Lily Fontaine. Welcome to Kansas."

The statuesque Roni Moore, whose curves and build were reminiscent of Jill Scott's, was dressed in nice pair of jeans, a summer sweater, and hikers. "Been looking forward to meeting you. Thanks for the invite."

Her husband stepped up to shake Bernadine's hand. As he introduced himself, he was so not what she'd been expecting. Medium height. Nerdish. Black-framed glasses with lenses thick as the proverbial Coke bottle, but his smile was warm and his handshake firm but gentle. She liked him instantly.

Sheila Payne, dressed in a simple white tee and brown twill pants, stood in casual contrast to her tall marine husband, in his crisp green uniform positioned by her side like a redwood.

"Thanks for flying us in," she said warmly. "I've been waiting to meet you too."

Her brown-skinned husband stuck out his hand. "Colonel Barrett Montgomery Payne. United States Marine Corps. Retired. Pleasure to meet you."

Bernadine kept her face neutral and returned the handshake. "Same here."

He gave her a curt nod.

"Well," she said a bit overwhelmed. "How about we go inside and get out of this heat?"

As the visitors headed up the steps and into the trailer, Bernadine gave Lily a look. Lily returned it, but neither of them said a word.

Inside the cool confines of Bernadine's well-appointed trailer, she gestured for everyone to take a seat in her living room. The singer and her doctor chose the sleek, comfortable gold-patterned couch while the Marine Corps chose the matching loveseat on the other side of the African carved coffee table. The living room was done in soft earth tones. The artwork gracing the walls were pieces she'd picked up on her worldwide travels.

Roni looked around at the room. "You know, this is gorgeous. Whoever thought a trailer could be this fabulous or this big. Wow."

Bernadine came in carrying a pitcher of cold lemonade and glasses on a tray. "Glad you like it."

"I may have to get me one of these," she said, looking around at the beautiful lamps and the African sculptures expertly showcased on a large black bookcase across the room.

When the others smiled, she added, "No joke."

Bernadine set the tray on the coffee table and began to pour. "How about I give you a tour later?"

"I'd love that."

Lily brought in a large crystal bowl filled with Ms. Agnes's prize-winning chicken salad, then returned to the kitchen to grab the tray of fancy crackers, some plates, napkins, and the rest. As she set everything down she said, "Not sure if you've eaten, so help yourselves if you'd like. We'll feed you real food this evening."

"This is fine," Sheila said, reaching for one of Bernadine's gold-rimmed salad plates and helping herself to the fixings.

After everyone had a plate and was settled in, the lighthearted small talk drifted back and forth over neutral topics like hometowns, colleges they'd attended, and siblings. Roni and Reggie had two brothers each and were the eldest in their families. Colonel Payne and Sheila were only children.

"We're both military brats," Sheila pointed out glancing over at her husband. "He grew up in the corps and I grew up in the navy."

"Lived all over the world," Payne added.

Bernadine had expected him to be standoffish and cool, but he seemed pretty regular.

Reggie said to Payne, "The kids would probably enjoy hearing about your traveling. Don't you think, Ms. Brown?"

"Please, call me, Bernadine. And yes, most of them have probably had little contact with people who've seen other countries. Be a great way to teach a little geography too."

Roni asked, "Do you have the kids picked out?"

"I do, but we'll talk about that later. After we eat, I want to show you around so you can get a taste of what you'll be getting yourselves into if you decide to sign on." It would also give her a chance to check them out; see how they interacted with each other, get a feel for anything that might throw up a red flag. Just because she only had two couples didn't mean she was going to give them an automatic pass in order to expedite the process. This was going to be serious business, and she needed them to be serious people.

So after lunch they all piled into Baby, and Bernadine drove to town. On the way, Colonel Payne said, "I've never seen the plains of Kansas. Got its own kind of beauty."

"I agree," Bernadine replied, surprised by his sentiment. "Roads are rough though."

"No kidding," Reggie said as they bucked and lurched over a particularly large rut.

"People keep telling me I'll get used to it," Bernadine said, bouncing around in the driver's seat, "but so far, not yet."

Bernadine took them on a tour of the old Henry Adams, then showed them the trailers, which were duplicates of her own. They seemed impressed by both stops.

They then went to the site where the homes were being built. The first five homes going up were now wrapped in Tyvek and actually looked like houses instead of a field of beams. The workers were buzzing over the site, doing their thing, but the noise of the construction was pretty much muted inside of the truck by the raised windows. Bernadine stopped but kept the engine running. "These first five homes will be finished in another three weeks or so."

Roni looked out the window at the open spaces surrounding the homes. "There is absolutely nothing else out here."

Bernadine chuckled. "I know, but it doesn't take long for the feel of the land to grow on you. Real peaceful, I'm finding."

Lily added, "When I was growing up here, I hated all this nothing, but after living in Atlanta, I'm loving it. As you get older, things change, I guess."

"Just the houses being built first?" Payne asked.

"No. We're putting up a rec center for the community just up the road. Give us all a place to meet. Have meetings, hang out."

Lily added, "Especially in the winter. The seniors can get pretty isolated."

Reggie asked, "What about health care? Is there a doctor here?"

"No. Right now, people go to a clinic over in Franklin, about fifteen miles away. If it's really serious, they have to drive down to the big hospital in Hays."

"You know I'm a pediatrician."

"I do."

He asked, "So are you planning on having some kind of clinic here for the children?"

"Soon as I can find a doctor willing to take the job. Lily and I have put out some feelers."

He nodded as if the answer pleased him.

In the mirror, Bernadine saw his wife give him a small smile, which he returned.

Bernadine said, "I know you're all cramped up back there. How about we get out and stretch our legs?"

Payne grumbled, "Thought you'd never ask."

Now they could hear the noise. She spied Trent in his hard hat looking over a blueprint with construction-boss Kelly. When he saw her, he handed the blueprint over to Kelly and came over to where she and the others stood.

Introductions were made, and they all shook his hand.

"Trent's the town mayor," Bernadine told the guests. "His family's lived here for generations. In fact, his great-great-grandmother was mayor in her day."

"A lady mayor?" Sheila asked curiously.

"Yep," Trent replied, "but we were also outlaws in those days, so don't let that fool you."

"Outlaws?" Payne asked.

Trent nodded. "When you meet my grandmother, have her bring out her pictures. She loves showing them off."

"I'll do that. My great-great-grandfather was a deputy marshal back in those days. Wonder if he arrested your ancestors. That would be something, wouldn't it?"

Trent studied him. "Where was he marshal?"

"Indian Territory. Town called Wewoka."

Trent went still. "What was his name?"

"Deputy Marshal Dixon Wildhorse."

Trent looked Payne up and down, then smiled and stuck out his hand again. With real warmth in his voice, he said, "Welcome home, my brother."

Payne looked confused, and so did everyone else. He shook Trent's hand warily. "What do you mean, 'welcome home'?"

"Your great–great-granddaddy and mine were good friends. So good that back in the day they fought on the same side during a shoot-out at the saloon here in town called the Liberian Lady. In fact," Trent was just grinning. "wait until Tamar finds out. Dix's descendant. She is going to have a fit. Man! It's great to meet you."

Payne still looked confused. "Are you saying Wildhorse was here? In Henry Adams?"

"Yep. More than a few times. Plus we share heritage."

Payne stared back blankly.

"Black Seminole," Trent said.

"Black Seminole?"

"You didn't know Marshal Wildhorse was Seminole?"

"No."

Roni whispered in an awed voice, "This is amazing."

Bernadine was riveted. She'd never seen Trent so animated.

"Let me get my truck," he said, excitement in his eyes. "Bernadine, we have to go see Tamar. I know you probably had other stuff planned but I—"

She held up a hand. "No, we can go. She was on my list anyway. That old saying about it being a small world for Black folks?"

"Amen," Lily chimed.

Payne still looked doubtful. "Are you sure?" he asked Trent again.

"Sure as my name is July and Tamar's got pictures to prove it. Meet you all there." He took off at a run to get his vehicle, leaving Bernadine and the others to stare after him in wonder. "Guess we're going to Tamar's."

The stunned Payne said, "Guess so." He looked down at his wife, who smiled up and said softly, "Told you this is where we're supposed to be."

What could he say?

Sure enough, Tamar came out to the porch with a battered old album that was lovingly wrapped inside of a pillowcase. Everyone looked on eagerly as she opened it. Colonel Payne was seated next to her on the sofa. She told him. "The folks in Nicodemus had a newspaper called the *Cyclone*, and the photographer took pictures everywhere. Some of these are from the paper and some from pictures he took of folks who lived around this way." She turned past sepia-colored photos and tintypes. When she got to the page she was looking for, she pointed her aged finger at one of the men in the photograph. "This is Deputy Marshal Wildhorse. His wife, Katherine, was a pioneering newspaper lady, but I don't have any pictures of her."

Payne peered down at the faded picture of a dark-skinned man wearing a double-breasted shirt and dusty-looking denims. He was posed with a long rifle in his hand. The star on his shirt was prominently displayed. "Wow," he whispered, awed.

"Yep. And that there is my grandfather, outlaw Neil July," she said, pointing to each person in turn. "Next to him, outlaw Griffin Blake. That man there is Griff's brother Jackson. He was a sheriff down in Texas. That's my great uncle Two Shafts. He was part Comanche, and that's my great aunt Teresa."

"She's dressed like an outlaw too!" Sheila exclaimed with surprise. She was seated on the other side of Tamar.

"That's because she was an outlaw too."

Sheila's mouth dropped.

Roni and Reggie edged closer to get a better look.

Bernadine had seen the pics before and took great pleasure in the wonder on the faces of the visitors. She was also pleased to see somebody else blown away by the history of the town and its residents.

Payne asked, "When was this taken?"

"Date on the back says 1889. This was after the big shoot-out over at the Liberian Lady."

Payne couldn't take his eyes away from his tall, stately looking ancestor. "And he was Seminole?"

"Yep," Tamar responded. "And proud to be. Was appointed marshal by Hanging Judge Isaac Parker."

"How do you know all this?"

"Because I'm the July griot. The keeper of the lore. You know what that means?"

He nodded.

"Once upon a time we all had griots in our families. I learned from my great-aunt Teresa starting when I was a little girl. She learned from her mother, the first Tamar, who learned from her mother. Now, most of the family griots are gone, which is why some parts of the race are in such terrible turmoil. They've forgotten."

They all thought about that for a moment, and Bernadine decided Tamar was right. Personally, Bernadine knew her grandparents had come north from Kentucky during the early part of the twentieth century but knew nothing about her great-grandparents at all. Her family had forgotten too.

Payne shook his head. "This is amazing."

Trent says, "So that makes you Seminole too, Colonel."

"I see."

Tamar said, "One day when you have the time, come back by and I'll tell you the whole story—from the Three Seminole Wars to the Great Walk."

"The Great Walk?"

"Yep."

"You mean the Trail of Tears?"

"No. That was the Cherokee. The Seminoles walked from Indian Territory to the Mexican border trying to get away from the slave catchers and the Creeks."

When he just stared, she smiled and patted him on the arm. "It's okay. We have plenty of time for all this later, but on behalf of the July family, welcome. Welcome to all of you."

It was apparent Payne wanted to know more, but he didn't ask anything else.

Bernadine was amazed by his soldier's discipline. Had it been her, she would have asked so many questions Tamar would have had to have her bodily removed. Bernadine also wondered how this startling revelation might factor into the Paynes' decision to become foster parents.

Trent was leaning against the porch rail, still pleased by the surprising discovery. Who would have ever imagined that the lines of Wildhorse and July would cross paths again more than a century later? Deputy Marshal Wildhorse had been very respected in his day according to all the stories he'd heard. He glanced over Lily's way and found her watching him. For a long moment, their eyes held. Time seemed to stand still. He studied the familiar lines of her face and thought back on all they'd shared and dreamed about. He looked away.

Tamar asked Bernadine, "You want me to start rounding up everybody for the video?"

"Would you, please? Then we'll have dinner."

Tamar nodded at the Paynes and Garlands. "I'll see you all in minute." She eased the photo album back into its protective pillowcase, and Bernadine led everyone else to her place.

Soon after the locals and the newcomers found seats, she popped in a DVD prepared by the state's adoptive agencies. It featured testimonies from both foster and adoptive parents on the kids they'd agreed to take into their lives.

Some were success stories, like the one told by a single mother in Oklahoma who'd adopted four toddler siblings. They'd grown up and were all college graduates. Others told of the heartache of raising children who in spite of being given love and stability never recovered from the tragedy imprinted on their early lives. Some wound up in jail or were drifting aimlessly. One young man who'd been fostered by a couple in Topeka committed suicide on his fifteenth birthday. The parents made it clear that the decision to say yes wasn't to be taken lightly.

When the DVD ended, the room was silent. Bernadine looked around at the seriously set faces but waited before speaking. She wanted them to digest what they'd seen and heard first.

Reggie broke the silence. "I'm glad we saw that."

The others agreed.

His wife added, "Gives us lots to think about."

Colonel Payne asked Bernadine, "When will we need to let you know what we decide?"

"Truthfully, before you leave in the morning. I'm scheduled to pick up the kids Friday. I need to know how many families I'll have for them. And one thing I need to make clear for everyone is that children like these do not bond overnight. It may be months, even years, before the real child opens up."

For a moment there was silence as the couples looked at each other. She said to the Paynes and Garlands: "If you all want to use one of the bedrooms to speak privately, please help yourselves."

They accepted her offer and walked to the back while Bernadine, Trent, and the others sat tensely.

The couples came back a short time later and the answer was yes. Outwardly, Bernadine thanked them graciously but inside she was doing her hallelujah dance.

CHAPTER
11

Speechless, Lily looked around the luxurious interior of the small private jet. It was done in white leather and trimmed in burnished silver. It sat ten and had a galley kitchen and a small bedroom in the back. The seats were so white they could have been made out of freshly fallen snow.

A smiling Bernadine fastened her seat belt. "Do you like it?"

"My goodness, yes. And this is yours?"

"Yep. It was a gift from one of my Bottom Women sisters."

"Who?"

Before Lily could explain, the lyrical voice of their Jamaican pilot, Katie Skye came over the speakers. "Ms. B, does it matter which city we fly to first?"

"Nope. Just so we hit all the spots today."

"Gotcha. Then we'll start with Dallas."

"You're driving."

They were cleared for takeoff from the Hays airport a

short time later and were soon airborne and heading south for Dallas.

After reaching cruising speed, the still-dazzled Lily asked, "Now, how did you get this plane?"

"I belong to a group called the Bottom Women's Society."

"*Bottom* as in hips?"

"No, as in pimps."

Her eyes widened.

Bernadine asked, "Do you know what a pimp's bottom woman is?"

"Yeah. She's his first money machine, shall we say."

"We shall, and he builds his empire on her back, right?"

Lily nodded. "Or so I've heard. She supposedly takes care of the other girls he brings in, handles the house, the finances, etcetera."

"Well, that's who my girlfriends and I are. Only our pimps sat in board rooms. We're all first wives."

"*Ah.* I get the name now. And one of your girls just gave this to you?" She couldn't stop staring around.

"Yep, it's how we Bottom Women roll. This plane was part of her divorce settlement. She hates to fly though, so she gave it to me in honor of my second divorce anniversary."

"Do you think you all could take in a poor Bottom Woman like me?"

Bernadine laughed. "Sure, why not. We can nominate our friends, and we are friends, right?"

"If you all pass jets around, I'm your best friend."

Both women laughed and settled in for the flight. It was so smooth and uneventful that Bernadine took it as a sign that the day would go well.

When they began their descent to a small municipal field outside of Dallas, Bernadine's heart was pounding with excitement and anticipation. She would be fostering the fourteen-year-old Crystal Chambers. According to the phone calls she'd had with Yvette Carr, the social worker, the girl had lots of issues, but Bernadine planned to give her all of the love and support she'd need to get a handle on her life and move forward.

After they landed, Bernadine pulled out her phone. Arrangements had been made in advance for Crystal and Ms. Carr to be waiting at one of the small hangars. She called to make sure they were there, and Katie taxied the plane to the meeting spot. Bernadine left the plane to meet them while Lily stayed on and observed.

The first thing she noticed was the terribly unkempt blond extensions the teenager had woven into her scalp. Lily had seen better heads on mops. The second thing she noticed was Crystal's sour face, but Lily supposed it was to be expected. The girl had no idea who Bernadine was or where she was going to live. After having been in the system as long as the papers in her file said she had been, one foster parent was probably just another foster parent. The thought tugged at Lily's heart.

She watched Bernadine and Ms. Carr end their conversation and Bernadine gesture Crystal toward the plane. The girl stopped, looked at the jet, and then back at Bernadine with wide eyes.

Bernadine smiled, the girl climbed the stairs with a look of wonderment on her face, and Lily smiled too.

Crystal entered the plane gushing, "I get to ride in this! Dayum! This is sweet!"

Bernadine said, "Crystal, I want you to meet Lily Fontaine. Ms. Fontaine is my assistant."

"Hey, Crystal."

"Hey," she replied, but her entire being seemed focused on taking in the plane. "Man. Wait until I tell my friends. They're going to think I'm smoking crack!"

The blond tresses looked even worse up close. The tight jeans looked sprayed on, and the sleeves of the worn white T-shirt were rolled up to show off the tattoo—a blunt with smoke rising from the tip etched on her thin bicep. *Lord have mercy.*

"Who'd you get this plane from, Ms. Bernadine? Your boo?"

Bernadine chuckled, "No. Got it from one of my girlfriends."

"Girlfriend? You lesbian?"

Bernadine blinked. "No, but a few of my friends are."

Crystal shot a look at Lily, "You one?"

"Lesbian? No, but if I were, would that be a problem?"

"Hell, yeah!" the girl said as if that was a stupid question and took a seat.

Bernadine knew this was not the time or place for a tolerance lesson, but one would be coming very soon.

Katie's voice came over the speakers asking everyone to buckle up, and the jet began the slow rollback to the runway.

"Where we going now? To your mansion, right? If you got a jet you gotta have a mansion to put it in, right?"

Bernadine and Lily shared a look before she answered, "We're going to Alabama to pick up an eight-year-old boy named Devon."

"Why?"

"Because he's going back to Kansas with us too."

"So it'll be just the two of us?"

"Nope. Then we go to Miami to pick up Zoey."

"Zoey? What kind of wack name is that?"

Bernadine overlooked that. For now. "Then to Detroit to get Amari. Last stop will be to pick up Preston in Milwaukee. Do you like flying?"

She shrugged. "Never been on a plane before."

Lily handed her a stick of gum. "Here. Chew this. It'll keep your ears from stopping up."

Crystal looked confused but she stuck the gum in her mouth and turned her eyes back to the view out her window.

Bernadine and Lily shared another look, then settled in for the flight to Alabama.

When they landed again, they taxied into another small airport and over to one of the hangars for their rendezvous with Devon Watkins and his social worker. This airport was not as modern as the one in Dallas. Dallas was technically considered part of the South, but this was *the* South. You could see it in the rural landscape surrounding the little airport and you could see it in the faces of the men and women going about their jobs.

Crystal asked, "Where are we?"

"Near Birmingham, Alabama."

"Okay." They were the first words she'd spoken since leaving Dallas, and Bernadine hoped it wasn't because she'd been terrified about being up in the clouds.

"What do you think about flying so far?"

"I like it."

"Good. I like to fly too."

Bernadine stood and looked out the windows at the gray corrugated metal hangars they were slowly passing. "I don't see anybody. Do you?"

Lily didn't either.

"Is that them?" Crystal asked, pointing a finger crowned with a long fake pink-and-white nail.

Bernadine saw a tall blonde white woman holding the hand of a small brown-skinned little boy wearing a dark suit, white shirt, and tie. "I think so," she called to Katie. "This is them, Kate."

"Okay."

When the jet halted, she got off and walked over to where the woman and the boy stood waiting. "I'm Bernadine Brown."

"Lorna Stevens," the woman responded, and extended her hand. "Nice jet."

Bernadine returned the shake and the smile and looked down at the boy holding Lorna's other hand. "You must be, Devon."

"Yes, ma'am."

"Pleased to meet you, Devon. I'm Bernadine Brown."

"Pleased to meet you, too, ma'am."

The flowered pillowcase near his feet apparently held his belongings "Are you ready to go?"

He looked up at Ms. Stevens with a solemn glance then replied, "Yes, ma'am."

He seemed so wooden and resigned, Bernadine wanted to hug him and never let him go.

Lorna Stevens bent down and said to him softly, "I'm jealous. You get to fly off in a fancy jet plane and I get to go back to my office and do paperwork."

He smiled a little.

She touched his cheek. "You stay well now Devon Watkins, hear?"

"Yes, ma'am. God be with you."

"You too, angel."

She stood and met Bernadine's eyes. "Take real good care of him, Ms. Brown. He's very special."

"I will. I promise."

She nodded.

Bernadine took his warm hand in hers. He picked up the pillowcase, and she led him over to the waiting jet.

If Devon was awed by the plane's luxurious interior, he didn't show it. Instead he stood silently in the aisle as if waiting for instruction. Bernadine introduced him to Lily.

"Pleased to meet you, Ms. Fontaine."

"Same here, Devon."

"This is Crystal Chambers."

The teen gave the little boy and his suit a critical once-over. "You just come from a funeral?"

Confusion filled his face.

"The suit," she explained. "Where I come from only time you wear a suit is to a funeral or to court."

"I wear this all the time."

"Why?"

He shrugged. "I just do."

Crystal wasn't buying it. "Ms. Brown, we're going to have to get him some real clothes. If we're going to be flying on jets and living in a mansion, he's gotta dress way more tight than this."

"I don't own a mansion, Crystal."

"Yeah, right." She then stuck out her hand to Devon. "Welcome to the family. Have Ms. Lily give you some gum so your ears don't pop. You ever been on a plane before?"

"Once to San Francisco and the other time to Washington, D.C."

Crystal looked impressed. "Well, get a seat and buckle up. We got three more stops to make." She then yelled into the comm console. "We're ready back here, Ms. Katie."

The pilot responded with a laugh. "Thank you, Miss Crystal."

Bernadine buckled her seat belt. She could have kissed Crystal for welcoming Devon the way she had. It proved that beneath the bad hair and the drug-thug tattoo beat a good heart. She vowed to remember that when times ahead with Crystal got hard, because she knew they would.

Next stop, Miami. This time the social worker was a young Black man, and beside him, standing no bigger than a minute was Zoey Raymond.

While Bernadine went outside to facilitate the transfer, inside the jet Crystal barked, "A White girl?"

Devon made his way over to Crystal's side of the plane so that he could see out too.

Lily, who'd known about Zoey's race, said, "Yes, Crystal, a White girl. She's got a lot of issues, and I expect you to be as nice to her as you were to Devon."

Devon said quietly, "She looks sad."

Lily agreed. The little face was as pale as milk, but the bowl-cut hair and bangs were so black they made her appear almost ghostly. She was a pretty little girl though. Bernadine would be pairing her with the Paynes. They thought Sheila would be the perfect foster mother to give the girl all the special love and attention she'd need.

Crystal asked, "So what's wrong with her?"

"She's mute."

Crystal looked confused.

"She doesn't speak."

"At all?"

Lily shook her head.

"That's rough."

They all watched silently as Bernadine and Zoey walked toward the plane. Devon quoted just loud enough to hear, "And when the demon had been cast out, the mute spoke."

Lily turned to him. Crystal did as well.

"Mathew nine, verse thirty-five," he said.

Crystal groaned like only a fourteen-year-old can, "Oh Lord. A Jesus boy."

Lily gave his thin shoulder a small squeeze and said reassuringly, "You keep quoting the Word, Devon. We're going to be needing all the Scripture we can get before this is over, I'm betting."

"Yes, ma'am."

Crystal must have taken Lily's warning seriously because when Bernadine and Zoey got on, she said, "Hey, Zoey. I'm Crystal. Back there is Devon. They told us you can't talk, so I don't expect you to say hi or anything. Welcome to the family."

Zoey dropped her head a notch in what could have been shyness or recognition or who knew, but she didn't act afraid, and that gave Bernadine hope.

Devon said, "Hey, Zoey, you can come sit with me, if you like."

She looked up at Bernadine, who replied, "Up to you."

Zoey let go of Bernadine's hand. Dressed in a battered pair of jeans and matching shirt, her pale feet stuck in green flip-flops, she went down the aisle and settled into the seat next to Devon.

Crystal was turned around watching. "She get her gum, Ms. Lily?"

Lily grinned. "I'm on it."

"Make sure she's buckled in, Devon," Crystal added.

"I will."

And once everything was done, Crystal called to Katie, "We're ready back here, Ms. Katie. Fire this baby up!"

"Aye-aye, Captain."

A few minutes later, they were winging their way north to the Motor City.

There was no social worker waiting with Amari Steele,

but there were two uniformed police officers standing to his left and right. Bernadine had never seen an eleven-year-old in leg irons and handcuffs before, and she stared stunned as she viewed the scene from the jet's window.

"Is that him?" Crystal asked.

Bernadine sighed, "I think so."

Obviously impressed by the shackles and the po-po escort, Crystal said, "Now that's gangsta."

Devon and Zoey looked out at the window and then shared a silent glance.

Bernadine left the plane and walked over and introduced herself.

The female officer said, "Sorry about the hardware, but he got away from us a little while ago. We wanted to make sure he was here when you came to pick him up."

Amari shrugged. "It was a Chrysler Prowler. I've never driven a Prowler before."

They went on to explain that he'd given them the slip once they arrived on the airport grounds. They found him behind the wheel of a Prowler.

"You can release him now."

Amari grinned. "Thanks, Ms. Brown. Excuse my manners. I'd shake your hand but I'm a little tied up at the moment."

She groaned inwardly at the pun. The mischief in his eyes equaled the wattage in his crooked white-toothed smile. Once he was freed, he stuck out his hand, "Amari Steele."

"Bernadine Brown." She knew right there and then that this handsome charmer was going to be trouble with a capital *T*.

"Whose jet is that?" he asked gesturing in its direction.

"Mine."

"How fast will it go?"

Bernadine studied him. "Why?"

"I'm into engines."

"You'll have to ask my pilot."

"Can I ride up front with him."

"Pilot's female and, no, all passengers have to sit in the cabin."

He looked disappointed.

The policemen were shaking their heads.

"Are you ready?" Bernadine asked him.

"You sure I can't ride up front?"

Bernadine gave him the same look her mama used to give her when the discussion was closed.

"Okay. I get it."

"Good."

The male police officer produced a small rolling suitcase. "Here's your stuff, Amari."

"Thanks."

He gave the officers a smile and wave and walked with Bernadine to the plane's lowered steps.

As he got on and took in the laid interior he whistled long and low. "Man! Now this is the shit."

"Watch your mouth," Lily warned sternly.

"Sorry. Didn't know this was a noncussing flight."

Behind him, Bernadine coughed to hide her laugh.

Lily fought to keep a straight face.

"I'm Amari," he said to Lily, and walked up and stuck out his hand. "Pleased to meet you."

"I'm Ms. Fontaine. I work for Ms. Brown."

He glanced at the other kids.

Crystal asked, "Why were you with the po-po?"

"Car theft."

Devon said, "And the thief shall make restitution. Exodus two, verse one."

Amari turned and stared at Devon then looked him critically up and down. "Who're you supposed to be, Creflo Dollar's Mini-Me?"

"I'm Devon. This is Zoey."

"She looks like that girl from *The Addams Family*. Tuesday? Wednesday?"

Crystal said, "Her name's Zoey. She's mute. Hurt her feelings and it'll be me and you."

Amari tossed back. "It ought to be you and a hairdresser. Those tracks look like something Amtrak runs on."

Crystal jumped up in defense of her blond weave. "You little mother—"

"Crystal!" Bernadine snapped.

Crystal had fury in her eyes. "He can't talk to me like that. He don't know me!"

Amari was grinning. He ignored her and turned to Zoey. "I'm sorry, Tuesday. Wasn't trying to play you. You, too, Creflo."

The young ones stared back but didn't respond. Amari shrugged and took a seat.

Lily and Bernadine shared a look that said silently, "Do you believe this?"

Crystal was still shooting daggers at Amari.

Bernadine said to her, "Sit down, honey. Tell Katie we're ready."

"Katie, we're ready," she snarled, and sat.

When they reached the small airport outside of Milwaukee, Bernadine was surprised to find a short, overweight kid with braids waiting alone at the prearranged pickup point.

When she approached, she asked, "Are you Preston Mays?"

"Yep. You Ms. Brown?"

She nodded and took a quick look around the hangar area in a search for his social worker. "Where's your worker?"

"She didn't want to be late for court, so she dropped me off."

"She was supposed to stay with you until I got here."

"Welcome to the zany world of foster care," he offered cynically.

"I'll be calling her supervisor."

"Doesn't matter. Nice jet."

"Thanks. Come on," Bernadine urged, still irritated that the child had been left to fend for himself. "Let's get you settled."

"Are we really going to Kansas?"

"Yes."

"You got cable?"

"Yep."

"Good."

On the plane, Preston looked around. "Nice," he said to Bernadine in an impressed voice. "Real nice."

He checked out the other passengers. "I'm Preston."

Amari introduced himself and added, "This here is Creflo and Tuesday."

Devon said, "Our real names are Devon and Zoey."

Preston nodded. He looked at Crystal, who was still sulking.

Amari said, "The blonde's Crystal."

"Hey, Crystal."

"Hey," she said disinterestedly, then turned back to the view outside her window.

Preston said, "Okay, then."

After his introduction to Lily, he asked, "Where should I sit, Ms. Brown?"

"Wherever you'd like."

Amari called out, "Back here, man."

Preston looked pleased and hurried down the aisle to take the seat next to Amari. Bernadine watched them exchange a handshake and grins. Pleased, she retook her own seat, glad to be heading home.

Once they were airborne and Katie had the jet leveled off, Bernadine and Lily passed out lunch. Sandwiches, with a choice of ham or turkey were joined by bags of chips, raw baby carrots, and juice boxes.

"Juice boxes are for babies," Crystal pronounced, turning down the drink. "What else you got?"

"Water," Lily replied flatly.

She huffed. "Give me the box then."

Lily handed it over and shook her head. Looking on, Bernadine did the same. While eating her lunch she discreetly checked out her kids. Zoey and Devon looked so small in the large white seats, but they seemed to be getting along well, as were Amari and Devon, who were talking a mile a minute about everything from sports to video games and wolfing down food right and left. Between them they ate three sandwiches apiece, went through four juice boxes, more chips, and all the rest of the carrots. From her social worker training and from the foster care videos she'd seen, she knew that children in the system often gorged themselves at meals because they weren't sure if there'd be another any time soon. Hopefully they'd find out that food was as plentiful as love in their new lives.

Crystal on the other hand ate nothing but the meat in her sandwich. She didn't like the lettuce, tomatoes, or the brown bread. She'd also not spoken a word to anyone since the terse greeting she'd given Preston. Until Hurricane Amari's arrival, Crystal had been in charge of their little adventure and had appeared to be enjoying her role. Bernadine doubted anyone had ever been in charge of Amari, and she guessed Crystal was having problems with not being able to boss him around. This was typical of teens, she knew, and that the pecking order issues would be resolved over time.

After lunch, she and Lily went to the small galley kitchen at the back of the plane to take care of the cleanup. When they returned to the cabin, all of the children were asleep, even Crystal.

Breathing a sigh of relief, Lily said, with soft emphasis, "Hallelujah!"

"Amen. Let's enjoy this peace and quiet for as long it lasts."

Bernadine had arranged for the kids to be taken back to town in a sleek stretch limo. She knew it was over the top, but she wanted them to feel special because there'd been so few special moments in their lives in the foster care system. Because the kids had slept during the last leg of the flight, Amari and Preston were energized by the sight of the long shiny black car, but Zoey and Devon were so groggy they had to be helped in. It was plain that Crystal was impressed by the vehicle as well but she played it off as if she'd had limos at her disposal her entire life.

Amari looked around the interior and asked, "Ms. Brown, you think anybody famous ever rode in here?"

"I have no idea, Amari, how about you ask the driver?"

The driver, an elderly gentleman with snowy hair replied with pride, "I had the governor a few years back."

"Naw, man," Amari said, "famous famous like Paris Hilton or Flava Flav or 50 Cent."

The man's puzzled eyes were reflected in the mirror. "Who?"

Amari waved him off. "Never mind."

Crystal drawled, "Boy, you are truly ghetto."

"Tell that to your hairdresser, Ms. Amtrak."

Amari and Preston rolled with laughter, making Crystal jump up and yell, "Shut the hell up!"

Lily grabbed the back of her shirt. "Everybody! Freeze!"

Lily's mama's voice impressed everyone. Even the once-groggy Devon and Zoey were sitting up at attention.

Lily looked around and upon seeing the rigid faces of the little ones, said softly, "Devon and Zoey, you two relax. You aren't in this. But you three," she said, turning flashing eyes on the main culprits, "Ms. Brown didn't go through all this trouble and spend all this money for you act like you don't have any damn sense. Crystal, you started it, so apologize."

She opened her mouth to protest but the look in Lily's eyes must have changed her mind. She mumbled a terse, "Sorry."

"Amari. Same thing."

His voice was clear, "Sorry, Crystal."

"Now," Lily said with finality, "Until we get home, we're going to play Peace and Quiet, understand?"

Bernadine figured they must have because no one made a sound.

However, a few moments later Amari started asking questions: *Ms. Brown, how come I don't see any MacDonald's? Hey, driver what kind of tractor is that? Ms. Fontaine, do any trees grow here?*

He must have asked ten questions for every mile they passed. It was so nonstop Bernadine could feel a headache starting, but she and Lily answered as many as they could, patiently and with a plastered-on smile.

When the questions finally stopped, a relieved Bernadine leaned over and said softly to the sullen Crystal, "You shouldn't let Amari push your buttons, otherwise he's gonna make you crazy."

"I hate teenage boys. Give me an old man any day. You know, somebody in their twenties."

Bernadine knew Crystal had no idea how naive and silly that statement sounded, so she just nodded.

"How come there are no houses?" Preston asked as they continued to pass acres and acres of open land.

"It's called the American plains. Not a lot of people live out this way."

"Looks like nobody lives out this way."

"I felt the same way when I first got here," Bernadine told him truthfully. She had no idea how the urban kids were going to like being out on the Great American Plains, but she couldn't worry about that now. She looked over at Devon and Zoey seated next to each other. "You two doing okay?"

"Yes, ma'am," Devon said, answering for them both. "Thank you for the plane ride."

"You're welcome."

"Zoey thanks you too."

"You're welcome, Zoey." The little girl and the little deacon seemed to have bonded, and Bernadine saw that as a positive sign. Something told her that Devon might be just the friend Zoey needed to get her talking again if it were at all possible.

When the limo turned into Tamar's yard and Bernadine saw all the people standing around, she looked to Lily in confusion.

The kids were staring out of the one-way tinted windows as well.

Amari asked, "Are we here?"

"Yes," she answered before asking Lily, "Is this part of Marie's birthday party?"

"Not that I know of. Party's not until tomorrow."

The driver parked. As he came around and opened the door, Bernadine stepped out and heard a band of horns begin playing, "When the Saints Go Marching In."

Applause broke out. She stared around at all the smiling faces, then froze at the sight of the long white banner strung above Tamar's porch that read in big letters: WEL-COME, along with the names of the kids. Tamar stood beneath it beneath wearing a big grin and Bernadine realized this was a party, but for the kids. She wanted to kiss everybody for this kindness.

Grinning over at the musicians, who included Malachi, Trent, and Clay all dressed in black and wearing shades, she motioned for the kids to get out, and as they did the applause started again.

"Wow!" Preston said, looking around. "This is crazy."

As she and Lily and the kids made their way to the porch, people Bernadine had never seen before came up to shake the kids' hands and welcome them to town. Others patted them on the backs and told the children how glad they were to have them there. The enthusiastic welcome left her speechless. By her guesstimate there had to be fifty or sixty people in Tamar's front yard, and they were all clapping and cheering.

Crystal tugged on Bernadine's sleeve. "Is this for us?"

Bernadine smiled, "Yes, ma'am. See your name up on the banner?"

Echoing Preston, all Crystal could manage to say was, "Wow."

Feeling like a mother duck, Bernadine shepherded her ducklings to the porch, where the band was playing. Malachi blowing on a sax caught her eye and winked. She grinned.

Lily said, "Is this cool or what? I had no idea they were going to do this."

Bernadine looked out over the crowd and was blown away, "You know I didn't, but it is cool. Real cool."

Tamar cut off the musicians and in the silence that followed said in a loud voice. "It's not often that we get new residents, so I want to thank you all for coming out to meet our new kids. They and Ms. Brown represent the Henry Adams of the future."

More applause. Tamar looked to Bernadine and said, "Would you do the honors and introduce them."

So one by one, she introduced the children, and when their names were spoken each was given another rousing round of applause. Devon and Zoey looked uncertain,

Crystal waved like a Texas beauty queen, Preston grinned and bowed, but Amari struck a rapper's pose, arms crossed, chin up. The crowd roared. All Bernadine could think was *Lord help us.*

Tamar rolled her eyes at him and said, "We're going to get these kids fed and home so they can relax. We'll see you all tomorrow at Marie's."

Still wondering where all the people had come from, Bernadine directed the kids over to her trailer, and they went inside.

Inside, they looked around. Crystal said, "A trailer? I thought you lived in a mansion?"

"I told you I didn't."

"It's nice though," she said, looking around at the beautiful furniture, the art on the walls, and the sweet light fixtures and lamps.

"Thanks, Crystal. Make yourselves at home. We'll be having dinner next door with Ms. July. After that, Crystal and Zoey will sleep here and the boys with Ms. July's grandson, Trent July." She saw Amari and Preston share a glance. Zoey and Devon shared one too, but none of the kids said anything.

She directed them to the restrooms and the bedroom where her big screen hung on the wall. "Go on in and get comfortable. And you older kids, nothing inappropriate on the tube. Devon and Zoey aren't old enough for drama."

Crystal shot a look at Amari, "Don't worry."

He rolled his eyes, and he and Preston headed off.

By the time everyone arrived for dinner, Tamar's house

was hot and bursting at the seams. Luckily the meal would be held outside, where it wasn't much cooler but at least there was a breeze. Joining the kids were Clay and Bing, Malachi and Trent, and Agnes and Marie. Trent brought in an old-fashioned ice cream churn and set it the shade near the house.

Introductions were made. The kids were polite but didn't say much, as if they were waiting to see what kind of people the old people were going to turn out to be.

Bernadine looked over at Devon sitting in a lawn chair next to Zoey. "Would you like to bless the food?"

"Ye, ma'am." He stood up and said, "Join hands, please."

Tamar and the others stared at him curiously for a moment but did as instructed. Crystal changed spots so she wouldn't have to hold Amari's hand and went to stand between Trent and Lily. She looked up at Trent and asked coyly, "Are you going to be one of the foster parents?"

Lily glanced over. "Change places with me, Crystal."

She poked out her heavily glossed bottom lip but did as she was told.

Preston snickered.

"What are you laughing at, Bubble Butt!"

"You don't want to mess with me," he warned her calmly.

"Why, you gonna sit on me?"

"Not unless I get shots first."

Amari hollered ecstatically, "Yeah!" He broke the circle walked over and gave Preston five. "My man!"

Malachi looked at Trent, Trent looked at Bernadine, who looked at Tamar, who asked, "Are you three done? Do you see this boy standing here waiting to say grace?"

The three shrunk.

"Apologize, Crystal," Tamar demanded.

"Why?"

"For calling Preston out of his name. And Preston, you apologize for that shots remark."

They both looked mutinous.

Tamar folded her arms. "We'll wait."

They mumbled apologies in voices that could hardly be heard.

Tamar wasn't through. "We are all family here in Henry Adams, and as family we don't dis each other."

"Did she just say, 'dis'?" Amari asked surprised.

Bernadine smiled and nodded.

He looked Tamar up and down. "Who are you, Tyler Perry's Madea?"

"Madea's fiction. I'm not."

"Oh." From the look on his face it was easy to see that he had no more questions.

"Anything else?"

"No, ma'am. Not from me."

Tamar turned to Devon. "Go ahead now, Devon."

"Dear God. Thank you for this gathering today. Bless the food that we are going to eat and bless the hands that prepared it. Please stretch out your hand to the poor and to those who lift them up, so that your blessing will be complete. Amen."

"Amen."

It was a great meal. Lots of barbecued chicken and ribs, coleslaw, Marie's prize-winning baked beans. Throw in some of Ms. Agnes's light-as-a-cloud biscuits and you had a meal the kids kept getting more helpings of. It was obvious to Bernadine that the senior citizens had been cooking all day, and she loved them even more.

The ice cream was a big hit.

"What is that?" Amari asked when Trent dragged the churn and its tub over to the table.

"Ice-cream churn."

"What?"

He took the top off and drew out the paddle, which was covered with the thick cold dessert. He grabbed one of plastic spoons and dipped out a small portion and passed it to Amari. "Taste."

With all the skepticism of his age, he asked, "What is it?"

Clay told him, "Ice cream, man. You think we're going to poison you your first day here?"

Bing tossed out. "The poison comes next week."

Amari grinned, and while the other kids looked on, he popped the spoon into his mouth. He swooned, "Oh, this is the shit."

"Amari!" Bernadine warned.

"Sorry, but this is good."

So good in fact, that when Preston tried to go back for his *third* helping, Malachi said, "You've had enough, son. Too much and it'll give you nightmares."

"I don't believe you."

"You ever had homemade ice cream before today?"

"No."

"I've had it all my life. Too much will give you nightmares."

It was easy to see why the twelve-year-old was overweight; the boy was a heavyweight eater, and because of his asthma he probably got very little exercise. The disappointed Preston walked slowly back to his chair. Bernadine caught Malachi's eye and mouthed a silent, thank you.

He nodded and put the top back on the churn. Tamar and the other ladies seemed taken by Devon and the silent Zoey, and so they spent most of the evening seated near the two, making sure they had enough to eat and were comfortable. They seemed to be, although with Zoey it was hard to tell. Bernadine had noticed the happy swing of her little feet in the green flip-flops when she'd been eating the ice cream, which let her know that underneath the traumatized surface was a child who could still be reached.

Crystal, on the other hand, continued to sulk. Marie tried to draw her out but was rebuffed, albeit politely, so folks just left her alone.

With the meal over, everyone pitched in to help clean up, and when they were done, everyone prepared to leave. Tamar had one last thing to say, though. "We're all glad you children are here. Everybody in town is going to help with your raising, so if you need something, just ask. See you tomorrow."

The kids said good night and Bernadine and Lily escorted them out.

Trent had the boys grab their stuff, and they left to

spend the night at one of the new trailers he'd claimed. Malachi, Clay, and Bing tagged along.

After Lily and Marie said their good-byes, Bernadine was left alone with Zoey and Crystal. "Guess that leaves us, ladies. Let's go see your room."

CHAPTER

13

Bernadine's guest bedroom with its cream and beige color scheme held twin beds. "There's a bathroom through that door with plenty of towels and soaps. Help yourself if you want to take a shower or wash up. Do you need anything?"

"Toothbrush. I try and take good care of my teeth."

Bernadine was glad to hear the teen had some measure of hygiene because you couldn't tell by the bad weave, tattoos, and all the makeup slathered on her face. "There are some new ones in the medicine cabinet." She'd asked Tamar to pick up a few when she and her friends did all the grocery shopping for the houses. "You need anything, Zoey?"

She gave a small shake of her dark head, which both surprised and pleased Bernadine. "Okay. I'll be down the hall. TV is on the wall over there if you want to watch something. I'll come back and check on you in a bit."

"What time is it?" Crystal wanted to know.

Bernadine checked her watch. "A little after nine."

Zoey yawned.

Crystal pointed out, "It's too early for me to go to bed."

"That's fine, but we'll be getting up at eight for breakfast. No sleeping in allowed."

"Okay."

Bernadine left them to themselves and walked down the hall to her own bedroom. The room had been decorated to reflect her stylish tastes, and like the other spaces of her home it was accented with the artwork and sculptures she'd collected on her travels. She came out of her heels and her black suit and sighed with relief. *Long day.* A quick shower gave her a second wind, so she donned a pair of lightweight silk-blend sweats and a tee and checked in on the girls. Zoey was in the shower. Crystal was watching TV.

"Do you have pajamas, Crystal?" She noticed the tatoos were gone, and was glad that they'd been only temporary ones.

"Nope."

"How about Zoey?"

Crystal searched through Zoey's little suitcase. "Nope."

"Okay. I have some T-shirts you can use."

Crystal said, "I'm good. I'll just sleep in my underwear like I always do."

"When we go shopping, we'll get you and Zoey pajamas."

"We're going shopping?"

"Yep."

"Why?"

"Because we can."

Crystal looked impressed. "I like that."

"Let me get the shirts. Be right back."

After leaving the shirts with Crystal, Bernadine headed back downstairs to relax a bit before bed.

She wound up outside. It wasn't fully dark yet, but the sun had already gone down and the breeze was a good one. She thought about the girls inside watching TV and hoped they were getting along. Although Crystal had seemed protective of Zoey at first, the teen was a loose cannon, so Bernadine hoped she'd be nice. All of the trailers were spread out on Tamar's vast property, and she could see the front of Trent's trailer clearly.

A few moments later, Malachi came out and seeing her walked over.

"Everything okay over there?" she asked when he got close.

"Seems to be. Devon's just sitting back and watching everything, but Amari's asking a thousand questions a minute. Trent may have to gag that boy so he can sleep. Amari and Preston both are real quick."

"Yes, they are. If we can keep them from setting Crystal off, we might live through this."

He waved it away. "They're kids. They'll work it out."

"Since when did you become such an expert?"

His mustache lifted in a smile. "Used to be a kid myself once upon a time."

"This has to be scary for them, though."

"Sure, but once they figure out they're safe, it'll be okay. How are you doing? After flying all over the country you have to be whipped."

"I am, but there's still miles to go. The Paynes and Garlands will be here sometime tomorrow. I hope they'll all get along. I so want this to work."

"It will."

She appreciated his support. "I'd like you to think about the kinds of renovations you want done to the D&C."

"Really?"

"We need a diner, and since we already have one, I thought we'd fix it up."

"Okay. When you get the chance how about we get together and do a walk-through and see what we can come up with?"

"Sounds good." In the silence Bernadine could feel his presence washing over her like the evening breeze.

"You know, what you're doing here is fantastic and I'll do whatever I can to help. I might be made out of snake oil, but I am a July. This means a lot."

The sincerity in his tone touched her as much as his presence. Bernadine had to admit she hadn't felt this kind of heat around a man in a long time, and because of that, this little interlude had to end. She stood and said quietly, "Thanks, Malachi. I appreciate that. Now, I'm going in to check on the girls. You have a good evening."

"Running?" he asked.

Bernadine chuckled at his insight. "Yeah. I am."

"At least you're honest."

"I am that, if nothing else."

The silence rose between them again until she finally said, "See you tomorrow, Malachi."

" 'Night, Bernadine."

He walked back toward Trent's place and she went inside.

Later, after all the lights were out in the new trailers and everyone was supposed to be asleep, Amari lying on a sleeping bag in the dark asked Preston, "What do you think about all of this, my man?"

Preston was in a sleeping bag close by. "Best first day I've had in new place, so for now, it's okay."

"My best too."

The two boys had opted for sleeping bags on the floor of Trent's guest bedroom. Devon was in the big bed.

Amari called to him softly, "Hey, Crello, you asleep?"

There was no response.

Preston raised up to look. "I think he is."

There was silence again and then Preston asked, "You think the foster parents are going to be wack?"

"Aren't they always? Wish I could stay here. Trent seems pretty straight."

"Yeah. We'll probably wind up with some crazy old bitch who'll feed us dog food."

"Been there."

"Me too."

For a few moments they each thought about the past. Finally, Preston said. "I'm going to sleep. Been good hanging with you today, Amari. See you in the morning."

"'Night."

Preston drifted off, but Amari lay in the dark thinking for a long time.

Over at Bernadine's, Crystal woke up and groggily looked around. Something had awakened her but she wasn't sure what it was. Lifting up, she saw the moon streaming into the room through the open curtains and Zoey sitting in a chair bathed in the light. "What's the matter, Zoey? Why you got the drapes open?"

No response.

Crystal slowly tossed aside her lightweight blanket and got up. She walked over and knelt beside her so she could see better. Zoey looked like a little ghost. Crystal placed her hand on her forehead. "You sick?"

But her forehead was cool.

Crystal knelt there for a moment looking at Zoey and trying to figure this out. She studied Zoey and then looked over at the opened curtains letting in the wide beam of moonlight. "Are you scared of the dark?" Zoey's eyes met hers, and the look in them told Crystal all she needed to know. "Okay," she said softly. "How about you come sleep with me? I won't let anything get you. I promise."

Zoey continued to hold her gaze.

"If you want to keep the curtains open, that's okay, but you can't stay up all night. You got a big day tomorrow. Come on," she urged gently. Standing up, she held out her hand. "Nothing's going to get you. Me and Ms. Bernadine will beat the hell out of anything that tries. Anything, I swear," she promised again.

Finally, Zoey, in the T-shirt that brushed her ankles, scooted to the edge of the chair and took Crystal's hand. Crystal could feel the little girl's trembling but didn't mention it. Together they walked across the half-lit room to the beds. "You get in. I'll get your pillow."

Zoey climbed in.

"And don't worry about kicking me or anything. I've slept with little kids all my life. I'm used to waking up with feet in my face." She put Zoey's pillow next to her own and got under the blanket.

"Okay?"

She sensed Zoey relax.

"Good girl. Now go on to sleep. If you need to wake me up that's okay. I won't yell at you."

Crystal threw a protective arm across Zoey's thin frame and a few minutes later they were both asleep.

The next morning was Marie's party, and Crystal came in for breakfast first. "Where's Zoey?" Bernadine asked.

"In the bathroom. She'll be out in a minute. Do you know that she's scared of the dark?"

Bernadine stopped. "She is?"

"Yeah. I woke up in the middle of the night and she had the curtains open and was sitting in the moonlight. She was shaking."

Bernadine sighed, wishing she knew what was going on inside her youngest child. "What did you do?"

So Crystal told her the rest of the story.

Moved by the teen's heart and spirit, Bernadine said, "She's blessed to have you in her life, Crystal."

"*Aw* come on. Don't go all mushy on me."

"It's a mushy moment, girl. Somebody else would have just left her sitting there and gone on back to sleep. Shows your good heart and your maturity." She had to remember to get the teen something nice as a reward for her kindness. "I won't forget this, Crys. Is it okay to call you that or do you prefer Crystal?"

"I prefer Crystal but Crys is okay too."

Bernadine looked at the ratty Day-Glo gold weave and wondered how she could convince the teen to do something different with her hair, but since they had a lot to do today, she set the thoughts aside for now.

Zoey entered looking sleepy.

"'Morning Zoey. We're going to a picnic birthday party today, are you ready for breakfast so we can head on over?"

Her face said she was. She climbed onto the stool next to Crystal and they began their day.

It took Bernadine a while to find a place to park on the road to Marie's, but once she did, she and the girls got out and started the long walk back toward the house. It had been a while since she'd hiked any kind of distance as evidenced by her increased breathing and the straining muscles in her legs, but the exertion felt good. She made a mental note to work some exercise into her daily routine; she had no idea where she'd find the time, but for her age and size she was in good shape and she wanted to keep it that way.

"Whose party are we going to?" Crystal asked. She was holding Zoey's hand.

"Marie Jefferson. She was the lady with the cat eye glasses last night at dinner. She's also going to be your teacher once we get school started."

"School?"

"Yep. You can't grow up and get a good job without an education. Any idea what you might want to be after college?"

"College? I'm not going to college!"

"And why not?"

"College is for geeks."

"I see."

Cars and trucks were still arriving so they walked close to the edge of the road. Folks waved as they passed them by.

"Do you know all those people?" Crystal asked.

Bernadine shook her head.

"Then why you waving at them?"

"They waved at me, I wave back. It's called being friendly."

"Where I live you don't just be waving at people you don't know. People'll think you're a crackhead or something."

"Small towns are different. People care about each other and want to say hi."

"I'm not going to be waving."

"That's okay. You may change your mind once you're here for a while."

The look on the teen's face said she didn't agree, but Bernadine didn't press. An old red truck she recognized as belonging to Malachi rolled up slowly beside them and kept pace. "Hey Ms. Brown. Hey ladies."

"Hey, Mr. July," she said, looking in at him and his dark assessing eyes. A smile played along the salt-and-pepper mustache crowning his lips. A young brown-skinned woman dressed in a yellow halter top and gold chains was in the seat beside him.

"Want you to meet Tarika Sims."

"Hi there, Tarika," Bernadine responded.

Tarika leaned forward and waved. "Nice to meet you, Ms. Brown. Hi, girls."

Crystal nodded. Zoey looked away shyly.

Bernadine knew it was not her place to judge, but she had shoes older than the girl with him and he probably did too. Directing her attention back to him she said, "Good luck finding a place to park. We're way down the road. Are Marie's parties always this packed?"

"Always."

Bernadine didn't know what else to say, so she said, "Ok. Well, we'll see you all there."

He flashed a smile. "See you later."

With a wave, he drove on. Bernadine shook her head and continued her walk up the road.

Crystal said, "He's kind of cute for an old guy. Is that his granddaughter?"

"No. I believe she's a friend."

"As in girlfriend?"

"Not sure."

"*Whoa*. Mr. Malachi's a player."

"I wouldn't know."

The weather was much cooler than it had been for the past few days and Bernadine was thankful for that. Nothing like arriving at a function a sweaty mess, but she was fine. The Jefferson place was a sizeable brick structure laid out on flat land just like most of the other places in the area and had a lone tree in the front yard. There was music in the air, along with the smells of meat grilling, and she could hear the distant sounds of voices.

As she and the girls approached, some of the folks immediately waved. She waved back.

"Do you know them?" Crystal asked.

When she responded that she didn't, Crystal rolled her eyes. "Is it just going to be old people here?"

Bernadine shrugged. "This is my first time."

"If me and Zoey get bored can we go back to your place?"

"Let's see how it goes first."

"I'm not going to have a good time and neither is Zoey."

"You don't know that Crystal."

"Yeah, I do."

The sight of Lily coming out of the front door carrying a carrying a large cookie sheet groaning with halved, seasoned chickens covered with a long sheet of waxed paper cut off further discussion. Bernadine could have kissed her.

"Hey, there. Hi, Zoey. Crystal. How are you?"

"Bored."

Lily replied, "Well don't let Tamar hear you say that, she'll put you to work peeling potatoes or something."

"What?"

"You heard me, so act like you're having a good time even if you're not."

Lily threw Bernadine a wink, then said, "Everybody's around back. Come on. Trent and the boys are already here."

14

Clay Dobbs was tending the grills. "I hear you steal cars, Amari."

"Yep."

Clay looked him in the eye. "You bragging?"

"I just thought you wanted me to tell the truth."

Trent rolled his eyes and shook his head.

"What's the fastest one you ever rode in?"

"Two thousand five Mustang. I buried the speedometer at one forty."

Trent, Bing, Clay, and Preston stared.

Amari said, "You asked. I got sent to juvie for thirty days that time, but it was worth it. The car belonged to a Ford engineer. He told me to look him up when I turned eighteen if I wasn't in jail and he'd get me a job test driving at the proving grounds because I didn't crash his car."

Trent had never met a youngster like Amari.

Preston looked out over the gathering and said, "Hey, Devon. Here comes Zoey."

The men watched the little deacon's face light up. Trent said, "You can go meet them if you want, Devon."

"Thank you, sir."

Trent thought the boy would take off running but he didn't. He walked.

Amari said, "Is it just me or is Creflo strange."

"Quit calling him that," Trent said pointedly.

"I give everybody nicknames. It's fun. You don't think he's strange."

"No stranger than you," Bing said.

Amari grinned. "Good one. I think I'm going to like living here."

By Bernadine's estimate the open field behind the house was filled with a good sixty people. There were blankets spread out, card games going on, and people sitting and laughing in lawn chairs. From speakers somewhere Stevie Wonder was singing "Signed, Sealed, Delivered, I'm Yours," and a few of the oldsters were up doing their thing. Coolers of all shapes and sizes were filled with ice and canned drinks. Canopies that appeared to be made of stitched together tablecloths held up by poles and then staked to the ground with lengths of plastic rope offered shade where nature provided none. There were dozens of them all over the field, fluttering like colorful flags, and the people camped beneath them looked to be having a good time.

She even saw children playing off in the distance. She hadn't seen any kids since coming to Henry Adams. It made her think of her kids and wondered if they'd find some playmates. "Do all of these people live here?"

"No. Most of them drove in or flew in from other places.

Marie taught school here for a long time before retiring.
A lot are former students and their families. When I was
growing up there was some kind of summer celebration
like this every year."

Bernadine noticed that some of the people were in period dress. The men had on long-sleeved old-time shirts
and vests and women were in high-collar dresses. They
made her sweat just to look at them. "What's up with the
old clothes?"

"There's a Henry Adams Historical Society and whenever there's an event the members encourage folks to dress
up, but in this heat that's insane."

Bernadine thought so too but was fascinated by the idea.
"Reminds me of the people at Colonial Williamsburg." She
wondered if duplicating that idea on a regular basis might
be a way to generate some tourism dollars. One of Agnes's
suggestions had been to build a museum to house all of the
Henry Adams artifacts. Bernadine wondered if maybe they
could hold some type of an annual Founding Days event to
show off the history.

Up ahead was a large purple and white canopy. Beneath
it were two extra-long tables covered with red-and-white-
checkered tablecloths.

"This is where we put all the food when it's time to eat,"
Lily explained. "Are you hungry? Mr. Dobbs just took some
hot dogs off the grill."

"Are you girls hungry?"

Zoey didn't appear to hear the question because she
was too busy smiling at the suit-wearing Devon coming
their way.

"You can go on ahead, Zoey." Still wearing her green flip-flops she hurried off to meet up with her friend.

Crystal was dressed in a pair of Daisy Dukes and a halter top. Bernadine could see the attention she was drawing from some of the men and the disapproval on the faces of some of the women. She was going to have to take Crys shopping as soon as it could be arranged.

The meat was being cooked on three huge oil-drum grills tended by the aforementioned Clay Dobbs. He was decked out in an apron that read "If You Can Shoot It—I Can Cook It!" and he was moving around the pits with a practiced efficiency.

Seated at a table nearby were Trent, Bing, Preston, and Amari.

Mr. Dobbs took the sheets of seasoned chicken from Lily and opened one of the drums. While he placed the pieces on an empty section, the sweet smell of the meat already cooking inside rolled out on hickory-laced smoke. Bernadine couldn't wait for dinner."

Lily said, "I'm going to head back inside for a minute. You going to be okay, Bernadine and Crystal?"

Clay waved his fork. "They'll be fine. You just go tell Ms. Agnes to hurry up with that sauce."

She saluted and barked, "Yes, sir," before hurrying off.

Bernadine saw Trent's eyes follow her departure for a moment. When he saw Bernadine watching him, he asked Crystal, "You sleep okay?"

"Yeah, but this is boring."

"Oh, really?"

It was Tamar. She'd just walked up and Crystal froze.

"You ever shuck corn?" Tamar asked

"No."

"Then I'll teach you. Come on." She handed Clay the large pot of sauce he'd been waiting on, but Crystal didn't move.

"I think Ms. Bernadine needs me to keep an eye on Zoey and Devon."

"I think Ms. Bernadine can do that herself. Come on."

Crystal turned to Bernadine. "Do I have to?"

"I think you do, Crystal. Might be fun."

Crystal's highly glossed pink lip poked out. She huffed out her displeasure, then followed Tamar back across the field.

Bernadine shook her head and took a seat at the picnic table with the men. Amari began asking Clay and the others a million questions, but some of the answers he received helped Bernadine learn things she didn't know, either, like Clay, Malachi, and Genevieve Curry all graduated from high school together and that Clay was Trent's godfather. Malachi and Clay had been friends since kindergarten.

Before long they were rejoined by the women from the kitchen, including Crystal, whose skimpy clothing was now hidden beneath a long T-shirt with a Kansas State University logo on the front.

Tamar explained, "Her top got all wet washing the corn."

"Ah."

Crystal sat down at the picnic table as if she was mad at the world. Hoping it might cheer her up, Bernadine said, "Thanks for helping Tamar."

"Not that I had a choice, but you're welcome," she grumbled.

All of the prep work in the kitchen was done, so now it was time for them to relax and enjoy the festivities. Bernadine could see Marie walking the field and holding court. She gave hugs to her former students, kissed grandbabies, and stopped and talked with everyone. It was obvious the schoolteacher was well loved. "What did Marie teach?" Bernadine asked Lily.

"Everything. English, science, math. You didn't play in her classroom either. If she had to call your parents because you were cutting up, forget it. She ruled. And Lord help you if you didn't do your homework."

Tamar cut in, "I remember the time Trent decided football was more important than algebra. Marie made him spend a whole weekend at her house catching up. He ate there, slept there. Grandson never missed another assignment. Did you?"

"No and neither did anybody else. She didn't play."

Before he could say more, the sound of jeers swept across the field and everyone at the table turned to see the cause. Riley Curry, Genevieve, and a tall skeleton of a man Bernadine didn't know had just arrived. Trotting beside them on a leash was Cletus, who was decked out today like a Green Beret complete with camo uniform and a small beret. Riley, dressed in that same black suit, was grinning and acknowledging the boos with presidential-like inclinations of his head.

"Good grief," Ms. Agnes said.

Bernadine had to agree. The hog was apparently ac-

customed to being in the spotlight because it seemed to be
showing off like a pure bred at a dog show. She noticed
mothers were holding onto their younger children, though,
and wondered what that was about?

"What the hell is that?" Amari asked. "Sorry for cussing."

"A hog," Trent said, his eyes hard.

"Looks like a big rat."

"He's mean enough and he bites."

"What's wrong with Zoey?" Preston asked with alarm.
"Look!"

Bernadine turned to see Zoey running toward the table.
She was looking at the hog with terror in her eyes. Crystal
stood and took off at a run and scooped her up. Zoey practically climbed Crystal's neck.

Holding the small child tight, the teen carried her back.
"She's shaking."

Everyone at the table could see the shivers coursing her
little body.

"Hand her here," Bernadine said, concerned. "It's okay,
Zoey. Nothing's going to hurt you."

By then the Currys were on them, and Zoey was clutching Bernadine so tight, she thought she might suffocate.

Clay snarled, "Get him out of here, Riley. The little girl's
scared."

Riley smiled. "Of Cletus? Oh come now, we all know
Cletus wouldn't hurt a fly."

Clay snapped, "Did you hear me? Get that hog out of
here or I'll gut him right here and throw him on this pit!"

Riley immediately placed his hands over the hog's ears.
"Hey. You know how sensitive he is."

Tamar had fire in her eyes. "Git!"

Bernadine said, "I'm going to take her in the house." Although she'd seen the hog a few days ago and knew it was big, up close and personal the true girth and size was jaw-dropping. It was a scary-looking thing and seemed to be surveying the scene with malevolent little eyes.

Riley pulled himself up to his full five-foot-four-and-a-half-inch height. "I just came to make sure the pieces he gets are done."

Bernadine wondered if all hogs were carnivorous but was too outdone to ask.

Clearly irritated, Clay said, "The meat'll be done just like it always is. Now get that thing out of here."

But he didn't leave. Instead he turned to Bernadine and said, "Ms. Brown. This is Morton Prell. He's a banker over in Franklin and a friend of mine."

Prell looked old enough to have known Frederick Douglass. His brown flesh seemed to have been stretched over his bones and his dun brown suit looked two sizes too big on his frail, thin frame, but his eyes were sharp as he took in Bernadine and held out his hand. "Pleased to meet you, Ms. Brown."

"Nice meeting you, but I need to take her inside."

"Riley's told me a lot about you. Are these the children?"

Bernadine waited. Zoey's silent tears were wetting Bernadine's cheeks. "If you'll excuse me."

He gave her a cadaverlike smile. "Says you got a lot of money."

Bernadine turned cool eyes on Riley, who simply raised

his chin as if daring her to deny the truth. "Good day, Mr. Prell."

"I have some investments you might be interested in."

"No, thank you." She began to walk away, and he had the nerve to walk with her.

"You haven't heard me out."

"I know, but I'm up to my eye shadow in investments right now and my accountants want me to stay pat. I'm sure you understand."

The eyes were shrewd as he checked her out. He nodded a head that had more liver spots than hair. "I understand. Keep me in mind though, if you would."

"It was nice meeting you."

Prell then looked over at Tamar, who was walking with her. "You all have a good time."

Inside, they got Zoey some lemonade and set her in a chair at the table.

Lily came in a few moments later. "She okay?"

Zoey seemed calmer but her hands on the glass still shook a bit.

"Do you think it was Cletus?"

Bernadine shrugged and took the now empty glass Zoey handed her. She brushed a hand over the girl's sweat-damp hair. "Do you want to stay inside for a little while?"

Her eyes said yes.

"Okay, then I'll stay with you." Bernadine could only assume it was the pig that had set her off, but why? She knew Cletus was scary looking, but Zoey's reaction bordered on the extreme.

Soon Agnes entered to check up on Zoey, and upon finding her much more settled, she appeared relieved.

Tamar asked acidly, "I couldn't believe Prell wanted you to stop and talk. When is somebody going to put a stake in that vampire's heart?"

Agnes responded, "What heart?"

Bernadine assumed there was a story behind Prell but at the moment she was too concerned with Zoey to care. The tears had ceased as had the shaking. She was still a bit pale though.

Devon came in next and with him were the other kids. "She okay?" he asked.

Amari knelt down in front of the chair Zoey was sitting in and said to her sincerely, "Zoey, you have three big brothers now, me, Preston, and Devon. We'll turn that hog into bacon if he even looks at you again, so don't be scared. Okay?"

He held out his hand, "Now come on. Some kids want to teach us how to play something called Red Light, Green Light, and we can't play without you."

To the amazement of the adults, she took Amari's hand, scooted off the chair, and let him lead her and the rest of the kids back outside to the party.

"I'll be damned," Tamar said.

"What she said," the outdone Bernadine replied.

It was finally dinnertime, and after they got the kids settled in at a nearby table, the adults sat and started in on their meals. They were eating and talking about everything and nothing when Malachi came strolling over. He had a piled-high plate in one hand and his off arm wrapped around Tarika, the girl who'd been with him earlier in his truck. She had a plate too.

Clay Dobbs took one look at Tarika and called out to his best friend, "She ride here on her tricycle, Mal, or did you drive her?"

Laughter rang out.

"Quit hating on my boo," Tarika quipped, smiling. "You all are just jealous."

"Tell 'em, baby girl," Malachi crowed.

Bernadine wondered why a girl who seemed halfway intelligent was hanging out with a man three times her age.

Bing said sagely around his grin, "Young girls are gonna kill you one of these days."

Malachi countered, "You know a better way to go?"

Tamar said, "Just get a seat. Welcome. I'm Malachi's mother, Tamar, and these are all friends."

Everyone introduced themselves. Tarika responded like she was well raised. "Pleased to meet you all."

Once that was done, everyone went back to their plates.

Bernadine noted that although Trent was sitting directly across from Lily, he made a point of not looking at her, and she wondered how long she'd have to be a resident before someone clued her in on why they acted like oil and water around each other.

After dinner, to work off all the fabulous food, there were sack races, egg tosses, and a huge sixty-person game of Ms. Jefferson Says—sorta like Simon Says. Marie wasted no time in whittling down the participants. Her quick terse commands eliminated a third of the players before the game was five minutes old, including Amari and the rest of the kids at the event. As she progressed in her crisp teacherly voice the remaining adult participants dropped like flies. The last person standing was Trent. No matter what she asked him, she couldn't get him to mess up, so she finally gave up and with a grin crowned him the winner.

As he basked in the cheers of the crowd, he proclaimed loudly, "She's been ordering me around my whole life. I'd better win."

After the laughter died they could all see that the sun was setting. It was time to bring the party to an end.

People lined up to give Marie one last hug, and it was vividly apparent that she cared as much for them as they did for her.

Morton Prell walked over to Bernadine. "I didn't believe Riley when he said you were bringing in a bunch of foster kids. Fancy yourself a philanthropist, do you?"

"I'm just Bernadine Brown, Mr. Prell."

"And humble too. Isn't that nice. If there's anything my bank can do to help you, just let me know." He handed her a business card.

"I'll be sure to do that."

"Nice meeting you."

"Same here," she lied.

As he moved on, she wondered if any of the local farmers grew garlic.

CHAPTER
15

The people from out of town were soon packed up. With the sun setting they wanted to get back to their hotel rooms before dark. Cleaning up would be handled by the Henry Adams locals, so once the others were gone they cranked up the music, grabbed a glass or a can of their favorite beverage, and dove in. First off, the tables were stored away along with the lawn chairs. Clay and Bing oversaw the dousing and cleaning of the pits with the help of Preston and Amari, who asked another one hundred questions about the process, while Tamar, Crystal, and the ladies dealt with the leftover food. It was Henry Adams's version of an after party.

Lily was shaking her thing to the syncopated percussion of, "Me and Baby Brother" by War as she pulled a full trash bag out of one of the many barrels and tied it closed. Glancing around to gauge how much more there was left to do, she saw Devon and Zoey helping out. Across the field was Bernadine in her 48-carat gold bangles and perfect nails hauling trash bags just like everybody else, and Lily's admiration for her employer rose even higher. Who would have thought a woman of her stature would happily volunteer for cleanup duty at a country birthday party, or that Lily would be tapped as No. 2 Sista in Charge of the project? Lily was genuinely enjoying helping Bernadine transform Henry Adams just as much as she was enjoying the transformations in her own life. Winston called almost every day, trying to convince her to come back to Atlanta, but she kept telling him no.

"Lily Fontaine! Cut out that daydreamin' and get to work," Tamar yelled.

"Yes, ma'am!" Lily called back with a laugh and moved on to the next barrel.

Once Lily finished her area of the field, she carried the trash bags to the central collection point over by the house. Eventually all the bags would be loaded into the bed of Bing's truck and taken to the dump. As luck would have it, she and Trent arrived at the spot at the same time. He had two large trash bags in his hands, and on his face that same unapproachable look he'd been wearing since she came to town. Common sense told her to just leave it alone, but she knew the drama between them had to be straightened out. "Can I talk to you for a minute?"

He dropped his bags. "Sure."

She had no idea how to begin, but looking up at him she could see him as he'd been in high school—his smile, the way he moved, the special moments they'd shared. Beneath all the anger was the young boy who'd been her first love. "I'm sorry, Trenton."

"For what?"

"Don't play with me. I'm trying to be honest here."

"And I'm trying to find out what you're sorry for."

They were half an inch from blowing up; she knew it, he did too, so she grabbed hold of her temper and said as earnestly as she could, "For hurting you."

He looked off into the distance for a few silent moments, then said stonily, "Thanks." And he walked away.

She wanted to throw something, curse, rage. She wanted to tackle him, snatch him up, and make him give her something besides that terse one-word response. Instead, she stomped off too, because in the end, the mess between her and Trent was still her fault.

Across the yard, Bernadine watched Lily and Trent as if they were actors on a stage. They were too far away for her to hear the conversation, but the way Trent turned away and the way Lily marched off in the opposite direction seemed to confirm that they were still at odds. She sighed. Her hope was that they'd get it together. They were going to be foster parents, and the last thing their kids needed was interpersonal drama negatively impacting their adjustment.

She pulled another trash bag out of the barrels Tamar had assigned her and took a moment to wipe the thin sheen of perspiration from her brow. The sun was going down but it was still hot. She noticed Malachi coming her way and wondered what he wanted. He and Tarika had disappeared after the meal, missing the games and dessert. He was alone now. She supposed Tarika had to be home before the streetlights came on. Chastising herself for the catty crack, she tied up the trash bag and set it aside.

"Brought you something," he said as he approached.

Somebody had put Etta James on the box. Her bluesy voice singing, "At Last," rolled over the openness like the rising dusk.

"And what is it?" she asked, hoping this wasn't going to be more of his foolishness. It had been a long day, a good day, but a long one.

He held up his hands to show her a can of grape pop in the left, and a can of beer in the right. Both looked ice-cold. "Figured you might be thirsty. Tamar can be a tough boss."

"Bless you." She chose the pop and wasted no time getting it open. The icy cold liquid slid down her throat like butter. Savoring that first sweet swallow she gushed, "That was good. I needed that. Thank you."

Noticing that he hadn't popped open the beer, she gestured to his can. "You're not going to drink with me?"

He met her eyes for a long moment, then looked out over the open plains. When he turned back to her, his voice was soft. "My name is Malachi July and I'm an alcoholic."

The confession startled her. She searched his eyes and saw only truth. Everything she'd assumed about the man was suddenly flipped on its head. "I'm sorry." She didn't know what else to say.

"No need to apologize. It's not like you knew."

He was right of course, but she felt like she'd put her foot in her mouth.

"I brought over a can of beer too because I wasn't sure which one you'd want," he explained.

It must have been easy for him to see that she was still

struggling to find words, because he smiled wistfully and said, "I'll let you get back to work. You take it easy."

And before Bernadine could force her brain to engage, he walked away.

After talking with Lily, Trent tore out of Marie's driveway like a bat out of hell. He knew he should have been more gracious with her apology, but all he'd wanted to do was shout at her, "Why?! Why'd you do me like that? I loved you!"

Maybe if he'd still been seventeen he'd have asked, but he was a grown man now, and grown men didn't bare their feelings, especially if they were hurting, so he was driving like a crazy person instead. The ruts and holes in the road were bouncing the truck like a spurred horse. The pounding had to be killing his shocks, but he didn't care. He just needed to drive.

He didn't realize he'd driven to the Dog and Cow until he got there. To his surprise, standing out front like a mirage in the desert was Rocky. At first he thought his anger at Lily was making him hallucinate, but it was her, and she looked as mad as he'd ever seen. Cutting the engine, he got out. "What's going on?"

"I need a ride to the airport," she said bitterly.

Confused, he glanced at the suitcase by her feet. "Where's Bob?"

"Home."

"Did something happen? You okay?"

"I don't want to talk about it."

He could see fury snapping like fire in her eyes. "Okay.

Is your sister okay? That why you're flying out?" Kristin, her younger sister lived in Boston.

"Krissy's fine. In fact, that's where I'm heading."

"For a visit or for good?"

"Not sure."

Trent was so confused he felt like a man walking around in a strange house in the middle of the night while wearing a blindfold. "I'll drive you to Hays. No problem. You ready to leave?" Her arms were folded and he could see the tension in her biceps. She seemed to be physically holding something inside that was threatening to make her blow sky high if she let it loose. "Talk to me, Rock. He didn't hit you or anything, did he?"

She shook her head, which came as a relief because he'd hate to have to hunt Bob down and kick his ass to show him the error of his ways. But Trent still had no clue as to why she was so upset. "Come on. Get in the truck. What time's the flight?"

She didn't move.

He sighed and waited.

When she finally confessed what was wrong, he thought he must have gone deaf because he was sure he couldn't have heard what he thought he'd heard her say. "Run that by me again?"

"You heard me the first time," she snapped, and snatched up the handle on her suitcase and stormed over to the truck.

Trent's jaw dropped. "You caught him wearing your underwear!"

Her head swiveled like Linda Blair's. If a look could

have killed, he would have been dead on his feet. "Laugh and I will kill you. I swear I will."

But Trent had already gone around the bend. He was doubled over. Howling. And for all of her anger Rocky was fighting hard not to laugh too.

She tossed her suitcase in the bed. "I paid fifty dollars for that bra and panty set. I walk into the bedroom and his fat behind is wearing my shit!"

Trent exploded. The anger he'd been carrying dissolved like shadows in sunlight. It was cathartic. Exhilarating. Freeing.

Rocky slid into the passenger seat and slammed the door. "Get in the truck, fool. You're going to make me late for my flight."

But the mental picture of Bob posing in her fancy underwear had Trent so totally possessed he dropped to his knees and laughed until he cried.

Lying in bed, Malachi looked out the window at the moon and wondered what in the world was happening to him. He'd never told a woman what he'd confessed to Bernadine Brown. Ever. Since going sober, the lie he always told as to why he didn't drink revolved around a made-up allergy to the grains used in the distilling process. He'd learned the hard way that some women wanted nothing to do with a drunk, ex or not, and frankly he understood, but rather than be dissed or pitied or in some cases both, he kept his recovery to himself.

So, why had he told Bernadine the truth? Her of all people. She'd called him pitiful—something else that had never happened before. Women loved him and always had. He certainly hadn't intended to show her who he was inside. Hell, he was only beginning to have nerve enough to look in there himself. Yet he'd told her the truth and didn't have a clue as to why. Letting the thoughts roll around in his brain for a moment it came to him that maybe he'd wanted her to know that there was more to him than snake oil; that he had with hard work and the good Lord's patience managed to put Satan alcohol behind him. Up from his memory rose the quote he'd carried around in his wallet during the early days of recovery, and still did today: *He who conquers the city is great, but he who conquers himself is mighty.* Now, with years of sobriety under his belt, he felt mighty indeed, but why did he want her to know that? If he were someone else looking at this conundrum from the outside, he'd say that deep down inside he was trying to impress her. That surprised him so much he sat straight up. Admittedly, he was attracted to her, and what man wouldn't be? She was gorgeous, classy. He'd never been mercenary when it came to the softer sex, so her money wasn't the draw. *She* was. He liked the way she carried herself, the way she spoke, and that she had a mind and heart that believed she could take old sow-eared Henry Adams and turn it into a silk purse.

Malachi had loved him some women over the course of his lifetime, but he never remembered being attracted to a woman on anything other than the physical level. So what in the hell did all of this mean, he wanted to know. Was he finally at age sixty-something maturing—finally wanting to be with a woman people didn't mistake for his granddaughter—finally growing up?

Realizing he was taking himself into some unknown and downright scary territory, he thought it might be better if he went to sleep, but it took a while.

Trent was on his way back from the airport. On the way there he'd called Tamar to tell her what he was doing for Rocky and asked if she'd keep an eye on the boys until he returned. She agreed without giving him the third degree.

Now driving home through the dark, he'd come to the conclusion that this mess with Lily needed to be put to rest. The ongoing feud wouldn't be good for the kids, Bernadine, or anyone else. Lily was going to be around for who knew how long, and hanging onto a grudge from the past couldn't be healthy. It was time to move on.

When he walked into Tamar's, the boys were watching TV.

Seeing him, Amari stood and asked, "Where'd you go?"

"Had to take a friend to the airport. You all ready to head home?"

Tamar came out of the back. "Yes, take them home and let an old lady go to bed."

They grinned.

She added, "And boys, thanks for your help with the cleanup. We all appreciated it."

"You're welcome," Devon said.

"See you tomorrow," she told them. " 'Night, Trent."

" 'Night, and thanks."

The boys took their showers, and while Preston and Devon climbed into their sleeping bags, Amari stepped outside, where Trent was sitting on the steps smoking a cigarette.

"You smoke?"

"Trying to quit. First one I've had in over a week."

"That's good. You stressed?"

Trent turned and studied him silently for a moment. "Maybe."

"I had a foster mother who was trying to quit, but every time she got stressed she'd light up. What's up with you and Ms. Lily?"

Trent stared at this remarkable boy. "Nothing. Why'd you ask?"

"Because you watch her all the time when you think nobody's looking and I saw you two arguing when we were cleaning up."

"You're pretty observant."

"When you steal cars for a living you have to be."

Trent chuckled and stubbed out the cigarette. "Tell you what. Can you keep an eye on things here while I make a quick run to talk to her?"

"You gonna be gone all night?"

"No. Just a few minutes, then I'm coming right back."

"Is it about what you were arguing about?"

Trent nodded.

"Okay then, sure, I'll hold down the fort. Ms. Lily's hot, you know."

Trent's shoulders shook with amusement. "Go inside."

"You don't think she's hot?"

"Go inside, Amari."

"You think she's hot too. You just don't want to admit it."

"Now."

Amari finally went inside, and the chuckling Trent walked over to his truck and drove off.

Agnes and Marie were already in bed, but Lily, still blue from her encounter with Trent, was mindlessly watching TV. When the knock on the door sounded, she stared at the time on her watch and got up to see who it could be.

Opening the door she saw Trent framed against the moonlit darkness. Her jaw tightened. "What do you want?"

"To talk. Can you step out here for a minute. Promise I won't keep you long."

She nodded and joined him on the porch. "What?"

He didn't speak for a moment, as if trying to get his thoughts together, then said, "Came over to apologize for the way I acted."

"I appreciate that."

"You were trying to set things straight and I acted like an ass."

She shook her head. "And you had the right. What I did—my friends did . . ." The memory came back and she was once again standing in her dorm room. He'd come up to visit. Her new friends ridiculed him for the way he dressed and spoke, but instead of coming to his defense she'd laughed right along with them. "It was wrong, Trent. So wrong."

He nodded. "Yeah, it was."

She had no defense and knew it. "My excuse, if you can call it that was, was that I was trying to fit in. I was hanging out with these big city kids, and I felt so cool . . . "

"And then I showed up."

Her lips tightened with her shame.

"Me with my high-water pants and country haircut."

Her heart broke. There was nothing she could say, except "I'm so sorry."

He sighed and whispered, "Loved you like I loved breathing back then, Lily flower."

The intensity in his gaze caused tears to well in her eyes. The endearment almost made her crumble. "I know."

He reached out and brushed away a tear sliding down her cheek. "Just wanted to apologize and to tell you I accept yours."

"Thanks," she breathed.

"See you tomorrow."

"You too."

He stepped down off the porch, but before leaving, he stopped, turned, and said, "Glad you're back."

"So am I."

He drove away.

As the silence of his leaving settled, Lily Fontaine sank into the chair on the porch, put her head in her hands, and cried like a baby.

CHAPTER

16

After lunch the next day, two big moving vans drove up to the two unused trailers, and the kids gathered on the back porch of Tamar's house to watch them be unloaded. There were boxes and pieces of furniture, exercise equipment, and more boxes. Some of the stuff went into one of the vacant trailers while the rest went into the one next to it.

A big black car like the one they'd taken from the airport rolled up and parked in front of the van. Four people got out. One was a tall, kind of heavyset lady with a short natural who stood with a short guy wearing glasses and jeans. They were joined by a brown-skinned lady of average height and a tall dude in a green uniform.

Preston announced, "I am not living with the army."

They watched Bernadine give the new people hugs.

Amari said, "Now, I'm really voting for Trent. Mr. Army looks like a hard ass even from here."

Devon and Zoey were looking on as well, and while

the older kids continued to speculate on the possible personalities of the foster parents, Zoey saw the movers bring out something from the back of the truck that made her go absolutely still.

Amari cried out, "Wow! Look at that piano."

"Reminds me of the big shiny one Alicia Keys sings with," said Crystal.

"That, my friends, is a baby grand," Preston tossed out proudly. "Somebody paid large cash for that."

Zoey watched intently to see which trailer the piano went into and which of the people went into it too. Once she knew, she settled back in her chair.

That evening, everyone, including the new foster parents, the kids, and the Henry Adams residents gathered for dinner in Tamar's front yard. Introductions were made and the kids and the Garlands and Paynes got their first up close look at each other. Afterward they all waited anxiously as Bernadine prepared to announce the pairings of children and parents. Bernadine prayed the matchups she and Lily had worked out would be a good fit.

Everyone, including the adults, was nervous.

Bernadine looked out over the gathering and said, "First, would the parents please stand."

The Garlands, Paynes, Lily, and Trent rose to their feet. She saw Amari's face widen into a grin when he saw Trent standing with the group.

"First, Amari, will you go stand by Trent."

She expected the boy to yell out his excitement but in keeping with the tone of the evening, he stood and walked silently to Trent's side. The two smiled at each other.

"Zoey Raymond." But before Bernadine could ask her to go stand with the Paynes, Zoey walked over to Reggie Garland and took his hand. Reggie met his wife's surprised but smiling eyes, then looked down at Zoey. She didn't glance up. She simply stood by him, then placed her free hand on top of the one already entwined with his as if to further stake her claim.

Bernadine was more than a bit taken aback. It was plain to see that Zoey had made her own choice, and Bernadine had no idea what might happen if she forced the girl to go with the original plan, which was to place her with the Paynes. So, she let it go.

Sheila looked disappointed, but she gave Bernadine a smile that seemed to say, it was okay, so Bernadine moved on.

"Devon Watkins," Bernadine called quietly.

Dressed in his suit and tie, he stood.

"Please go stand by Ms. Fontaine."

The responding smile lit up his little brown face. He walked over and took Lily's hand. Lily smiled down warmly.

"Preston Mays."

Preston stood up, his face was void of emotion.

"Please stand with Colonel and Mrs. Payne."

Disappointment flashed across his face but was gone so quickly Bernadine thought maybe she'd imagined it. He walked over, shook both their hands, and stood between them.

"Last but not least by any means, Miss Crystal Chambers."

Crystal stood. Beneath all the makeup she was a pretty young woman, and folks could see that now that Bernadine had convinced her she only needed two layers of paint as opposed to the six she usually buried her skin beneath.

"Come stand by me."

Crystal's hand flew to her mouth. Disbelief widened her eyes. She walked over to Bernadine and grinned before placing her hand over her mouth once more.

Everybody had a home now. One that Bernadine hoped would be permanent, loving, and nurturing.

"Tamar."

Dressed in flowing robes of red and black, her wrists heavy with silver bracelets, Tamar stood. "Form a circle if you would please. Agnes, come stand by me."

Malachi was passing out fat white candles to the people in the circle.

Tamar lit her candle and used its flame to light the one Agnes held, before saying, "Many years ago, our ancestors came to Kansas and founded this town with a lot of hard work, perseverance, and dreams. Now, we pass on those dreams to another generation of pioneers. Would each of the children come forward and light their candle from mine or from Agnes's, then light your parents'."

One by one the children stepped up. Bernadine watched Amari and Trent. Their twin smiles filled her heart. Then came Zoey. In the light from the candle the determination on her face could be seen as she lit the candles held by the Garlands. Preston lit the ones held by the Colonel and Sheila, who had tears in her eyes. Devon lit Lily's, who gave his shoulders a loving hug. Bernadine held up her own so that Crystal could light hers while she offered up a silent prayer that all would go well. Soon they were all standing behind wavering points of flame, and the darkness around them glowed.

After a moment of silence, Tamar said, "Any time there is doubt or worry or pain call up the memory of this night to remind you that you are not alone. We are your family, you are our family, and we hold each other up. May the spirit of the ancestors see that all of our dreams come true."

She blew out her candle, and everyone followed suit.

The short but moving ceremony seemed to have touched everyone. Amari and Preston shared a long, involved handshake, and the adults congratulated each other. Crystal standing beside Bernadine asked, "Did you really want me?"

"Why wouldn't I?"

Crystal shrugged. "I don't know. Nobody wants teenagers."

"Do I look like your average everyday nobody?"

She smiled and shook her head.

"Good. Go and see if Tamar and the ladies need help with the dessert. You're the big sister around here now, so get to acting like it."

The gentleness of Bernadine's tone made the girl look in her eyes for a moment more, then, smiling, she went into the kitchen to see if Tamar needed help.

The new families went home after dessert.

When Preston and the Paynes entered the place they'd be calling home for now, he looked around. Boxes were piled up everywhere. Even though the couple seemed nice, he figured life had given him the short stick again. Why couldn't Trent have been his foster dad instead of the U.S. Army?

Mrs. Payne's voice interrupted his thoughts. "Preston, we're very glad to have you here."

"Thanks, but I don't know why you picked me. All you're gonna do is send me back."

"Why?"

"Because that's the way it works. I act out, you can't handle it, you send me back. I've been in eight different homes in the last year. Proud of myself."

Sheila looked at the boastful young man, then at her husband, who'd taken on the icy glare of the drill sergeant he'd once been. "Why are you proud?"

"Because I won and they lost. All they wanted out of me was the money anyway. How much are you all getting?"

"Not a dime," Barrett replied.

Preston seemed stunned. "Stop lying."

"I'm not. Ms. Brown isn't paying anyone to do this."

"No way you're doing this and not getting paid. If you are, you're crazy."

Sheila saw her husband smile the smile of a crocodile, but he didn't bite, instead he said. "Let's show you your room, Son. We'll talk more in the morning."

"Whatever." Grabbing up his old suitcase he followed the colonel out of the room.

Sheila watched them leave and shook her head. Preston had no idea what he was in for, but on the other hand, she didn't think her husband knew either.

Barrett Payne said to Preston, "We'll put you in here for now. I know it's kind of bare, but soon as we move to the new house, we'll fix it up the way you like."

"Thanks." Preston looked around. The room held a bed and a dresser and a nightstand with a lamp.

"So what kinds of things do you like to do?"

Preston shrugged. "Play video games."

"*Ah*. Anything else?"

"Nope."

"Somebody your age should have more than video games in their life. Once we get you settled we'll see about broadening your interests."

Preston didn't think his interests needed broadening, but he kept that to himself. "Look, I'm real tired. I'll see you in the morning. Okay. Thanks for taking me in."

"You bet. See you in the morning."

As Preston lay in bed, he wondered why he always wound up with the wack foster parents? He couldn't wait to be eighteen so he could lose the foster care system and chart his own life.

Because Lily was staying with Marie and Agnes, Devon was given the guest bedroom upstairs. Lily was thrilled that Bernadine had decided to let her and Devon have one of the five new homes being built, but for now they'd stay with the Jeffersons. Devon was lying in a four-poster bed, and she noted that he'd put the old flowered pillowcase on the pillow beneath his head.

"Is this a special pillowcase, Devon?"

"Yes, ma'am. Belonged to my grandma."

"I see."

"How long do you think I'm going to live with you?" he asked.

"Until you get big enough to go to college."

His eyes widened. "I'm going to go to college?"

She nodded. "Or trade school or the military. It'll be up to you. Would that be okay?"

"Yes, ma'am."

Lily could almost see his young mind trying to wrap itself around the concept. "But that's many years away. Right now, just know that me and Agnes and Marie and everybody in Henry Adams is your family now, and we're going to love you and look out for you from now until now on."

He smiled. "Yes, ma'am."

"How about we go shopping tomorrow?"

"What for?"

"Anything you might need. Socks, shoes. That kind of stuff."

"Okay, but I don't have any money."

She caressed his cheek. "I know, baby. You won't need any. Me and Ms. Bernadine got your back."

Lily thought about the semiprivileged upbringing her son, Davis, had been given once her life started moving up. Whatever he'd needed, whether it had been a baseball uniform for Little League, a new backpack for school, or help with his homework, she'd provided it, along with love, trips to the library, and lots of discipline. *Every child should be that fortunate*, she thought, so Devon had nothing to worry about. Gifting children with experiences and with as much of the world as a parent could offer was a mandatory thing. "You get some sleep now. I'll see you in the morning."

"Can I give you a hug?"

Lily felt tears sting her eyes. "Sure, if you want to."

"My grandma always gave me a hug before I went to sleep."

So he gave her a strong hug. "I know God is watching me, but I was scared after my grandma passed."

She held him close. "I know, baby."

"I'm not scared anymore. God bless you."

"You too, Devon. Now go on to sleep. My bedroom is right across the hall. If you need anything, you just let me know."

"Thank you, Ms. Lily."

" 'Night, Devon."

" 'Night."

Lily turned out the light, wiped at the tears running down her cheeks, and quietly left the room.

Reggie and Roni sat in the bare living room after putting Zoey to bed and looked into each other's eyes. "She's a sweetheart," Roni said.

Reg nodded. "She really surprised me the way she claimed us."

"Me too. Maybe she knows something we don't."

"Apparently. I felt bad for Sheila Payne, though. She looked so disappointed."

"I noticed too, but you know I'm a believer in things happening for a reason. We'll just have to see what the reason is. You gonna be okay being mama to a little white girl?"

"Yep. Like you said. Stuff happens for a reason."

Reg looked down at his wife cuddled against his side. "Did I tell you today how much I love you?"

"I think you did, but no harm in telling me again."

"Good. I love you, baby."

She kissed him. "I love you more."

Malachi asked Trent. "Do you think that boy asks questions in his sleep?"

They were sitting outside on the trailer's steps. "I hope not. I understand now why curiosity killed the cat. I'm going to want to shoot myself before this is over."

"Malachi chuckled, "He's something."

"Yes, he is."

"We'll be good for him, though."

"If he doesn't talk us to death, but I like him, Dad. I always wanted to be a father."

"And you'll be a whole lot better at it than I was."

"You weren't so bad."

"Quit lying. If it hadn't been for Tamar and Dobbs . . ." his voice trailed off.

"That's the past. We can't change it so let's just focus on what we have now, which ain't too bad."

"You're a way better son than I deserve, Trent."

Trent shook off the clouds of the past and grinned. "I know."

Malachi chuckled. "I'll be heading to Vegas in the morning."

"You're not leaving me here alone with Amari."

"Got to. The honeys are calling."

"You're a mess."

"I know. You think Amari will have run out of questions by the time I get back?"

"How long are you going to be gone?"

"Week. Ten days at the most."

"Then probably not. In fact, I'm going to tell him to save some just for you."

"Hater."

"I love you too, Dad."

They spent a few more minutes talking, and when they were done, Trent went back inside, hoping Amari was asleep, while his father drove home to his place at the D&C.

The new families spent the next few days shopping in Hays for clothing for the kids and attempting to forge a bond. It wasn't easy, at least not for Preston.

Barrett Payne was accustomed to rising every morning at 4:00 a.m. Now that he'd retired, his wake-up time had been dialed down to 6:00 a.m. Sheila entered the small kitchen at 6:30 to begin preparing breakfast, and by 6:45, the smells of coffee and bacon filled the trailer aromatically.

By 7:15, because Preston still hadn't made an appearance, Barrett went upstairs and stopped for a moment in the bedroom he and Lily shared to pick up the old boom box he'd unpacked last night. With it in hand, he walked down to Preston's door and knocked.

Nothing.

He knocked again and called out in a loud voice, "Preston. Time for breakfast."

Still nothing so he opened the door. The overweight kid was sprawled on the bed and was out like light at night. Barrett jostled him gently. "Time to get up, Son."

Preston opened one eye. "Go away."

"Time for breakfast."

"Too early. Go away," he repeated crossly while turning over and drifting back into slumber.

The former drill sergeant reached down and snatched the covers back. Smiling, he pushed Play on the boom box. The sound of reveille, loud as the engine of a jet filled the room with its trumpet call. Preston bolted awake like the bed was on fire.

The *rata-tat-tat* of the trumpeting continued loud and long. Preston yelled angrily over it, "What the hell's the matter with you!"

Payne cut the music. "You awake now?"

In the silence, sullen eyes met the Colonel's. "Yeah I'm awake. I'm deaf too. That was mean."

"Mrs. Payne gets up every morning and cooks breakfast. What's mean is if we don't respect her enough to eat it when it's ready."

Preston was in no mood for logic.

"So get washed up and come to the table." He walked back over to the door. "Good morning, Son," and he exited.

With a snarl on his face, Preston murmured a profane two-word reply that told the colonel exactly what he could do with himself. However, he knew further resistance was futile, so he left the bed and went into the bathroom to wash up and brush his teeth.

Tamar, Marie, and Agnes had volunteered to take the kids to Hays to the movies, and after they left, Bernadine stopped in to see Lily, who was working on setting up a Web site for the town. "I'm going into town. Is there anything I need to take to Trent?"

"I have some work orders, so is it okay for me to ride with you?"

Since Bernadine never remembered Lily actually offering to seek out Trent's company, she wondered what this meant. "Okay when we get back I want you to see about ordering something to drive. Truck. SUV. Something so you can get around in. I'm paying."

Lily had sold her car back home rather than have the fancy import tortured by the terrible roads. "I can pay for it."

"I know that, but consider it my gift. Okay?"

And before Lily could argue, Bernadine said, "Let's ride."

CHAPTER
17

Bernadine's vision for Henry Adams was beginning to take shape like a lump of clay on a potter's wheel. In addition to the homes being built, the new neighborhood center the residents wanted would be the first municipal building to go up, and it was almost finished. Once it was, the town's residents would have a sumptuous new place to hold their gatherings. As it stood now, the only places available was the church basement or the Dog and Cow, neither of which was large enough to accommodate everyone comfortably.

They found Trent up on a roof.

"Hey, Bernadine. Hey, Lil."

Bernadine stared. She heard the quiet affection in Trent's voice along with the shortening of Lily's name. She also saw that Lily was smiling like a shy teenager. Had she missed something?

Trent came down to them. "How are you ladies doing this morning?"

"Fine," Bernadine said.

"Fine," Lily echoed. "You?"

"Spent the morning answering Amari's' questions but I think I'm surviving."

Bernadine looked between the two again. She had missed something. Damn! Putting that thought away for now, she walked with them as they toured the site. Standing next to Trent as he pointed out various details on the building, Bernadine considered him a blessing. Since heading up the operation he always had time for her many questions and didn't seem to mind helping her understand the stuff she knew nothing about, like heating and cooling installation, plumbing lines, insulation methods, and the rest. When she first began putting her dreams together for this endeavor, she was glad she hadn't known just how much work it was going to be or how much she didn't know. If she had, she might have said, "Never mind," and flown off to Nepal or the Bahamas instead.

But here she was, wearing a hard hat, construction boots, and her gold bangles, watching her hopes come to life.

"Another few days and they should be ready for occupation."

The sound of that was like music to her ears, but she could barely hear it over all the sounds of hammering, drills, saws, and heavy equipment filling the air. Accustomed to seeing her on site, the busy workers acknowledged her with waves and smiles.

"Is everybody around here always this friendly?"

Trent nodded. "Yes, but these folks are more friendly

than most because you're providing jobs. Not much call for new construction around here these days. Economy being what it is, many of them would be working out of state this summer were it not for you. Their families are probably pretty happy with you too."

"Never thought about that."

"In your own small way, you're helping a lot more folks than just us. Crew Chief Kelly told me that some of his people were a season away from losing their homes. Not anymore."

Her heart tightened with emotion. She hadn't thought about there being a ripple effect to any of this. She wondered how many more people would be blessed by what she was trying to do. She had no answer but hoped the numbers would soar into the thousands.

"What the hell do those two want?" Trent asked.

Walking up were Morton Prell and Riley.

"No clue," she said with irritation.

"*Ah*, Ms. Brown. Trent," Prell said in his Karloff voice. "How are you on this nice sunny day?" His loose-fitting brown suit fit him like the walking skeleton that he was.

"Fine, Mr. Prell. And you?"

"Doing well."

Bernadine turned to Riley. "Mr. Curry."

He nodded to her and to Trent and Lily. Bernadine swore she saw an evil gleam in Riley's eyes, which was more than enough to warn her to watch her back.

Prell was looking at the construction. "I see that things are moving along well here."

"I'm pleased with the progress." Bernadine hadn't seen

him since Marie's birthday party, and seeing him today was way too soon for her liking.

"Riley tells me you're also putting up municipal buildings, like a recreation center?"

"Yes."

"I'd like to invest in some of what you're doing."

"In exchange for what, may I ask?"

He gave her the cadaver's smile. "A small say in how things go."

"No thanks."

"You're a hard woman to negotiate with, Ms. Brown. You turned down my invitation to invest in some of my ideas, and now you're turning down my request to invest in yours?"

"That sounds about right."

"I'm not accustomed to being told no, Ms. Brown."

"Sorry to hear that." She could tell by his tone that he was not liking the way this was going; she was sorry about that too. *Not!* "Will there be anything else, Mr. Prell?"

"Yes, since you're being so difficult, you can move those trailers you have squatting on my land off my land and tell Tamar July I'm calling in her mortgage for violating the no-renters' clause in her contract."

Trent stiffened, as did Bernadine. "What?"

"You heard me, Ms. Brown," he repeated with a snake's smile. "I've owned that land of hers for over ten years. It says specifically that there will be no other housing structures of any kind erected without my expressed approval."

Trent said, "Let me get this straight. Just because she

won't let you in on the project, you're going to take it out on my grandmother?"

"I'm just exercising my rights as the landowner."

"Which means, yes," Bernadine replied, looking him up and down like the pitiful excuse for a human being that he was. "Who else do you plan to mess with because of me?"

"Let's see, we could involve Dobbs and Shepard. Their combined two thousand acres went into foreclosure five years ago, but out of the goodness of my heart, I haven't evicted them. Then there's Agnes Jefferson. That poor old woman owes my bank over fifty-five thousand."

"So in total, they owe you what?"

He thought for a moment. "About seven hundred and fifty thousand, give or take a dollar or two."

"That much?" she asked.

He nodded and seemed to be pleased with apparently having the upper hand.

"And what's the name of your bank?" Bernadine asked while digging around in her Hermès tote for her phone. Bernadine held title to the town proper, but the surrounding landowners owned their own acreage.

"First Franklin Savings and Loan," Riley offered proudly, speaking for the first time. "Been in business for going on fifty years." He looked pleased as well.

She noticed that Prell seemed annoyed with Riley for butting into the conversation, but that wasn't any of her concern at the moment. She was focused on the number she was punching into her phone. "Excuse me for just a moment."

With Prell and the others looking on, Bernadine waited for the connection to ring through and when it did, she said to her friend on the other end of the line, "Hey, Tina girl. How are you?"

"Fine," came the response in Bernadine's ear. The two women chitchatted for a couple of seconds, then Bernadine asked, "Need you to do me a favor. Got a bank I want you to buy."

Prell's eyes grew big as saucers.

"Yeah, the head cheese is a bastard and threatening to put some senior citizens that I know out in the street. Need you to buy it, then send me their mortgages so I can pay them. Hold on a minute." Bernadine turned to Prell. "First Franklin Savings and Loan is the name of your bank, right?"

He looked like he was about to choke to death.

Bernadine ignored him and resumed her conversation and then ended it, saying, "Okay, hon. Thanks a million. I'm sure he'll put up a fight, but do what you need to do to acquire it. I'll fax you the names on those mortgages later today. See you soon. Love you too."

She closed the phone and turned to the ashen-faced Prell. "I am not somebody to mess with. You may be a big fish here in this small Kansas pond, but in my world you are plankton. Is there anything else you'd like to threaten me with?"

Prell was clutching his chest as if his heart had stopped, but Bernadine was too angry and too through to care.

"Have a good day, gentlemen. Let's go, Lily. Trent, we'll see you later."

He appeared pleased. "Yes, ma'am."

In the truck, Bernadine pushed the stick into first and drove away. She was so angry she was shaking.

"Remind me never to get on your bad side," Lily joked. "That was Oscar-winning material there."

"Asshole. I should have had Tina buy his damn house too. Threatening me."

"Did you see his face? I'm sure he wet his pants. Riley looked like he'd swallowed his tongue. Tamar is going to want to adopt you."

"Good, because I've already adopted her." Bernadine couldn't believe the nerve of the man. He actually thought she was going to be intimidated. Maybe if this had been 1945 when women were powerless . . . She wanted to turn the truck around and go back and run him down.

"Will your friend really buy his bank, or were you just kidding?"

Bernadine turned to him, "Do I look like I'm kidding?"

Lily sat back against the seat and beamed with joy. "After he gets through having that heart attack, he's going to be real mad."

"Good, because he made me mad."

"So who is your friend Tina, or am I being too nosy?"

"Nope. She's one of my Bottom Women sisters. Blonde, blue eyes, lives in Connecticut. Love her to death. She collects independent financial institutions like some folks collect sea shells. Her husband was Mitchell Craig."

"The big banker guy that went to jail last summer?"

"Same one. He divorced Tina about fifteen years ago. She threw a party the night he was sentenced."

"Not a friendly divorce, I take it?"

"No, he divorced her to marry their son's nanny, who drained him like a vampire. He was embezzling for her, which is how he wound up doing ten to twenty at Club Fed."

"Karma is a bitch."

"Amen."

Lily thought about her own divorce and how painful it had been. Her ex was on his fourth wife at last count, each one younger than the last. The only positive thing to come out of her short marriage was her son, Davis. The rest was crap. "Do you think you'll ever get married again?"

"Not if I can help it. I'm enjoying running my own table." Bernadine looked over. "What about you?"

Lily shrugged. "Don't know. I do know that Winston won't be the one, though."

"Is he still calling?"

"Almost every day. He can't believe I threw over a college professor to come back here. Says he's going to keep calling me until I come to my senses."

"Think that'll happen any time soon?" she asked, amusement in her eyes.

"Not while I'm drawing breath. He's so damn boring. I want to kick myself for even thinking about settling for him. And that's what I was doing. Settling."

"What's your son saying about all this?"

"He's all for the new me. Told me my life was stagnating in Atlanta and that it was about time I got off my butt and started living." She smiled. "Can't wait for you to meet him. Told him all about you. You'll like him."

"Can't wait to meet him either." Bernadine wanted to ask her about Trent but didn't feel she and Lily had known each other long enough to talk about the truly private matters in their lives, but she hoped their relationship would reach that point eventually. There wasn't that much of a difference in their ages; her being the older one of course, but she thought it might be nice to have someone in town under sixty-five she could talk with and relate to. "You know, even though we're technically employer and employee, be nice if we could be friends too."

"Thinking the same thing."

Their eyes met.

"Then girlfriend, me and you."

"All righty now."

Later, back at the office, Bernadine's phone rang. It was Tina.

"Hey, girl," Bernadine said. "What's up?"

"Are you sure this Prell person owns this bank?"

"Fairly sure, why?"

"If he does, he's in big trouble."

"Hold on a minute. I want to put you on speaker."

Lily came out of the back with a sandwich in her hand.

Bernadine said, "You might want to listen in."

Lily nodded and took a seat.

"Ok, Tina. Go ahead."

"There's nothing on file anywhere that indicates this is a registered and viable financial institution. According to what I could find, the First Franklin Savings and Loan has been defunct for years."

"What?" Bernadine and Lily shouted in unison.

Tina laughed at the reaction and asked, "Who's that with you, B.B.?"

"My assistant, Lily Fontaine."

"Sounds like the name of burlesque queen from back in the day. Hi, Lily."

"Hey, Tina."

"Hope I didn't offend you."

"Nope."

"Good."

As Bernadine and Lily listened in, Tina explained that all records showed that the Feds had sent Prell a notice back in '03 that his savings and loan was being investigated because of poor record keeping and insufficient deposits. Tina explained, "The auditors said Prell couldn't produce any of his records, nor did he have copies. Everything he did show them was on paper."

"I'm not surprised, really," Bernadine offered. "Old as he is, he probably wouldn't know a computer if it ran over him in the street."

"But get this. The Feds closed him down six months later. So if he's been taking money from folks as a mortgage lender and he's not one, I'm pretty sure that's a felony."

Bernadine and Lily shared a look.

Bernadine asked, "So what's that mean?"

"I'm going to talk to a few lawyers and you should do the same, but in my mind it means, what mortgages? If he's not a banker and doesn't have paperwork backing up the contract he supposedly has with them, his claims are null and void."

Lily asked, "But wouldn't the state have some kind of record?"

"You'd think they would, but they can't seem to find anything current either. Either he didn't file anything with the state, or everything was lost years ago. One of the clerks told me that lots of documents fell through the cracks when agencies switched from paper to computers in the seventies and eighties." Bernadine asked, "So how are my friends going to prove they own their land?"

"The clerk said if they have their original deeds, fax her copies and she'll see what can be done. She made it seem like she was just going to plug them into the system and pretend like they were already there, especially when I explained to her that these were old people who'd been scammed."

Bernadine had no doubts as to why she considered Tina Craig one of her best friends.

"She's going to look into the property taxes, but as far as she could tell, none of the mortgages exists. At least not in his name."

"Interesting."

"I thought so too. Like I said, get those documents faxed and let's hope your friends can catch a break."

"Okay, thanks Ms. T. I owe you one."

"No problem. Nice talking to you, Lily."

"Same here."

"BB, is Lily a Bottom Woman?"

Bernadine laughed. "She's divorced and was a first wife, so I guess she qualifies."

Lily called out, "I'm a little light in the Benjamin department compared to you all, though."

"We don't care," Tina assured her. "We've got enough Benjamins for every female on the planet. Have BB bring you to the next meeting so we can meet you. That okay, B?"

"Fine with me. Thanks again, Tina."

"Love you, girl. Ciao."

In the silence that followed, Bernadine said, "Well. We thought Prell was having a fit because we were going to take his bank, but the real deal is he has no bank, and that's probably what he didn't want anyone to know. If I didn't think it would splash on Tamar and her buddies, I'd call the FBI on his skeleton-looking behind right now."

"So they have been paying him all these years for no reason?"

"Apparently so, and he certainly wasn't going to tell them he'd been shut down."

"You'd think someone would have known, but this is a small town. If he was opening the place up every day and pretending like he was still in business, who would know the difference? That's cold."

"Yes, it is."

That evening, after Tamar and the kids returned, Bernadine told Tamar about Prell's threats, and all Tamar could say was, "That skinny bastard."

"Why'd you all deal with him in the first place?"

"Back in the fifties the white banks wouldn't loan to us, so it was Morton Prell or nobody."

"So he was legitimate back then."

"He was, and made loans to most of us out here. Foreclosed on a lot of land too when folks couldn't pay him back."

"You have your original deed?"

"Sure do."

"Then get it to me tomorrow along with Ms. Agnes's and the others and we'll fax them to the lady in Topeka."

"Sure thing." Then she said, "Bernadine?"

"Yes, ma'am."

"How many more blessing are you going to bring?"

She smiled. "I don't know."

"Well keep them coming."

"Doing my best."

CHAPTER
18

Crystal was having a ball. She and Bernadine were using Bernadine's laptop to surf stores for stuff for Crystal's bedroom at the new house. The room she had now was pretty generic and basic. Although it was nice, Bernadine wanted the teen to have a space that reflected Crystal's own tastes and choices.

It was difficult at first, because Crystal had never been given carte blanche before on anything, and even at fourteen she knew a high price when she saw one.

"I know it's expensive, Crys," Bernadine kept reminding her, "but it's a quality comforter and it will last you for years."

Crystal didn't seem convinced, but after a while, she got into the sprit of it and before long had ordered everything from bedding to curtains to towels to throw pillows in colors and designs of her own choosing.

They were looking at shoes when Lily rapped on the door and called out, "Hey in there. Anybody home?"

Bernadine called back and invited her in and was pleased to see Devon with her. He was wearing yet another suit and tie. Lily had purchased him a ton of regular boy clothes and was hoping to wean him into them sometime soon, but she didn't want to push him into anything before he was ready.

"Morning," Lily said. "Devon has some questions for you."

"What can I do for you?"

"When can we go to school?"

She studied him. "I thought we'd get you all settled in with your new families first, let you play for the rest of the summer, and start school here in the fall when all the other kids go to school. That way Ms. Marie can order all the things she needs to teach you all the things she wants you to learn. Is that okay?"

He nodded.

"Do you have another question?"

"Yes, ma'am. Where's the church and who's the pastor?"

Bernadine gave Lily a quick glance before answering. "The church is downtown, but there is no pastor."

His face lit up. "Can I be it?"

Bernadine was stumped by that one. "Well, I don't know, Devon. Being pastor is a big responsibility."

"I know."

"Can I think about it and get back to you?"

"Yes, ma'am."

Crystal was shaking her head the entire time, and after Lily and Devon departed, she said, "That little boy needs a life."

"Why do you say that?"

"He's eight, Ms. Bernadine. He's supposed to be doing kid stuff, not getting up every day and dressing like he's going to a funeral."

"I'm sure that'll change, but for now he's being who he was raised to be. We all are."

Crystal thought about who she'd been raised to be— certainly not a preacher. "You ever go to church?"

"Back home I went most Sundays. It's good for the spirit. What about you?"

She shook her head. "I only been a couple of times. I don't think God listens to people like me."

"Why not?"

"Because when I was little I prayed all the time for my mom to come and get me, but she never did."

"How old were you the last time you saw her?"

"Six? Seven?"

"About Zoey's age, then?"

"Yeah. I want to find her. I know she's looking for me. Wouldn't you look for your daughter if the state took her away?"

"If I was an upright mom, sure, but when the state takes a child from its family it's usually in the best interest of that child. It's not a decision the judge makes without giving it a lot of thought, Crys."

Crystal, like most kids in her situation, didn't care about logic or judges. "I know she's looking for me, and when I find her, I'm going to help her get off crack, and we're going to get us a house and live together again. That would be da bomb, don't you think?"

"Yep, I do." Bernadine knew from her social worker experiences that children who'd been taken out of the home because of drugs or abuse often fantasized about finding the parent and saving them from themselves so that life would be normal again. Crystal was not the first nor would she be the last to imagine such a scenario because children's hearts were filled with hope. In reality few of the dreams came true, and if Crys's mom was a crack addict, there was very little chance of there being a happy ending. It saddened Bernadine. She didn't want her foster child to suffer any more hurt ever again but knew she would, especially if she was bent on finding her mother. "You know I'd like you to consider doing something else with your hair. That weave is breaking off your hair on top."

"Really?" She rushed to the mirror in the bathroom and Bernadine stood behind her and watched as Crystal tried to see the crown of her hair.

"It is, isn't it? Do you think I'll be bald?"

Bernadine shrugged. "Hope not, but think about changing up just in case."

Crystal scratched because her scalp itched. "Okay."

If the truth be told, Bernadine wanted to wrestle her to the ground and take a sharp pair of scissors to the girl's awful blond extensions, but like Devon and his suits, Crystal was only being who she'd been raised to be, and Bernadine would just have to play along.

The Currys were just sitting down to breakfast—at least Riley was. Genevieve had been up since six, feeding Cletus and mopping the floor in the back room Riley used as a barbershop on the weekends. Cletus had been in there and left a putrid mess behind.

"What happened to your hand?" Riley asked, seeing the tea towel she had wrapped around it.

She set the plate of turkey bacon on the table and took a seat. "Cletus bit me. Again," she said stiffly, unfolding her napkin and placing it across her lap.

"What'd you do to him?"

"Nothing."

"You must have."

"He's getting harder and harder to handle, Riley."

He took a sip of coffee. "You're imagining things. You bought that new perfume—"

"My perfume is upstairs in the bottle. It's the hog, Riley Curry. Not me. I was bleeding pretty good too." She didn't expect him to ask to see the bite and sure enough, he didn't. "Something's gotta be done."

"Like what?" he asked eyeing her over his cup.

"I don't know, but something. Soon."

"I'm not getting rid of him, Genevieve, so don't even think about that."

Her lips thinned. "Do you know why we don't have company come around anymore or why no one gets their hair cut here anymore except Clay?"

"Yes. It because of that Brown woman," he grumbled in reply. "Her and her big ideas. I still say that money of hers is from ill-gotten gains, and Morton's gonna prove it."

"What? How?"

"He's looking into her. You know she got him cheated

out of his bank. Every cent he had, gone just like that." He snapped his fingers.

"Then maybe Morton should let sleeping dogs lie, and Ms. Brown is not the reason we don't get company."

"No? Then what is?"

"Because this house smells like a septic field, that's why. Feeding Cletus the way you do? All he does is pass gas all day long, not to mention the droppings."

"He's housebroke."

"He used to be, but he's so mean now he does it inside, out of spite. You've been spending all your time with Morton. I've got the mess cleaned up by the time you get back, so you don't see it."

He shook his head. "Not getting rid of him, Genevieve. I'd sooner you leave than him. That hog's gonna make me rich one day. Richer than even Bernadine Brown."

Angry and hurt, Genevieve tossed down her napkin and stomped out of the room.

Riley helped himself to more grits. "Women."

Outside on the porch, Genevieve wiped away the tears threatening to run down her cheeks and drew in a deep breath. She was not going to cry. She looked out at Cletus wallowing in the mud hole in the middle of the yard. At one time it had been a beautiful yard, filled with roses and lilies and stands of sunflowers. There'd even been a few mature trees, but hogs root, and Cletus had rooted everything up no matter what kind of fencing she put up. Clay and Malachi had suggested running a strand of electrified wire through the fencing like many hog farmers did to keep their stock away from stuff they had no business messing with, but Riley deemed the solution too expensive and he didn't want Cletus to get shocked, not even once.

Her jaw tightened. Hadn't her father warned her not to marry Riley? Hadn't he called him a chicken hawk, all mouth, no action. Until the day her father died, he'd been convinced Riley was only after his money, but she hadn't listened. She'd been in love, or so she thought, dazzled by Riley and his big golden dreams. Now the dreams were proven to be fool's gold and she was playing servant to a damn hog, and an increasingly mean one at that. Tears filled her eyes again and her wrapped hand began to throb.

She got up to get her first aid kit. At the door she stopped and looked back at Cletus wallowing in his mud hole in her devastated front yard. Something had to be done, she just didn't know what.

By noon the next day, copies of all the deeds in question were faxed off to the helpful clerk in Topeka. When she had them in hand, she called Bernadine and promised to get back with her as soon as possible

Also by noon, The Franklin Savings and Loan was closed down—closed down as in plywood covering the windows and padlocks on the front doors. Trent reported the news after a morning run into Franklin to pick up ply- wood. Nobody had seen Morton Prell since his visit to the building site yesterday, but no one cared enough about the old extortionist to ask Riley if he knew anything. Every- body figured they'd get answers soon enough and went on about their day.

Marie made sure the kids had something to do almost every day that was quasi-educational but it was fun stuff. Today they were down in Hays along with the Paynes and Garlands and Clay Dobbs taking a look at Historic Fort Hays, which had once been home to the Buffalo Soldiers. While they were gone, the houses were being inspected for the big move in. They were now complete, and Bernadine and Trent were waiting and watching the state's inspection teams make what she hoped would be their final sweep. She hoped Lily was somewhere filming, because this would be a historic event. However she didn't see Lily anywhere about. It wasn't uncommon, with work going on at two construction sites, but she wondered about her absence.

"Is Lily over at the rec center?" Bernadine asked Trent.

"Nope. She had to make a run to the airport."

"Airport? Why?"

"Pick up some guy named Winston. I let her take my truck."

"Winston? He's here?"

Trent shrugged. "Guess so."

"Lord. Okay."

Lily drove up to the terminal and looked around for Winston. The idea that he'd shown up here unannounced was not playing well. One minute she and Trent had been going over contracts and the next minute her phone was ringing. When she saw the familiar number on the caller ID, she almost let it go to voice mail but grudgingly picked up only to hear him say he was at the airport.

She drove down to another set of doors and there he stood, luggage beside him. Maneuvering Trent's black truck to the curb, she threw it into park and got out.

Upon seeing her he said, "When you said forty minutes, I thought you were joking."

She could see that he was peeved. *Join the crowd.* "How was the flight?"

He picked up the two generic-looking suitcases and followed her to the truck. "Long, and of course, they didn't feed us."

"I wish you had called first to let me know you were coming."

"Thought maybe the shock of seeing me again would jolt you back to reality."

"Your reality or mine?" she asked with a fake smile.

"Ours." He hoisted his bags into the bed. "Nice truck. Yours?"

"No. Belongs to a friend. How long are you staying?"

He shrugged. "Haven't decided yet. Purchased two return tickets in case you come back to your senses, though."

"Not going to happen. Haven't you been listening to anything I've said to you for the past few weeks?"

"I have. I just don't believe it."

She looked away and tried to keep her voice calm. "Winston. I'm not coming back to Atlanta. I have a great job here and I'm doing great work. This is where I'm going to be."

"I'm not into long-distance relationships, Lily," he said, warning in his voice.

"Neither am I."

Her response seemed to surprise him, "So, you're willing to dump years of a relationship like it meant nothing?"

Guilt grabbed her and then clashed with the dreams she had for her own future. "Look, Winston, we've had a great time together but I don't see us going any further. I'm trying to be honest."

"Who is he?"

"Who's who?"

"The man you're sleeping with?"

"I'm not sleeping with anybody."

"Is this his truck?"

She threw up her hands. "You should probably fly back home, Winston. This is getting stupid."

"Who is he? At least tell me the truth!"

People walking past them were looking on curiously, but she ignored them and tried to keep her voice down. "Why does it have to be another man? Why can't it be just me wanting to change my life?"

"Is he one of these farmers from around here? Sixth-grade education, hay in his ears? Living on farm subsidy welfare?"

She snapped. "That's it!" Storming to the back of the truck, she stood on the bottom of the tailgate, reached in and threw his bags out onto the sidewalk. "Have a good flight home."

His eyes were large. "What the hell are you doing?"

Lily answered by getting into the truck, locking the doors, and starting the engine. Steam was pouring from her ears as she gunned it and peeled out. She didn't look back.

Trent was heading over to the house that would soon be his when he saw Lily drive up. When he walked over to her, he could see fire in her eyes. "What's wrong? Where's your friend?"

"Left him at the airport."

"Why?"

"Because he's a jerk and an asshole."

"Okay." This reminded him of the last time he'd seen Rocky. He hoped Winston hadn't shown up wearing her underwear.

"I need to run home for a minute."

"No problem, but why don't you let me drive. You look a little hot."

She didn't argue and took the passenger seat while he got behind the wheel.

He drove out to the road, silent at first, then asked, "Besides him being a jerk and an asshole why'd you leave him there? Didn't he fly out to see you?"

"Yes, but I've been telling him for weeks that I'm not coming back to Atlanta and he won't listen. Thinks I've lost my mind."

"Is he a friend, boyfriend, fiancé?"

"Some place in the middle. He's been trying to get me to marry him for a while now."

"I see."

Lily looked over at the closed face and shook her head. *Men.* "But I've decided I didn't want to settle just because he was the only man in my life. Of course, he thinks I'm breaking it off because I'm sleeping with somebody. Which

I'm not. Accused me of sleeping with a farmer with a sixth-grade education, hay in his ears, and, on welfare."

"Covered all the bases, did he?"

"Threw his suitcases out of the truck and into the street."

He chuckled softly. "First time he's seen your temper?"

"I don't have a temper."

"Bullshit. Remember Oliver Johnson?"

"No."

"Liar. Took three of us to pull you off of him the day he wrote, *Lily gives it up!* on the blackboard in chemistry class."

"I wanted to kill him."

"Thought you didn't remember him."

"Thought you were driving."

He smiled but didn't say another word.

CHAPTER
19

The next morning, the helpful clerk looking into the mortgages of Tamar and her friends called Bernadine and said everything was cleared. In spite of her investigation she could find no liens on their properties. As far as her office was concerned the land continued to be in the hands of the original owners, and she'd be sending back all the original documents by courier. Added to the good news, now that the titles and deeds were clear, she was siccing the authorities on Prell. A warrant for his arrest on fraud and a number of other charges would be issued by the end of the day. Bernadine shouted "Hallelujah!"

That evening while the kids were inside playing the video games they'd hooked up to Tamar's new TV, and Lily and the other foster parents were over in Franklin enjoying a nice quiet dinner that didn't involve hamburgers in a bag, the seniors celebrated their freedom by starting a big fire in the barbecue grill and feeding Prell's so-called mortgage papers to the dancing flames.

Watching his grandmother and her friends burning their papers, Trent couldn't have been happier. Seated next to Bernadine in the lawn chairs set up by the house, he thanked her for her role.

She waved him off. "It was no problem. Glad I could help and that everything turned out the way it did. By the way, has anyone seen Prell?"

He shook his head and took a swallow of his lemonade. "No. I asked Riley when I ran into him at the Franklin Post Office yesterday, but he told me to mind my own business."

"He's such a nice little man."

"One of a kind."

"What is his problem?"

"Besides being a pain in the behind?"

She smiled.

"The rumor is that he was going to get a big fat kickback on the annexation deal he wanted us to do, but when you stepped in and bought the place, that was that."

"So it's about the money?"

"Partly. The other part is he's just a pain in the behind."

The reason no one had seen Morton Prell was because he was holed up in a rundown motel on Highway 183 just outside of Hays, registered under the name Miles Peterson. Thanks to the Brown woman, not only had it been necessary for him to close his bank, but all the snooping done by her and her friends made him certain the Feds were going to come calling sooner or later, and he was betting

on sooner. He hated her. Seated at his desk, in the small
cheerless room, the TV behind him playing with the sound
muted, he wondered what he was going to do now. Most
of the people who owed him favors were either dead or
in nursing homes, as were his old connections at the state
capitol in Topeka. He didn't know anyone anymore who
could dig up the dirt he needed on her, or stop her licens-
ing and building permits from going through, or audit her
operation. With one phone call she'd sent a decades'-old
scam crashing to the ground—one phone call and there
was nothing he could do to pay her back.

In the old days when he'd been in his prime, this
wouldn't have happened. Back then his reputation alone
would have made her heel. You didn't cross Morton Prell
because your stock would be poisoned or you'd be black-
mailed or beat half to death by the thugs on his payroll.
The only person loyal to him now was Riley, and he wasn't
worth a damn—him and that stupid hog.

Bent with age, Prell walked slowly over to the closed vi-
nyl drapes and peeked out of the dirty window at the parking lot below for any government sedans that might have
shown up since the last time he checked. Seeing nothing
suspicious he secured the drapes again and sat down on the
worn pink flowered spread covering the bed and tried to
come up with a plan.

The new houses were finally ready for occupation and Bernadine couldn't tell who was happier, the parents or the
kids. The new rec center was also finished, and that week-

end they'd scheduled a celebration, but today it was moving day and they started early.

Barrett Payne asked Preston, "Can you grab that box there, Son? It has Mrs. Payne's good dishes inside and I need to have them carried out to Mr. Dobbs's truck ands set on the front seat for the ride to the new house."

"I can't carry heavy stuff. Asthma."

Barrett looked at him. "Not asking you to carry the truck, just the box."

"How much do you make in life insurance if I die of an asthma attack?"

"Get the box."

Preston got the box. It wasn't as heavy as he imagined and he felt a bit silly for complaining as he carried it outside to Mr. Clay's truck, but physical labor was not his forte and he avoided it whenever he could.

Roni and Zoey were walking hand in hand through their new house. "I have this really big piano, Zoey. Where do you think we should put it?" Not that Roni planned on playing it any time in the near future, but Reg refused to let her get rid of it, so it needed a spot. "How about over there by that window? I know this is supposed to be the living room, but it's such a big space I think all of our furniture will still fit."

She watched Zoey look around as if assessing what Roni had said, then looked up at her and nodded. "Great, then that's where we'll put it."

*   *   *

Amari ran his hands over the brand-new mattress standing against the wall of his brand-new bedroom and liked the way it felt and how clean it looked. "Never had a new bed before."

Trent looked up from the bed frame he was putting together. "No?"

"Every bed I ever slept on had a pee-stained mattress somebody else had used."

Trent studied him and wondered what else his new foster son had never experienced. Personally, Trent had never slept on a used mattress, being an only child and grandchild, he'd pretty much gotten whatever he'd wanted, within reason, and it had always been new. "Everything's going to be new from now on."

"That's cool," Amari said quietly. "Real cool."

"Come here and let me show you how the rest of this frame goes together. Grab that socket wrench out of the tool chest."

Crystal couldn't believe how beautiful her bedroom looked with all the great stuff Bernadine had let her order to furnish it with. Nobody she knew had a room as hot as this. Nobody. Nobody had a foster mother like her either. Ms. Bernadine was R-I-C-H and Crystal wasn't mad about it. When they went shopping down in Hays last week, not only had Ms. Bernadine bought her a whole new wardrobe, she had also gotten her a small pair of diamond studs that Crystal planned on wearing the rest of her life. The studs were a reward for being so nice to Zoey the night she got scared. Crystal went to stand in front of the short dresser with the big mirror attached and looked at the sparklers in her ears. They weren't the biggest diamonds around, but they were real and they were hers. After she found her mom, Crystal thought she might want to grow up and be just like Ms. Bernadine, but not if it meant going to college; everybody knew that only booji geeks went there, and she wasn't either of those.

While Crystal was at the new house putting her room together, Bernadine was packing up the trailer with Tamar's help. At the moment, Tamar was on the phone. When the call ended she said, "Malachi says hello."

Bernadine felt heat rise into her cheeks. "Is he enjoying Vegas?"

"Since his women paid for everything, I'd guess, yes."

"Women? As in more than one?"

She nodded and wrapped a sheet of newspaper around the glasses they were packing. "One lady paid for the first week and a different lady the second. He's gonna wake up covered with hot grits one of these days."

Bernadine shook her head. "I am too scared of him."

"He ought to be scared of himself. Still thinks he's in his thirties," she added disapprovingly. "I stopped trying to get him to grow up a long time ago. Better for my blood pressure."

"He told me he doesn't drink anymore. Was he telling me the truth or was that just snake oil?"

"No, it's true, and nobody was prouder than Trent and I. Had poor Trent running crazy trying to keep him out of bars, bailing him out of jail, searching for him every Friday and Saturday night from here to Hays and back, whole time praying he didn't kill somebody on the road before he could find him, snatch away his keys, and drive him home. It was terrible," she said in a heavy voice. "It wasn't till he almost killed Cletus that he let the alcohol go."

Bernadine held onto her giggle, "He almost killed Cletus? How?"

"In a way, it was funny, but Cletus had some kind of infection and Riley asked Malachi to look at him. Well, Mal was drunk as a skunk when he got there and shot Cletus up with a tranquilizer instead of an antibiotic. That hog was out cold for a straight forty-eight hours. Riley had a fit. He just knew Cletus was dead."

"But he wasn't?"

"Unfortunately, no, some folks would say."

"So Malachi felt guilty? Is that why he stopped drinking?"

"No, he stopped because Riley called the state and the vet board took Malachi's license."

Bernadine nodded understandingly.

"He'd been the vet here since he graduated from college, but when they took his certification he had to go work in the Oklahoma oil fields. Made good money but it was the doctoring he'd always loved and it wore on him how much he missed it."

"So he got sober."

"Yes indeed. Reapplied for his license, got it back a few years later, and hasn't touched a drop since far as I know."

For Bernadine, the story added more flesh to the man. "But he hasn't sworn off the women."

Tamar started on another glass. "Nope."

"Are he and Trent's mother divorced?"

She shook her head. "Never married. The girl was the daughter of a lawyer over in Franklin. She was seventeen when he got her in *trouble* as we used to call it back then. Family moved to California. Year later, a big car drives up to my door. The girl's mother gets out carrying a baby. 'Here's your grandson,' she says to me and drives away."

Bernadine was speechless.

"Never heard another word. I don't know if Trent's mother is alive or dead, but I raised him. Mal was still a teenager. Only thing he knew about a baby was how to make one. Had to give it to him though, he never made another one far as I know, and never married either."

Bernadine could now add more flesh to Trent too. "That's quite a story."

She nodded. "I'm glad she brought Trent to me though. She could have given him to the state, and we would've never known. He may have wound up like those children you're trying to help."

And Bernadine was glad he hadn't.

She and Tamar loaded as many boxes as they could fit into Baby's bed, and after a wave and a thank-you, Bernadine headed to town. She'd made a monetary arrangement with Mr. Kelly's crews to help with the moving, and many of them had volunteered for the overtime. While they unloaded the truck, Bernadine went inside and called up the stairs for Crystal. The teenager came flying down, grabbed Bernadine's hand, and dragged her back up. "You have to see my room!"

Once there, Bernadine looked around and gushed, "Oh,

Crystal, this is gorgeous." The hot pink and bright orange room was a knockout.

"All the bedding fit. I had one of the workers put my bed frame together and help me hang the curtains."

Bernadine eyed the crazy Day-Glo orange-and-pink pattern on the big comforter and knew the dizzying color would have made her crazy inside of a day or two, but this was Crystal's room, and Bernadine's opinions didn't matter.

She glanced around at the matching drapes and at the walls adorned with posters of Crystal's version of the teenager's hall of fame: Rhianna, Beyoncé, Tyra, and Mary J. "Like the way you put up the posters."

The desk in the corner that was supposed to be reserved for homework looked more like a makeup counter, but Bernadine didn't fuss. "You did a great job."

"Come look at the bathroom," she said, grabbing Bernadine's hand and pulling her along. "I put up the shower curtain too."

The bathroom was way more sedate, at least the walls were, but the towels and the shower curtain, café curtains on the window, and rugs were a deep rich purple. "The curtain matches real well."

Crystal was beaming.

"It looks good, girlfriend."

"For real?"

"For real."

Like everyone else in town, Riley Curry had heard about all the hubbub going on with the Brown woman and wondered if maybe the time had come for him to cut his losses and start sucking up, too. He'd been supplementing his income for the past ten years with the payoffs Morton Prell gave him for incriminating news or gossip about people behind on their mortgages, in trouble with the law, or in need of financial assistance of any kind. Prell was for all intents and purposes a loan shark, and once the victims were targeted, he would step in and play savior, charging so much interest they never were able to break free. Anything Riley could find out that could put someone in Prell's clutches had been worth cold hard cash. Now, with Prell hiding out in a shabby no-tell motel out on Highway 183, Riley was on his own. Trying to wheedle his way onto the Brown gravy train would be difficult at this point, considering all the grief he'd been giving her, so instead, he'd been toying with another idea he wanted to pitch to the networks.

It would involve Cletus and the Brown woman's junior felons. The kids and the hog would all live together in a house. Cletus, wearing a housedress and a wig would be the mother. Riley could already see Cletus fixing breakfast, getting them off to school and helping with homework. It could be like the old *Donna Reed Show*. Of course it would be hard to get Cletus in a pair of high-heeled shoes, but he'd let the network's special effects people worry about that. The more he thought about it, the more of a hit series he thought it would be. "Hey, Genevieve!"

About an hour ago, they'd had another fight over Cletus and she was upstairs in her room sulking; something she'd been doing a lot of lately. It wasn't his fault if she kept wearing perfume and lotions that set the hog's dander up. He'd told her a hundred times or more that her smell was the reason Cletus kept chomping on her.

He walked to the steps and yelled up the steps. "Genevieve! Come here. Need you to help me think of a name for this new show I'm going to pitch next time the TV people come."

A few minutes later, she came down the steps. He stared at the pink suitcase she was carrying. "Where're you going?"

"Some place where I don't have to live with a hog."

"What?"

"You heard me." She walked past him and headed to the front door.

He hurried to catch up. "Have you lost the last of your simple mind?"

Apparently she had, because that remark earned him a slap so hard his head rang. "Don't you ever call me simple again!"

Holding onto his throbbing face, Riley stared at her with wide eyes.

She took a moment to pull on her good cotton church glove before saying calmly, "A while back, you said you'd rather I leave than Cletus. Well, you're getting your wish."

"You're leaving me?"

"Yes, Riley. I am."

"Because of Cletus?"

"Because of you, Riley. I have put up with your crazy-as-a-bedbug schemes, your friendship with that nasty Prell, and that hog, but no more. I should have listened to my father. He warned me."

"Your father was—" he began, but seeing the hard look in her eyes he quickly shut his mouth to keep from getting smacked again.

She pushed through the door and stepped out onto the porch.

He followed, adding hastily, "If you're going, don't expect me to take you back."

She started down the steps and across the yard, all without a word.

"I'm not taking you back! You hear me, Genevieve. You'll be back before nightfall, but I'm not taking you back!"

Her answer was to keep moving. She cast a baleful eye at the six-hundred-pound hog wallowing in his mud puddle and set out up the road.

Twenty minutes later, she rang Ms. Agnes's bell. When Marie came to the door she took one look at the hard set of her high school friend's face and the suitcase in her hand and shouted, "Hallelujah! It's about time. Come on in here, girl."

CHAPTER
20

The houses they'd moved into were close enough together that they were able to walk between each other's homes. Trent and the Paynes were on one side of the
street while Lily, Bernadine, and the Garlands were directly
across on the other side.

Amari and Preston couldn't have asked for a better situation because they were in and out of each other's houses
all day long.

Sheila was in the kitchen cooking dinner when they
burst in through the patio door heading for the refrigera-
tor and yet another video game match. From behind the
opened pages of his latest edition of the Marine Corps magazine *Leatherneck*, Barrett said, "Wash your hands before
you touch anything."

"You got it, Colonel," Amari called back. He and Preston headed to the first-floor powder room.

Barrett slid the magazine down just far enough to see

his wife's face and the happiness softening her features. He was sure it was his imagination but she looked younger. "You're liking this, aren't you?"

"I am. I like the kids, the adults at least so far, the towns-people, everything. This is utopia for me."

He put the magazine back up. "Pretty strong word to be using, *Utopia*."

"It's better than *hell*."

The boys came in, grabbed some juice boxes, shook some popcorn onto two papers plates from a flour-sack-sized bag Tamar had brought them from Sam's Club, and trooped up-stairs to Preston's room to grab their controllers.

"Why don't you act like you're scared of Captain Amer-ica?" Preston asked as his character stole a car and began to tear down the street, running through red lights and knocking pedestrians in the air.

"Because I'm not scared of him," Amari said, smiling as his car went up over the curb, hit a couple of prostitutes, then bounced back on the street while cops screamed be-hind him.

"Why not?"

"Because I don't live here, Pres. He's not my dad."

"Thanks."

"No problem."

Amari watched Preston's character walk down a dimly lit street. "Now, be careful, this is where that ho came out and took your money."

"Stabbed and killed me, too, remember?"

"Yeah. Just didn't think you wanted to be reminded."

"I didn't."

Preston focused his entire being on the game and the controller in his hand.

"Ten hut!"

They froze. Neither had the stomach to turn around. It was the colonel. They didn't have to turn around because he came to them. "I'll take those."

They handed over the controllers, and to their amazement, he knew what to do to turn the game off. "Stand up."

Their legs shaking, they complied.

He was wearing the pressed short sleeve brown shirt and the knife-creased brown pants he always wore. Standing with his arms behind his back, he waited for their eyes to rise and meet his.

"Where'd you get a copy of Grand Theft Auto?"

They swallowed.

Preston said, "At the mall in Hays, sir."

"How'd you buy it?"

Preston knew that this was the tricky part. "*Um.*"

"The truth, Son."

Amari jumped in. "Trickery, sir."

"Trickery."

"Yes, sir. We bamboozled Ms. Agnes the last time she and Tamar took us shopping. Told her they were educational."

"Did Tamar know about this?"

"No, sir."

"Shall I tell her?"

"No!" they shouted in unison. Amari might not have been scared of Captain American, but he knew not to get on the bad side of Madea.

"Give me the game and any other ones you know you aren't supposed to have."

Preston popped the game out of the console and fished the other contraband games out of the backpack under his bed and handed them over.

"Is that it?"

"Yes, sir," said Preston.

"Amari, let's head over to your house."

His eyes widened.

Barrett barked. "Move it, gentlemen! Now!"

The boys jumped and hustled past him to the door and down the stairs. Barrett followed.

Sheila was at the bottom of the stairs when he came down. "What's going on?"

He tossed her the case that held GTA. He looked into her wide eyes and said, "Be right back."

Bernadine was on her porch reading the newspaper and Crystal was leafing through a decorating magazine when they saw Amari and Preston come marching out of the front door with the colonel walking briskly behind them.

"Somebody's in trouble," Crystal said in a pleased singsong voice.

Bernadine thought so too, but she didn't interfere. Whatever it was, Amari and his partner in crime, Preston, were probably guilty, and it looked like Colonel Payne had everything under control. She went back to her paper.

Trent was making himself a sandwich when the boys marched in with Payne. He took one look at the marine's sternly set face, then at the guilty faces of Amari and Preston, and sighed. "What did they do?"

Payne handed him a bunch of video games. Trent's eyes popped as he read some of the titles.

"Preston had those stashed in his room. Amari's here to get his."

"I see," Trent said. "So what are you waiting on, Amari? And make sure you bring down all of them. You don't want me to have to toss your room. I grew up with Tamar, so I learned from the best."

Amari sighed and headed off. He returned a few minutes later with six games, all rated Mature. He handed them to the colonel.

"Thank you. I think Trent and I will agree that there will be no more video game playing."

"For a while. Maybe until Christmas."

Both boys looked stunned.

Barrett then made them explain how they'd gotten the games.

At the end of the tale, Trent eyed them both sternly. "You tricked an elder of your community?"

Amari asked, "Are you going to tell Tamar?"

Trent ignored the misery in his voice. "That depends on how well you handle the punishment you're going to be on."

Trent turned to Barrett. "Since the two of them are guilty, I say they get two punishments. One from me. One from you."

Barrett smiled for the first time. "I agree, and I'm going back home to get mine."

While he was gone, Preston asked, "Are you going to send us back?"

"Nope. Family doesn't get sent away, but you might wish you were somewhere else when I get through with you."

"You can't hit us, you know. We're wards of the state."

"Quiet!"

They both shrank.

Barrett returned carrying a small brown leather case. "You ever heard of backgammon?"

The boys stared.

"Yes? No?"

He got a yes from Preston and a no from Amari. "It's an ancient game and I play very well. You are going to learn to play very well too, because there will be no more video gaming until you can beat me."

Their eyes popped wide.

"But we don't know how to play," Preston protested.

Barrett reached into his back pocket and pulled out a rolled-up paperback. He thrust it at Preston. "Learn. This will teach you. Your turn, Trent."

Trent's punishment involved them all piling into his truck and taking a ride to the Jefferson home, where Agnes and Marie lived. As they got out, Marie came outside to meet them.

"Hey, there." The sullenly set faces of Amari and Preston told the former teacher all she needed to know. "What did they do?"

Trent said, "Let's just say they've volunteered to whitewash your fence."

"That bad, huh? Okay."

Trent turned his attention to the boys. "Do you see that fence?"

They looked out at the fence that ran the length of the property on both sides. It was gray and weathered and stretched nearly a quarter of a mile down the road.

"All that?" Amari cried.

Trent nodded.

Barrett smiled.

Preston said, "But I'm not supposed to be around paint. I have asthma. I could die."

"I'm sure Doc Garland can keep you alive," Trent said, and directed his attention back to Marie. "I'll provide the paint. They'll be here first thing in the morning."

Agnes came outside along with Genevieve Curry and asked, "Something wrong, Trent?"

"No, ma'am. The boys have volunteered to paint your fence."

"Really? You boys are so nice. Thank you."

They got back into Trent's truck and he drove them home.

After dinner, Preston went up to his room to continue his sulking and Barrett sat on the patio with Sheila and told her about the twin punishments he and Trent meted out.

"I like the creativity."

"I wasn't sure Trent was going to back me up, but he did. His punishment surprised me as much as it did the boys, and the way Marie acted when he told her they were going to paint, made me think it wasn't the first time the fence had been used for that purpose."

"Maybe it's some kind of Henry Adams tradition."

"If it isn't, it ought to be."

"So admit it. You had fun being a father today, didn't you?"

He looked over at his smiling wife seated on the other side of the table and nodded. "I did."

She raised her glass of tea. "Told you."

Barrett went up to Preston's room to check on him and found him seated on the floor with the backgammon board open. He was reading the book Barrett had given him and was attempting to set up the pieces by looking at the diagrams. Barrett walked over, looked down at the setup, and pointed out what he needed to change. "Move that one there, and the white one over to this spot."

Preston did as he was told and said, "Thanks."

"Glad to see you're getting started on this."

"What choice do I have?"

"None really."

Preston looked up.

"You think I'm pretty harsh, don't you."

"Truthfully, yeah."

"I grew up with an alcoholic father. He didn't care what I did, where I went, or who I was with. When he got angry, he hit me with his fists. Did the same thing to my mother, but because he was a good soldier the army did nothing to protect us."

Preston searched his face.

"*That's* harsh, Son. If you need help with the backgammon, let me know."

"Yes, sir."

Barrett turned and walked out of the room.

When it was time for Amari to be in the bed, Trent walked upstairs and knocked on his bedroom door.

"Come in."

He wasn't in bed though. He was seated in his video game chair watching TV.

"Did I forget to mention no TV either until further notice?"

"Yeah," he replied accusingly.

"My bad. Turn it off."

Amari snapped the remote and set it down on the floor beside the chair. "I take it you're still mad."

Trent shrugged as he walked over. "Not really. I did dumb stuff when I was your age too, but you took advantage of an old lady, Amari, and that's a concern."

He acted as if he were too ashamed to look Trent in the face.

"I know we've just met and there's lots we're going to learn about each other, but I need to know here and now who I'm dealing with. Are you somebody who preys on the weak? Are you a predator, Amari?"

An echoing silence filled the room while Trent waited for a reply.

Finally, Amari looked up and said softly, "No, sir, I'm not. And I'm real sorry about what we did to Ms. Agnes. I never thought about it being predatory. GTA's just a hot game and we wanted it."

"Try this. Think about you being Ms. Agnes, an old lady wanting to do something nice for two boys she's pledged to help raise. Then the boys run game on you and play you for a sucker. If you found out, would you ever trust them again?"

"No."

"Tamar used to call the dumb stuff I did, Stupid Boy Tricks, but this runs deeper than that if it's about taking advantage of someone."

Amari seemed to think that over for a few moments, then conceded. "You're right, and you know, you're pretty good at this."

"Think so?"

"Yeah."

"Just repeating the same speeches Tamar gave me whenever I screwed up. How do you think I came up with the idea of the fence?"

"You had to paint that fence too?"

"One summer, twice. The second time, she made me sand it down, prime it, and then paint. Took me almost until school started to finish. And at least you'll have company. I was by myself."

"That's rough."

"That's Tamar."

"You aren't going to tell her, are you?"

"Only if you think you're going to do something like this again."

He shook his head quickly. "No."

"I'll take you at your word then. Now head to bed. You've got a long day ahead of you tomorrow."

He got up. "I know."

Trent still liked Amari a lot. "Set your alarm for six."

He stared.

"Good night."

Trent came downstairs just in time to hear a light knock on the front door.

Lily.

"Hey," he said, glad to see her. This was the first time they'd been alone together since the day she threw Winston's luggage into the street.

"I know it's late, but Bernadine wants everybody to make a list of anything that's not working correctly; dishwashers, sticky doors or windows. Things the crews may need to redo."

"Does that woman sleep?"

"I'm not sure."

"Come on in." He opened the door so she could step inside. He tried to ignore how her being near made him feel seventeen all over again. "I haven't found any problems yet." Unless he counted being fascinated by the curve of her lips.

"Okay. This is all pretty exciting, isn't it? The new homes, the kids."

He gestured for her to take a seat in the living room. She took a seat on his couch, he sat in a chair across from it. "Yeah, it is."

"The rec center's ready for the grand opening this weekend. Who'd have ever thought this sleepy little town would be this alive again?"

"Not me, for sure."

"I never thought I'd be signing up to raise another child,

though. Devon is as sweet as he can be, but the idea of having to go through those teenage years again when boys get allergic to soap, and their rooms smell like funky sports jerseys, and they're eating you out of house and home. I'm probably going to have nightmares. I may be too old for this the second time around."

"You'll be fine."

"I know, and so will you. Amari already in bed?"

"Yeah. Will you have dinner with me?"

She looked caught off guard for a moment.

"If you don't, it's okay."

"No, I will." She replied studying him slowly, as if searching for something. When?"

"Tomorrow, maybe. Day after?"

"Okay. Let me find out who can keep Devon, and I'll let you know tomorrow which day works best."

"Sounds good."

She stood. "I need to get back; I left Devon sleeping."

He walked her to the door and out to the porch. " 'Night, Lil."

" 'Night, Trenton."

He nodded and watched her cross the street and go inside. Inviting her to dinner hadn't been something he'd planned. The words just sort of rushed out before he could snatch them back. It was done now though, and he was looking forward to spending some private time with her.

He was in the kitchen getting himself a bowl of ice cream when another knock sounded. The seventeen-year-old within hoped it was Lily coming back for something but it was Malachi instead, and with him were Clay Dobbs and Bing Shepard.

"What are you doing here. Thought you were still in Vegas."

"Got bored. I hear Bernadine put big-screen plasma TVs in the houses, so we came over to break it in right. KC's playing the Dodgers tonight."

Before he could invite them in they were already in.

"And we come bearing gifts just like the Magi," Clay told him, indicating the large grocery bag in his arms.

"I'm allergic to frankincense"

"So am I," Bing said, "So we brought beer."

Malachi looked around and pushed a six-pack of Pepsi into his son's hands. "Put those in the fridge for me. Where's the plasma?"

Tickled and wondering how boring life would be without the three old lunatics in his life, Trent led the way.

Roni Moore Garland was dreaming that she was onstage again, playing the piano. Standing at the backup mikes were Zoey and Reggie, but Roni wasn't playing any of her standards. The distinctive sweet notes of a Brahms lullaby lifted from her fingers on the keys and floated like gossamer over the empty concert hall, then she woke up. Still half asleep she was disoriented for a moment by the dark and the new bed, but the warmth of her husband's body beside her and the sound of his gentle snoring immediately set things to right. With the music still floating in her head, she settled in to go back to sleep, then sat up again. The hairs on the back of her neck stood up as she realized the beautiful music wasn't in her head. As it filled her ears and the quality of the playing pierced the darkness, she gently shook Reggie and whispered, "Baby. Wake up."

"What?" he asked thickly.

"Wake up. Sit up. Listen."

Scrubbing his hands over his face, he struggled to do as she asked, and once he was sitting up, she said again, "Listen."

"Did you leave the CD player on. What is that?" he asked finally, as fully awake as he could manage after being awakened from a dead sleep.

The unknown pianist had switched to another composer. "It's Mozart." Roni threw aside the bedcovers. "Come on." She had no idea why or how her baby grand was playing, but she was very curious to find out.

"What if it's somebody robbing us?"

She rolled her eyes. "Way out here? And I don't think a thief would take the time to test a piano first if they were gonna steal it, but grab your 8 iron if you think you might have to clock somebody."

He did just that and the two crept down the hall to check on Zoey first. The little lamp Roni had left on for her use was still on. Bernadine had told her as they were leaving her house earlier that the little girl was afraid of the dark, and Roni and Reg had hoped it would help her with her fear, but the bed was empty.

Her not being in the room made both their hearts beat fast with worry and fear, so they headed to the stairs. The first thing they noticed was that every light on the first floor of the house was turned on. It was as bright as midafternoon. Next, they saw Zoey seated on the piano bench, her back to them.

Reg's eyes widened with surprise. Roni made a move to enter the room, but he stopped her gently and shook his head. He didn't want her scared by their sudden appearance. He mouthed and pantomimed, "Call Bernadine."

Five minutes later, Roni met Bernadine at their back door and silently led her in. Zoey's music filled the house with its beauty.

Bernadine looked on astounded. Reg was still watching and smiled when he noticed her standing with his wife. They all listened for a few more moments then tipped out to the deck so they could talk freely and without disturbing Zoey.

"Did you know anything about this?" Reg asked Bernadine.

"Does this face look like I knew? My Lord, where'd she learn to play like that?"

Roni cracked, "If you don't have an answer, you know we don't. I've heard classically trained grown musicians who don't equal her skill. Her little legs can't even reach the pedals."

Bernadine was at a loss for an explanation and she desperately needed one.

Reg asked, "The social workers didn't say anything about this?"

She shook her head. "But I'm going to start digging soon

as the sun comes up. There are too many missing pieces on this child, and we need to find them."

Zoey played until dawn, at which point she curled up on the highly polished piano bench and fell into an exhausted sleep. Reg gently picked her up in his arms and carried her upstairs to bed. He hoped she'd finally found peace.

CHAPTER

21

There was no peace and quiet in Riley Curry's life and
hadn't been since Genevieve's leaving a few days ago.
His attempts to duplicate her great cooking fell way short,
so he was forced to eat basic stuff like boiled eggs and sandwiches. Because she'd always managed the household tasks,
he had no idea how much detergent she used to do a load
of wash. Only later, when suds started rising out of the top
like foam, and the machine began shaking and bouncing
around, did he it occur to him that maybe he'd put in too
much soap and too many clothes, but it was too late. Praying the thing didn't blow up, he left it whining, screaming,
and bucking in the basement laundry room.

His attempts at cooking had left every dish in the house
dirty, and more than a few pots were black on the inside
from all the food he'd burned. Wishing he'd gone ahead
and let Genevieve buy the dishwasher she'd nagged him
about wanting ten years ago, he'd valiantly washed up the
plates, glasses, and silverware, but the burned pots were

still on the stove because he had no idea how to remove the black crust inside.

Pleased that the kitchen was relatively clean, he was on his way to watch some TV when he heard Cletus's trademark snuffling. Years ago, much to Genevieve's displeasure, Riley had removed a section of the wall from the back of the house so that a swinging door and a ramp could be installed to allow Cletus to go in and out as he pleased. He was coming inside now. The hog was so large and weighed so much that the house's floor groaned under his weight. Like a child returning home from school, Cletus lumbered slowly into the living room. He was light gray in color and had a tendency to sunburn if he wasn't careful, which was why Riley made Genevieve slather him with suntan lotion.

"Hey, big fella. How are you? Pretty hot out there, ain't it. You need lotion?"

Cletus snuffled as if answering, and Riley smiled. "All righty. I'll get it. Come on in. Just sitting here waiting on the news."

Usually Genevieve shared the couch with him, but because he was mad at her, he refused to miss her company. "Who needs that damn Genevieve anyway? We're doing just fine without her, aren't we fella?"

Cletus came farther into the living room. His bulk sideswiped an end table and sent one of the fancy-dancy porcelain lamps Genevieve had inherited from her mother crashing to the floor. "Aw, Clete!"

The pig snuffled with high-pitched noises as if explaining it wasn't his fault, and Riley apologized. "I'm sorry.

Genevieve taking off has got me so mad I'm taking it out on you. Let me get the broom. Damn table was in your way, wasn't it?"

Riley did know where the broom was kept so he got up. When he came back Cletus had pushed aside the coffee table and hunkered down in the space where the table had been, between the couch and the color TV. His bulk filled the room.

Riley swept up the broken pieces of the lamp, put everything in the trash, and sat again. "How 'bout we watch a little Animal Planet until the news comes on?"

He switched channels, navigated around Cletus to grab a seat on the couch, and stopped. A stench that could only have come from Cletus filled his nose. Looking down he saw a pile of hog poop. "Dammit, Cletus. You were supposed to do that outside. What the hell's the matter with you?"

Cursing, he went to get some newspaper, gloves, and a shovel. When he came back, he said, "Move so I can clean this up."

Cletus didn't budge. In fact, if Riley hadn't known better he would've sworn the hog was ignoring him. "Move big fella and let Daddy clean up."

This time the hog did glance at him, but in a peeved sort of way before turning his attention back to *Meerkat Manor*.

Riley poked him gently with the end of the broom. "Move, would you please?"

Nothing.

"Move, dammit!"

Finally, the hog lifted his bulk and got to his feet. He

moved closer to where Riley stood and began to pee. Had Riley not jumped away his shoes would have been soaked. "Cletus!" he scolded angrily. "Get outside. Now!"

But Cletus turned, walked back to his spot in front of the TV, and settled down again.

For the next little while, Riley wheedled, cursed, and tried reason in an attempt to get Cletus to obey but was summarily ignored. Mad as all get out by then, he yelled louder, threatened, even tried to bribe him by dangling a snack cake under his snout.

Nothing.

So finally, he got behind the hog and tried to push him up. Straining and shoving for all he was worth, Riley set his feet for better purchase, but he slipped in the pool of waste, lost his balance, smacked his head on the coffee table, and was out like a light on the floor before he knew what hit him.

For a moment or two, Cletus observed him lying there unconscious, then turned his massive head back to the television to await the next show.

Malachi was going to try and wrangle an appointment with the always busy Bernadine Brown so they could talk about renovating the D&C.

Las Vegas had been great. Not having to fork over a dime had made it even better. His first week had been paid for by a woman he'd met at a vet conference last year. The second part was to have been courtesy of a waitress he'd met while visiting Kansas City back in the fall. It had been easy to send the vet, whose name was Diane, to the airport in a cab at the end of their stay, then grab a cab of his own over to the second hotel, where he sat in the lobby of Circus Circus to await the arrival of Karen, the waitress from Kansas City, as if he'd just flown in. He'd cut the Karen part short, however, by claiming to not feel well and came home.

As far as he knew, neither lady knew about the other, and if they did it hadn't been an issue, which suited him just fine. He was tired though. *Not as young as you used to be*, the sage voice inside his head whispered, but Malachi ignored it like he always did and kept driving.

He drove over to Trent's place first and found him inside watching *SportsCenter* and sipping on a cup of coffee.

He poured himself a cup. "Didn't get to ask last night, but did anything happen here while I was gone?"

"Not much. Amari and Preston are over painting Ms. Agnes's fence."

"What did they do?"

So he told them.

"Dummies," Malachi said. He took a seat on the couch with Trent. "What else?"

"As you can see we're all moved in."

"I like the houses."

"Me too."

"Do you know whether Bernadine is home or not? Want to talk to her about the D&C."

"Haven't seen her this morning, but give her a call."

Malachi studied his son. "And you and Lily?"

Trent shrugged. "We've signed a peace treaty."

"Good. Now you can see about marrying her the way you were supposed to in the first place."

"Don't start, Dad. Weren't you the same one on me about marrying Rocky?"

"That was before Lily came back."

Trent shook his head. "Instead of matchmaking you ought to be seeing about a new cook."

"Nobody wants the job. Can't blame them. Place is a dump. Pay's not much better."

"So you're tearing it down?"

He gave a small shrug. "Maybe. Want to see what Bernadine has in mind first. Maybe I'll just walk over and knock on her door."

"Suit yourself. I'll be heading out to check on the painters soon as I'm done here. Call me on my cell if you need to catch me."

"Will do." Coffee in hand, Malachi walked across the street.

She was coming out of the house just as he arrived.

" 'Morning."

"Hey there. I didn't know you were back. How was Vegas?"

"Great. Had a good time. These houses you've built are something."

"Aren't they fabulous? They're the concrete manifestations of my dreams. Trent's been a great boss. I'm going to buy him a 24-carat-gold baton when everything's finished for the way he's been conducting this building opera."

"You're kidding right?" he asked, chuckling.

"One never knows, does one?" she replied with a catbird smile. "So, what do you want to do about the D&C?"

He shrugged. "How about I drive you over there and talk about it."

"How about we drive?" she said pointedly.

He grinned and saluted her with his cup. "Can't fault a brother for trying."

Amusement danced in her eyes. "I'll meet you there."

When they arrived, Malachi opened the door and politely let Bernadine enter first. The silence inside echoed cavernously.

"Lot of memories in this old place," he voiced in wistful tones. "Graduation parties, birthday parties, a ton of retirement parties over the years. We watched ball games here, had *Soul Train* lines, and told a lot of lies inside these walls."

Bernadine looked around with the eyes of a woman who now knew more about renovation and construction than she had on her first visit. "Ideally, what would you like to see?"

"To have it up and running like it used to be. It's never been a fancy place, but it was ours."

She took a slow stroll, visually evaluating the walls, ceiling beams, and the two holes in the roof. "How about we gut it and start over?"

"If you're paying, I'm all for it."

"Every town needs a place where you can sit and eat, so yes, I'm paying."

Braced against the edge of the one of the tables, arms folded, he asked, "What man would be crazy enough to divorce you?"

She grinned. "*Ah*, here we go."

"No, I'm serious. You're smart, good-hearted, not to mention gorgeous. Was he doing crack?"

"No, his secretary. He didn't divorce me. I divorced him."

He nodded understandingly. "How many years did you put in?"

"Thirty."

"That's a shame."

"Tell me about it."

"Many men, present company included, do a lot more thinking from the waist down than from the brain down unfortunately, but in your case—the brother was insane."

She dropped her head. "Do you get up in the morning flirting?"

He shot her a grin, "Depends on the lady."

Their eyes met and held.

She broke the silence. "Can we go back to talking about the Dog and Cow? And who names a place that, anyway?"

"Dogs and cows were mostly what I treated in my practice. I was also drinking in those days."

She shook her head. "You are something."

"So are you."

At that moment, Bernadine had to admit she was very attracted to Malachi July, so she gave thanks for the voice that shattered the vibe.

"Malachi?" It was Clay Dobbs. "You home?"

"Yeah."

Clay entered. He looked surprised to see Bernadine standing across the room. "Sorry," he said apologetically.

"Didn't mean to interrupt. Just came by to see if we're playing cards tonight?"

Bernadine replied reassuringly, "It's okay. I was on my
way out anyway." She looked to Malachi. "If you'd do up a
list of the things you want included in the design, I can get
the architect started."

"Will do."

She nodded good-byes to the men and strode out.

After her exit, Malachi said, "That kind of woman could
make a man go straight."

Clay said, "Forget it. You couldn't catch her if she was
walking and you were flying a Stealth Bomber."

"Put your money where your mouth is."

"It's like that, is it? Well, tell you what. We'll take up
the bets tonight at the card game, but I got fifty says she
makes you cry in your Pepsi before the first snow falls."

"You're on."

"Warning you, Bernadine Brown is going to break you
down."

"Just bring your money," Malachi countered, grinning.

"Speaking of breaking down. Genevieve's left Riley.
She's staying with Marie."

The two old friends looked at each other and Mal asked,
"She going to divorce him?"

Cal shrugged.

"You've been waiting a long time."

Clay sighed. "I know, but I'm not low-down enough to
hit on another man's wife. I still love her though."

"I know."

"I'm just going to wait and see what happens. It's all I got."

"Yeah. I'll see you tonight."

Cal waved and was gone.

Up the road apiece, it was bit hard for Riley to see, what with a swollen-closed black eye and the big gauze bandage he'd had to place over the gash he'd gotten from hitting his head on the coffee table. He still had no idea how long he'd been knocked out, but it was dark when he'd come to, so he guessed a couple of hours. After waking up, he'd staggered to his feet, slipped in Cletus's offal again, went down again, and hurt his shoulder. As a result his right arm was in a sling he'd made out of one of Genevieve's scarves.

Since the day of Riley's fall, Cletus had been in front of the television watching Animal Planet, and it didn't appear as if he was planning to leave anytime soon. Riley had asked the hog a hundred times what was wrong, but Cletus continued to act like he'd never seen Riley before in his life. Riley didn't know what to do. Because of his limited vision and aching shoulder, cleaning up the messes Cletus kept making was becoming harder and harder, and the stench was unbelievable.

Yesterday he'd made up his mind to stop feeding Cletus inside the house in hopes he'd wander outside where his bowl was. The only problem was, years ago when Cletus was a piglet, Riley had taught him a trick where he'd stomp his right hoof to let folks know he was hungry. It had been cute back then, and for Riley, a measure of the hog's sky-high intelligence. Well, after having his foot stomps ignored all day and being told the food he wanted was outside—go out there and get it, Cletus had apparently had enough. He stood up, looked Riley in the eye, and stomped and stomped and stomped until the windows rattled, pictures danced on the walls, and the knickknacks in Genevieve's curio cabinet jumped up and down. It was like something out of an old Stephen King novel. The whole thing scared Riley so badly he hustled out, brought in the huge bowl of rice cereal and milk Cletus liked to eat with late night TV, and left the room.

So now, his house was wrecked, the place stank to high heaven, and he was no closer to getting Cletus out from in front the TV than he had been when this began. He went outside and sank down onto the old couch. He'd been spending more and more time outside because it was next to impossible to breathe inside due to the incredible stink, even with all the windows open. He shook his head mournfully. He had no idea what to do. Genevieve came to mind. *This was all her fault. If she hadn't taken off in a huff . . .*, he thought crossly. He'd be willing to bet she could get Cletus out of the house, though. All Riley had to do was talk to her, convince her of the errors of her ways, and she'd be so happy to be forgiven she'd come back. Once she did, she'd get Cletus out, clean up the house, and he could go back to watching the nightly news in peace.

With that in mind, he went in and got his car keys. He could hardly see to drive, and managing the steering with his injured shoulder was difficult, but he was on a mission and refused to be denied.

When he pulled up into the Jeffersons' yard, he saw two of Ms. Brown's junior felons whitewashing the fence. He ignored them and turned his limited vision toward Marie's car. Inside sat Genevieve. Marie was behind the wheel.

He got out and walked over.

Genevieve took one look at the bandage and sling and asked, "What happened to you?"

"Little accident. Nothing big. I need to talk to you a minute."

"About what?"

Riley hated that Marie was listening in. He'd never liked her. "Can we go back to the house and talk there?"

"No, say what you have to say. You're going to make us late."

"I need you to come back home. There I said it."

She sat back against the seat. "Why?"

"Because I can't get Cletus out of the living room. He's in front of the television and he won't go back outside."

"Having a few problems with your pet, are you?"

"No need to be snippy, Genevieve."

"Maybe it's the cologne you're wearing, Riley."

His lips tightened. "Genevieve," he replied with warning in his voice.

"You want me to come home not because you love me or want to apologize for what you said, but because you can't get your damn hog out of the living room?"

"But he's tearing up the place and he's shitting everywhere, and—"

Marie cut him off. "You ready, Genevieve?"

She nodded and told her husband as she powered up the window. "Go home to your hog, Riley."

Marie gunned the engine and Riley jumped away in surprise. Without so much as a word they drove away.

Genevieve could see him in the passenger-side mirror, dancing around in rage in the yard. Preston and Amari had stopped painting to watch him. She figured he was probably cursing her to heaven and back, but she didn't care. She wasn't going home again until Cletus was turned into an Easter ham.

CHAPTER
22

Lily and Trent had dinner at a cozy little Italian restaurant in Franklin. They'd placed their order and were enjoying the breadsticks and a glass of wine while they waited for their food to arrive.

"So how are the paint kings doing?"

"At the rate they're going, they might be done by Halloween."

She laughed softly. "Kids."

"Tell me about it."

Trent couldn't believe they were sitting across from each other again after the passing of so many years. "You look nice."

"Thanks." She'd spent a great deal of time worrying over what to wear because she'd wanted to look just right, and so settled on a little black dress that showed off her shape and her legs in the heels Bernadine had insisted she purchase on their last shopping trip. "Been awhile since I've been on a date. Not counting Winston, of course."

"How's he's doing?"

"Who cares," she said, taking a sip of wine from her flute. "He hasn't called, so he must have gotten the message."

"Throwing his suitcases out of the truck was probably a good clue."

The waiter arrived with their meals, then drifted away soundlessly.

"This is very good," she said, sampling her fettuccine and shrimp. "How long has this place been open?"

"About a year. First time I've eaten here, though."

They made more small talk, sticking to neutral subjects as they felt each other out. "I'm glad we can do this kind of thing again," he said to her, while taking in just how gorgeous she was to him.

"Me too; been awhile."

"Yes it has."

Their eyes lingered for a long moment, then as if realizing they were staring, they both looked down to their plates.

"Tell me about LA," Lily said.

"Not much to tell. Two marriages. Two divorces. I came back to lick my wounds."

"If I can ask, why'd they go bad?"

He lifted a fork of his spaghetti in marinara sauce. "Timing, careers, the fact that neither of them wanted kids. By the end, I didn't get along with either one of them any better than they got along with me."

"Then why'd you marry them?"

"Seemed like a good idea at the time," he offered with a shrug, "But it's okay. I'm getting my chance at fatherhood now, and who wouldn't want a carjacker for a son?"

She shared his smile.

He asked, "If I'm not being too nosy, why'd you get divorced?"

"Got tired of Randy coming home stinking of sex and other women's perfume night after night."

"Ouch."

"Yeah. It wasn't pretty. Made me grow up, though. Had to take care of Davis."

Trent understood. What he didn't understand was how any man could cheat on her. Memories of their being together and what they'd shared and the fun times they'd had began to surface, and he pushed them down.

Lily looked over at him and saw him as he'd been at seventeen, all dark good looks and muscles. He'd loved her as if she'd been the most precious thing in his world, and she'd loved him in the same way. She stuffed the memories inside of her heart and went back to her meal.

After a dessert of spumoni and some tasty little Italian cookies, they left the restaurant and headed home. Being parents they had kids to check on. They drove through the dark up Highway 183 listening to jazz on his CD player and silently relishing each other's company. They were also checking each other out when they thought the other wasn't looking.

When they got to her house, he turned to her and said, "I'll walk you to the door."

"That isn't necessary."

"Sure it is. First date, the man always walks the lady to the door."

Amusement in her eyes, she nodded. "Okay."

He came around and opened her door. Giving her his hand, he helped her step out. Together they climbed the steps and stood in the soft glow cast by her porch light.

"I had a great time," she told him.

"Me too."

Neither said anything about a repeat of the evening. It wasn't necessary.

She leaned up and gave him a quick kiss on the cheek. "'Night, Trenton."

"'Night, Lily."

By the time he walked away and drove the short distance to his place across the street, they each but separately came to the same conclusion that they were still very much in love.

Out on Highway 183, the pounding on the door startled Morton Prell awake. Panicked that it might be the police, he moved as quickly as he could to the bathroom and hid there. The deadbolt and its chain were in place on the door leading to the outside, so whoever was knocking wouldn't be able to get in with the motel's pass key. That they might break the door down was a possibility and he'd be a cooked goose if they did.

"Peterson! Open up. I know you hear me!" It was the motel manager, a cheerless old woman with a red wig and bad teeth. "You promised me rent three days ago! If I don't have it in my hand by 9:00 a.m. tomorrow morning, I'll be calling the sheriff!"

When she didn't say anything else he assumed she was gone. He cursed her and he cursed Bernadine Brown. Were it not for the Brown woman he'd be able to access the money in his numerous accounts, but a hold had been put on them the day after she'd made the call to her friend. Luckily he'd had two hundred dollars in his billfold and had been using that to pay for his stay in the sorry excuse for a hideout, but the jig was up because he was out of money. Common sense said he should have left town, but how far could he have gone on two hundred dollars? He'd planned on having a solution to the mess that was now his life before he was broke, but he didn't.

He was sure the manager wasn't bluffing and would call the sheriff, but where could he go? He had a couple of children somewhere in the country but he hadn't cared enough about them to keep in touch, so therefore had no idea if they were alive or dead. Were he a reflective man he might have looked back on his life and seen the things he might have changed or regretted some of the decisions he'd made, but he wasn't. All he cared about was finding a way out and getting back at the woman responsible.

He picked up the phone and called Riley Curry.

When Riley finally answered and Prell told him what he needed him to do, Prell wasn't in the mood for any excuses. "I know what time it is," he barked. "I need you to come and pick me up. Now."

Listening as Riley tried to squirm out of the assignment, Prell snarled threateningly, "Unless you want your wife to know you've been dipping into her trust, I suggest you get in your truck and get out here as soon as possible!" and he hung up.

Riley arrived at midnight. Prell made his way over to the old truck and got in. When he looked over at Riley's bandaged face reflected in the lone light of the parking lot, he asked, "What the hell happened to you?"

"Accident. Where do you want to go?"

"Your place."

Riley's good eye widened. "Why?"

"Because I can't stay here any longer. Drive."

Steering as best he could with his distorted vision and bum shoulder, Riley headed up for home. "Why can't I drop you at your place?"

"Because there's a warrant out for my arrest. It's the last place I need to be." Deciding silence was the better part of valor, Riley shut up and concentrated on getting home in one piece. He had no business being on the road at night in his condition. Would his troubles never end, he wondered. First Genevieve, then Cletus, and now this. Of the three, Prell was the most tricky. Because the old geezer knew he'd been making unauthorized withdrawals from Genevieve's account, he had Riley by the balls, and in Genevieve's present state of mind, if she were to find out that he'd helped himself to her trust fund to the tune of twenty-five thousand dollars, he wouldn't put it past her to call in the law and have him thrown headfirst into jail. *Why do these things happen to me?*

He'd given the twenty-five grand to Prell over the past few years for investment purposes, or so Prell had said, but so far there'd been nothing to show for it in terms of profits or dividends. He'd planned to replace the "borrowed" money with the kickback he'd been in line to receive had the annexation of Henry Adams by the town of Franklin gone through. He and the Franklin town fathers had had the deal all worked out, but they'd needed Riley's help to deliver the town to them, but Ms. Money Bags, Bernadine Brown, screwed that up.

Riley made it home without running the truck off the road or hitting anything. He cut the engine. Now came the task of explaining to Prell why he wouldn't be able to sleep inside. Riley knew the reason would probably make Prell blow a gasket, but there was nothing he could do. "You'll have to sleep in the truck or on the porch sofa. We can't go in the house."

"Why not? If Genevieve's mad about me waking you up, I'm sure I can charm her into a better mood."

"It's not her, it's Cletus."

Prell looked confused, so Riley explained, "He's taken over the place and I can't get him out."

"The hog?"

Riley nodded.

"You let an oversized pig run you out of your home?"

Offended, he didn't answer.

"God, Curry? What kind of man are you? Come on."

Riley got out of the truck and followed him to the porch. The stench wafting out into the night from inside was immediately apparent. It was so bad it could have been used as a weapon of mass destruction.

"What is that smell?" Prell demanded.

"Cletus."

The moonlight showed Prell's astonished face. When he recovered, he pulled a handkerchief out of his pocket and put it over his nose. Riley grabbed up the tea towel he'd been tying bandit-style around his face every time he had to go inside. It was difficult tying the ends behind his head due to his injured shoulder but once he had it secured he was ready to go.

Prell asked, "Where's the hog?"

"Living room in front of the TV. Let me go in first and turn on the lights so we can see."

And what the lights revealed was mind-blowing and gag inducing. Feces covered the floor like a carpet. Food of all kind was strewn about; hot dog buns, huge metal mixing bowls of Cheerios and Rice Krispies lay tipped over, their contents pooling beneath them. Twinkie wrappers and the ends of half eaten hot dogs added to the mess as did broken lamps and pieces of wood that had once been coffee tables and end tables. A curio cabinet lay on its side, the glass in it shattered. And in the middle of it all, lying in front of the muted TV, was the sleeping and snoring loudly Cletus. Another episode of *Meerkat Manor* was on the screen.

Unable to believe the state of the room or the overpowering stench, Prell asked from behind his handkerchief, "How long has this been going on?"

"You don't want to know. He'll let me mute the sound so I can sleep, but he won't let me turn the television set off, or unplug it."

"He's a hog, Riley. Wake him up."

Riley didn't see the sense in that. The house wasn't going to be habitable tonight or any other night in the foreseeable future, plus, he knew for a fact that Cletus didn't like being awakened from a sound sleep. "He's not going to like us waking him up."

"Who cares? He's a hog!"

Riley knew that Cletus would care, but if Prell had a plan that would succeed in getting Cletus outside again, he was willing to try. Shoot, at that point, Riley was willing to try just about anything.

He lifted the edge of the tea towel tied over his face just long enough to call out in a soft but cajoling voice, "Cletus. Wake up, big fella. We got company."

Prell removed his handkerchief and yelled, "Get up, hog!" as loudly as eighty-six-year-old lungs would allow.

It was enough. Cletus came awake with a series of snuffles, then turned to see what or who had disturbed his dreams.

Prell pointed toward the door and barked, "Outside, now!"

Cletus gave him a look, turned his head back around, and settled down to resume his sleep.

Next thing Riley knew, Prell had picked up one of the shattered legs from the end table. Realizing it was just the right size for club, he yelled, "Hey! What're you doing?"

"Teaching this animal some respect."

"Wait a minute, now, I don't want him hurt."

"This isn't a child, Curry. It's a damn hog."

Before Riley could blink, Prell advanced on the hog,

careful to keep his footing in the slop, and lowered the club. The blow came down hard on the hog's back. Cletus's head immediately spun around.

"Got your attention, do I?"

Prell had everyone's attention.

Riley grabbed his arm. "Quit that!"

Prell felt all the anger that was pent up inside over his financial situation boil to the surface. Now that he had a way to release it, he pushed Riley aside and sent the shorter man sliding in the muck.

Cletus saw all this, and although he'd been running roughshod over Riley for almost a week now, Riley was his food source, and animals no matter the species will protect their source of food.

So when Prell clubbed him across his rear end again, Cletus stood, turned toward him and began to advance. The hog weighed over six hundred pounds. No matter how mad Prell might be, at his advanced age he lacked the physical strength to really inflict any lasting harm and the look in the hog's eyes reflected that.

"Get back!" Prell ordered swinging the table leg. He brought it down on Cletus's head. The strike stopped Cletus just long enough for the hog to shake it off and squeal in anger.

"Leave him be!" Riley shouted in alarm. "He's mad. He'll hurt you!"

But Prell wasn't listening. "Damn piece of pork." He raised the wood to bring it down again and the squealing, angry Cletus charged.

Using his snout, he pushed the slipping and yelling

Prell all the way to the living room wall, then turned and pinned the man against it from the chest down. He ground his weight against the body to flatten him for extra measure, then sat down. Caught between the wall and the hog's crushing girth, Prell screamed and pounded the pig's back in a vain attempt to free himself. Soon his movement's slowed. Blood trickled from the side of his lips and then his nose and ears as the pressure of the hog's tremendous bulk forced the life out of him. Finally, he slumped over dead.

Riley staggered outside, threw up, then went back inside and called 911.

Trent's cell phone rang at 2:00 a.m. Blindly reaching for it in the dark, he placed it against his ear and mumbled, "Yeah."

Hearing the voice of the county sheriff Will Dalton on the other end, he sat up, "Hey, Will." A phone call in the middle of the night was always a bad sign, but as Trent listened to what Dalton was saying about Prell's death he shouted, "What!"

Dalton explained further, and Trent, shaking his head in disbelief, said, "Okay. I'll pick up Malachi and we'll be there soon as we can."

At 2:07, Malachi's phone rang. He looked at the caller ID and mumbled sleepily. "Did Amari already steal somebody's truck?"

"I wish, but no. Some kind of way, Cletus has killed Morton Prell."

Malachi burst into laughter. "You're kidding?"

"Not funny, Dad."

"The hell it's not."

"Okay, officially it's tragic, but Dalton needs you to bring a tranq gun so they can get Cletus out of the way and retrieve the body."

"Man, karma is a bitch."

"Just get dressed. I'll be there in a few."

Not sure he wanted to leave Amari alone, Trent called Lily to see if he could bring Amari over. He didn't tell her why, just that it was some police business. She sleepily agreed. He woke Amari, who of course had a million questions as Trent handed him a sleeping bag.

"Why can't I go with you?"

"It's official business."

"In the middle of the night. Did somebody get shot?"

"No. Come on. I'll tell you all about it when I get back."

"Square business?"

"Cross my heart."

"You know you can't lie on square business?"

"I know. Come on, Lily's waiting."

She met them at the door, and the sight of her all tousled and softened by sleep did something to Trent that was so physical he didn't want to think about it. "Thanks for the help."

"No problem. Now what's this about?" she asked stifling a yawn.

"Tell you later. I gotta go." It was either that or stand there contemplating how warm her skin must be.

She stepped aside so that Amari could enter. After he disappeared, she asked quietly, "This isn't something dangerous you're going to do, is it?"

"No, but I don't know how long I'll be."

"Just so it's not a late-night booty call."

He smiled. "No. Go back to bed. I'll pick Amari up when I get back."

"Okay." She closed the door softly and was gone. After standing there for a few seconds with his mind focused solely on her, he suddenly remembered what he was supposed to be doing. Cursing himself he drove off to pick up Malachi.

When they arrived at the Curry place, it looked like every official vehicle in the county was parked in the yard. They spotted cars belonging to the Medical Examiner, the Morgue wagon, a ton of county and state law enforcement cruisers, an EMT ambulance. Uniformed men and women were crawling over the place like ants on powdered donuts.

They got out and walked up to the house. Portable lights had been set up and the area was lit up like a miniature Vegas.

Dalton met them at the porch. The sheriff was in his midfifties but still had the bulk and size of the young man who'd been an all-America linebacker at the University of Kansas back in the seventies. "Thanks for coming."

"What's that smell?" Trent asked.

The sheriff gave them a couple of hospital masks.

"What're these for?"

"Put them on, then come on in and you can see for yourself."

After following his instructions they followed him inside.

Trent didn't know what was more shocking, the home's putrid-smelling, totally demolished interior or the sight of Prell's lifeless body slumped over Cletus's back like an old male marionette.

Seeing the way Cletus had the corpse pinned against the wall, Malachi whispered, "Damn."

Dalton explained, "The problem is we can't get the hog to move his big ass out of the way."

Trent looked around and asked through his mask, "Where's Riley?"

"EMTs are treating him. He's got a broken collarbone."

"Cletus again?"

"No, at least not directly. He says he fell down in all this crap."

Trent didn't doubt it. He hoped he had another pair of boots in his truck, because no way was he going to be able to wear home the ones he had on his feet now. He continued to be amazed by the destruction. "How'd the house get this way?"

"How about we get the hog out of the way first, then I'll answer your questions best I can."

Malachi walked over to Cletus and did his best to ignore the dead Prell and the hog's stench. "Cletus, you know we don't get along, never have, but I'm going to give you two choices. Either move, or I shoot you with this," and he showed him the tranq gun. "You decide."

What Malachi didn't tell him was that he was going to be tranqued either way. Officially the hog was a murderer. What the county planned to do with him once he was knocked out wasn't Malachi's concern. Even though the hog had rid the world of a certified parasite in Prell, no good deed goes unpunished and Cletus would probably be put down.

Cletus looked at the tranq gun. Being a fan of Animal Planet he'd seen a lot of them, and as Riley would testify later at the trial, Cletus, like most of his kind, was very smart.

Malachi didn't have to ask twice. Cletus stood up and moved away from the wall. As Prell's corpse slid to the floor, the hog slowly trotted off in the direction of his special door and exited the house.

Outdoors, Malachi hit Cletus with a couple of tranquilizer darts and the hog went down. The authorities waited until it was safe to move him before using chains and a tow truck's winch to guide the snoring hog onto a flatbed. After he was secured, the truck rolled out and disappeared into the night.

CHAPTER
23

Genevieve and Marie watched the local
reports on Morton Prell's demise and
by the circumstances surrounding it. They we
stunned by the conditions shown inside the
Genevieve couldn't believe the filthy room
room. Hands to her mouth in shock and de
rendered speechless by what came across the
her beautiful things had been demolished.
lay in pieces. The drapes she'd made herself
proudly were filthy and dangling from rods
attached to the walls. The curio cabinet she
catalog from California to display the little p
rines she'd inherited from her mother was lyi
broken and splintered, as if it had been ord
county dump instead. The place was in sha
filled with filth that according to the repor
wearing a mask to protect his breathing, th
partment had determined the house to be

CHAPTER
23

Genevieve and Marie watched the local morning news reports on Morton Prell's demise and were stunned by the circumstances surrounding it. They were even more stunned by the conditions shown inside the Curry home. Genevieve couldn't believe the filthy room was her living room. Hands to her mouth in shock and despair she was rendered speechless by what came across the screen. All of her beautiful things had been demolished. Her furniture lay in pieces. The drapes she'd made herself and hung so proudly were filthy and dangling from rods only partially attached to the walls. The curio cabinet she'd ordered by catalog from California to display the little porcelain figurines she'd inherited from her mother was lying on its side, broken and splintered, as if it had been ordered from the county dump instead. The place was in shambles and so filled with filth that according to the reporter who was wearing a mask to protect his breathing, the Health Department had determined the house to be a public haz-

the hog had rid the world of a certified parasite in Prell, no good deed goes unpunished and Cletus would probably be put down.

Cletus looked at the tranq gun. Being a fan of Animal Planet he'd seen a lot of them, and as Riley would testify later at the trial, Cletus, like most of his kind, was very smart.

Malachi didn't have to ask twice. Cletus stood up and moved away from the wall. As Prell's corpse slid to the floor, the hog slowly trotted off in the direction of his special door and exited the house.

Outdoors, Malachi hit Cletus with a couple of tranquilizer darts and the hog went down. The authorities waited until it was safe to move him before using chains and a tow truck's winch to guide the snoring hog onto a flatbed. After he was secured, the truck rolled out and disappeared into the night.

ard and by week's end planned to have the place razed. She shook her head and tears rolled down her cheeks. The lovely home her father had purchased for her as a wedding gift was gone forever all because of Riley and his hog.

The report went on to say that Riley Curry, the hog's owner, had suffered a broken collarbone and was staying with friends. A hearing to determine the killer hog's fate would be held later, but Genevieve didn't care about any of it. All that mattered for her was the grief she felt for the place she'd once called home.

Tamar parked her truck, and when she and Barrett Payne got out they walked slowly into the old cemetery. "My parents and grandparents are buried here."

"How old is this place?" he asked, looking around at stubby stones weathered away in size and shape by time.

"As old as the town. The first colonists came in the fall of 1880. Many of the old families had plots here: the Jeffersons, the Reeds, Sophie Reynolds who'd owned the original Henry Adams Hotel, her common-law husband, Asa. They're all together in death as they'd been in life."

The hems of her faded emerald-and-black robes lifted gently with the breeze as they advanced deeper into the field. The longer they walked, the farther back in time they traveled, and as a result the names and dates on the stone markers became more and more difficult to decipher. Some were so battered and worn that whoever was buried beneath them was now lost from memory.

"We're here to pay homage to her, my great-grandmother, the first Tamar, the woman I'm named for. Today is the one hundred and thirteenth anniversary of her death."

He looked surprised.

"She was one of the Old Ones. A member of the Black Seminole tribe born in the lush green of Florida, forcibly removed to the hardscrabble land of Indian Territory by a president of a nation that could not keep its word."

Having been a military man most of his adult life, and having sworn to defend the country in peace and war, he wasn't sure how he felt about her bitterly worded comment, but if his heritage was intertwined with hers, he guessed he understood. The country had not dealt honorably with the native tribes. "I looked online for more information on the Seminole Long Walk you told me about."

"What did you learn?"

"That it was led by the great Seminole chiefs Wild Cat and John Horse and that it began in Indian Territory and ended on the Texas-Mexico border."

"Very good. The grandfather of your great-great-grandfather Dixon took his surname from those chiefs when he came to Indian Territory."

"You're kidding."

"The combined names of Wild Cat and John Horse became your family's name: Wildhorse."

Barrett was amazed. He'd lived his entire life not knowing about his past, but now, after being in Henry Adams, he felt changed and he didn't know why. It was almost as if knowing his past had altered the way he looked at the world. "Tell me about your grandmother."

"She'd died in Henry Adams while visiting her son Neil

and his wife, Olivia. According to my aunt Teresa, the first Tamar was a woman of magic, song, and wisdom and had the power to walk in her children's dreams."

"I don't believe that."

"It doesn't matter. Her children did and so do I."

Tamar found the headstone she'd been looking for and bent down to brush away the Kansas dust and bits of detritus that had blown onto it since her last visit. "When the time comes for me to be laid to rest I'm not going to be able to do it here, and neither will my children or grandchildren because the county closed this cemetery down decades ago. It's a shame."

She stood up and looked around. "Time will claim it all, anyway, but as long as one July walks this earth, they'll come here and honor her on the day of her death because it's tradition, and without it we'll forget just like everybody else."

"Is that why you wanted me to come out here with you today?"

"Yes, you need to know how you came to be, Colonel. Tradition."

Barrett was so moved he didn't know what to say, so he didn't say anything as he walked with Tamar back to her truck.

Bernadine was on the phone. She'd promised the Garlands that she'd get busy on the Zoey mystery, but she'd gotten sidetracked, what with the news about Morgan Prell's death and all the thousand other things on her to-do list. She was on it now, however, and talking with the PI firm she'd hired to do the background checks on the foster parents. Their new mission was to find out everything they could about Zoey Raymond and report back. She also asked that they look into the whereabouts of Crystal's mother too.

She and the Garlands were in their kitchen. When she ended the call, she said, "Now we wait."

"I'm still so blown away by all this," Roni admitted, remembering how pale and small her foster daughter had looked against the big piano. "Be nice if we could hear back quick so we can try and figure out what help she needs."

"I know," Bernadine agreed.

Reg added, "The trauma Zoey suffered, whatever it was, had to have been powerful to make her stop talking."

Bernadine asked, "Do we assume that whatever it was, it happened to her at night?"

Reg shrugged. "Probably, though it's not a given."

"How long did she sleep after her concert?"

Roni looked to Reg for verification. "Quite a while. She came downstairs around 10:30. Smiled at me when I asked her if she wanted to eat. She's sweet as pie. Helped me do some unpacking, helped me load the dishwasher. I just wish she'd talk so we can help her." The honesty in her face showed how much she cared. "Devon came over and got her a little while ago. They're playing over at Lily's."

Reg heard the emotion in his wife's voice and wondered if maybe by helping the girl, Roni could be helped as well. Although he and his wife had been prepared to foster Preston, they'd wound up with Zoey instead. Fate? God? He didn't know, but he did know that she'd been placed in their life for a reason.

"Babe."

He came back to the present to see Roni waving a hand in front of his face.

"You with us?"

He grinned apologetically. "Sorry. I was out on Jupiter somewhere."

"I was telling Bernadine about your clinic idea."

"Yeah. I'd like to set up my practice here. Is there a building I can use?"

"No, but there might be room to do something small scale in the new rec center until we can come up with a permanent space. We can look this evening during the opening and see if any of the rooms would work."

"I've already checked into becoming licensed to practice here. Should know something on that soon."

Bernadine loved initiative. She stood, pleased. "Okay. I'm going to take off; got a thousand things to do. I'll keep you in the loop on what the firm finds out on our Zoey. Having you two in her life is going to be good for her."

"She's going to be good for us too," Reg said as they walked her to the door. He gave his wife's waist a quick hug, and she smiled up in agreement.

Bernadine sensed they had a good marriage. "I will see you all later at the opening."

"We'll be there."

With a wave of good-bye, Bernadine made the short walk back to her place.

The new recreation center was a big hit. Everyone invited, including some of the local dignitaries from surrounding towns *oohed* and *ahhed* over the amenities like the video game room, the pool, and the galley kitchen with its stainless-steel appliances. There was an indoor gym with an adjoining weight room that Barrett Payne seemed particularly taken with but scared the sedentary Preston to death when the colonel looked his way and smiled. There were two large meeting rooms, one of which had already been booked by the Black Farmers Association for its monthly gathering next week. The other would serve as a temporary classroom for the Henry Adams private school until a real building could be built next spring.

A tour of the media room was given to show off its state-of-the art big-screen projection system and its fifty stadium seats. A lot of money and thought had gone into the design and construction of the beautiful facility and it showed.

As Trent stood by the wall and watched the crowd milling about, he was having second thoughts about the whole foster parent thing. After having lived a solitary life, having a sidekick was taking some getting used to. Especially a sidekick with a gift for asking questions. Granted, a questioning mind was a good mind, but Amari was making him nuts, and this was only the what, second week? He assumed that when school opened, Marie would give the questioning mind plenty to do, but until then Trent had to learn to adjust.

"So who's that man over there looking like Guy Smiley?"

For a moment, Trent was confused.

Amari seeing it, repeated questioningly, "Guy Smiley? *Sesame Street*."

"Oh, okay. You mean the one talking to Bernadine with all the hair and teeth."

"Yep, him."

"That's Digby Kettle. He's a car dealer down in Hays." Trent nodded a greeting to one of the construction workers and his wife as they passed by. Bernadine had especially asked that the men and women who'd built the place be invited to join the celebration.

Amari sipped his punch and asked, "What the hell kind of name is Digby Kettle?"

"Stop cussing."

"Sorry."

Trent gave him a look and then shook his head. He was convinced that some kind of way the ancestors had put Malachi's genes into the boy. He reminded Trent so much of his father it scared him to death. "Digby's a Mennonite."

"What the—heck is a Mennonite?"

Trent was pleased to hear the self-check. "They're a religious group from Europe. First people to plant winter wheat in this area back in the Pioneer days, and before you ask me about winter wheat, how about we look this stuff up on the computer when we get home? That way you can get answers to all of your questions."

Amari sipped again, shrugged, and said, "Sure, that'd be nice, but I can't read."

With that he strolled off into the crowd, leaving the stunned and wide-eyed Trent behind.

Amari kept walking until he got outside. He found Preston sitting at one of the picnic tables. "Hey, man. What are you doing out here?"

"Avoiding the Marine Corps."

Amari sat on the tabletop, "Why?"

"I think he's going to make me start exercising."

"What's wrong with that?"

"I got asthma. I could die," he said.

"I don't see Ms. Bernadine letting him kill you, so I think you'll be okay."

Preston looked up into Amari's face. "The colonel's crazy. Woke me up so early the first morning it was still dark. Then turned on that damned reveille when I wouldn't get up. Stuff was so loud it gave me a hearing loss."

"What's a reveille?"

"That wake-up tune the army guys play on the horn." Preston vocalized the familiar notes.

Amari nodded. "Okay. I know which one you're talking about."

"So, why'd you come out here?" Preston asked. He'd noticed how pensive Amari appeared to be.

"Trent wants me to look up some stuff on the computer."

"Is that a problem?"

"It is when you can't read."

"Damn," Preston replied, looking at Amari with sympathy.

"I know. Hey, you know how it is. Nine hundred different schools, new teachers, never catching up, kids laughing, so I gave up. I know my ABCs, and little words, but a computer? Please."

"And I have the opposite problem."

"What's that mean?"

"I'm smart. Scary smart. My IQ is probably higher than everybody's in this town."

"Wow."

"Yeah, well, in my old schools I caught a lot of teasing about it, so I stopped showing it. People think you're wack when you know stuff. I can help you with your reading if you want. Not trying to get in your business or anything."

"I know, thanks, but I'm okay. Made it this far, but I promise I won't tell anybody about your big brain."

Preston smiled, "Same here for you."

"Thanks, man."

"Think Tamar will let us have more ice cream?"

Amari grinned. "I don't know, but let's ask." He scrambled off the table, and they bounded to the door.

Back inside, Genevieve was behind the punch bowl and had just handed Zoey and Devon a second cup when she saw Riley come in. She'd heard from Tamar that he was staying with somebody over in Franklin.

As the children moved on, she scanned him up and down. Someone had replaced the ridiculously large bandage he'd been wearing the last time she's seen him with one that appeared to be professionally applied. His arm was in a real sling and he looked tired, worn, and old. She supposed the whole mess with Cletus was wearing on him, not to mention having no place to stay now that the house was going to be bulldozed. In many ways she felt sorry for him and in many ways she still loved him, but she was tired too. Tired of being ignored about what mattered to her, tired of catering to the windmill dreams. She was sixty years old and on the downslope of life, was it wrong for her to want more?

He came over to the table. "'Evening, Genevieve."

"'Evening, Riley."

"Guess you heard about Cletus and Prell."

"I did."

"Cletus is locked up."

"I heard that too." Seeing him brought back all the sadness. "They're going to tear down my house," she whispered emotionally.

He looked down at his shoes.

She knew that if she stood there a moment longer, she'd break down. "I have to go and see if Tamar needs my help in the kitchen," and she left him standing there, alone.

When the party ended, the families walked back in a group to their homes down the road. Roni watched Zoey, who was paired up as always with Devon and wondered about this child she was fostering. How could she, a woman fighting her own demons, be there for the little girl when Roni couldn't even be there for herself? The shootings that had driven her into seclusion seemed to have happened ages ago, yet the memory of all the blood and screaming and people running remained so vivid it could have happened yesterday. Reg had accused her of using this fostering as another excuse to run away, and he'd been right. Her producer was trying to get her to go back into the studio. He'd promised her she wouldn't have to tour to support the project if she didn't want to, but she knew what the fans would be expecting. They'd been waiting for her to resume her career for so long, and not touring wouldn't be fair. So instead of dealing with all the things she needed to deal with to try and make it happen, she'd told her producer no, because she wouldn't have time due to the commitment she and Reg had made to being foster parents.

It was a cop-out; he knew it and so did she. Roni missed her music and she missed performing, but the memories of that terrible night in Boston were still so raw and painful she was afraid that when she opened her mouth to sing again, the only sounds that she'd make would be screams.

Lily tucked Devon in and looked down on his sweet face. "Did you have a good time, tonight?"

"Yes, ma'am."

"How are we doing, as a family, you and I?"

"We're doing okay," he replied softly. "I like it here."

"Good to know. Did you know that I have a son, named Davis?"

"No, ma'am."

She sat down on the edge of the bed. "He lives in California and he wants to meet you."

"Why?"

She shrugged. "He wants to ask you if he can be your big brother. He's never had a brother before."

"For real?" he asked, his accent prominent.

She laughed. She'd never seen him this animated. At that moment he was pure eight-year-old. "For real. He wants me to get a Web cam so you two can talk and see each other on the computer. Would that be okay?"

He nodded excitedly.

She gave him a motherly caress across his brow.

"Never had a brother either. Just my grandma."

"And she's looking down smiling, I betcha."

"I miss her."

"I know you do, honey, but she sent you to me and Davis and Tamar and Ms. Bernadine and everybody here so that you'd have somebody to keep loving you."

"You think so?"

"I know so." She gave him another soft touch. Feeling the way her heart swelled, she knew she'd made the right decision taking him in. "You get some sleep."

" 'Night, Ms. Lily."

" 'Night, Devon."

The Garlands weren't sure how to handle the night ahead and worried over the same questions they worried over every night since they discovered Zoey playing the piano. Would she want to sleep in her room? Would she get up in the middle of the night and start playing the piano again? Should they bed her down in their room? Would that help to keep her fears at bay? They didn't have a clue.

"Well, Doc," Roni said, "you're the resident child expert. What should we do?"

They were outside sitting on the porch. Zoey was inside watching her last Nickelodeon selection for the evening.

"Wish I knew," Reg confessed.

Before Roni could reply, Malachi drove up. When he got out of the truck they waved, he waved back. They expected him to turn toward Trent's house but he came up their walk carrying the largest stuffed animal they'd ever seen.

"Got something for Zoey," he said, struggling a bit with the thing.

Once they were inside, they could see it was a tiger.

A smiling Reg called, "Hey, Zoey. Come look."

She appeared, wearing her green Disney Princess nightgown. When she saw the tiger her face widened with astonishment.

Malachi was encouraged by her reaction. "This, little button-nosed girl, is Tamar."

Mirth flashed in Zoey's eyes.

"Yep, named after that crotchety old lady up the road."

The Garlands grinned.

Malachi then knelt beside the giant tiger and spoke directly to Zoey. "I saw this Tamar in the store this morning, and she asked if I knew a little button-nosed girl named Zoey." He paused a moment to look her in the eye and ask, "You do know that I'm an animal doctor and that animals talk to me?"

She shook her head.

"Well, I am and they do. She said she wanted to meet you because she thought you might need her."

Zoey's dark eyes met his. He smiled kindly, "So, here you go. She's real strong and she's real fierce. Tigers get hungry a lot and she'll eat anything that scares you. Make sure you feed her lots of that kind of stuff because the more she eats the stronger she gets. Okay?"

To his surprise she gave him a big hug, then grabbed up Tiger Tamar. It was almost as big as she was, but she managed to carry it to the stairs and up them to her room.

"Thank you so much," Roni said, giving him a fervent hug. "Thank you so much."

"No problem. Thought it might help."

Malachi walked back to the door. Reg shook his hand. "Thanks again."

"No thanks needed. I know what it's like to be alone in the dark."

With that said, he departed.

Upstairs, Zoey was making Tiger Tamar comfortable in the bed. She got her a pillow for her head and tucked the green-and-white top sheet over her so she wouldn't get cold, then she climbed in too. The bright orange striped fur was soft and the whiskers tickled her hands. Zoey liked it that the tiger had big white teeth because they looked like they could eat lots of rats.

A few minutes later, when her new folks came into the room, she sat up, gave them both a gigantic hug, and Mama Roni started to cry. Zoey wasn't sure why, but she thought they looked like happy tears. Daddy Reg ruffled her hair.

Mama Roni opened the curtains so the moon could get in. She turned on the light in the little bathroom and then the Tinkerbelle lamp over on her new green desk.

They whispered good night and after they left, Zoey put her arm around Tamar's soft, warm neck and tumbled into a soundless sleep.

Sheila Payne hated menopause. If it wasn't the hot sweats giving her fits, it was the insomnia, but tonight it was both. She looked over at the lighted dial on the clock on her nightstand: 1:00 a.m. Barrett was beside her, sleeping like the dead. Admittedly jealous she lay there in the dark. Hoping a dry shirt would help, she crept out of bed and tipped into the bathroom.

She'd learned over the course of this craziness her body was going through to keep extra shirts at hand, so each night she left two in the bathroom in case she needed to change.

She rid herself of the damp one and wriggled into a dry one with the Marine Corps crest in the center. She turned off the light, opened the door, and tipped back into the dark bedroom. Thinking maybe a small glass of juice or water might help her get to sleep, she quietly left the room and soundlessly closed the door.

In the hallway, the crack of light showing beneath Preston's door caught her attention, so she went to see if maybe he'd fallen asleep with the light on. She knocked softly. "Preston?"

She heard scrambling, so she opened the door just in time to see him stuff a book beneath his pillow. Closing the door softly behind her she viewed the guilty-looking face and said kindly, "You should be asleep, Son."

"I know. Just getting ready to put out the light." He reached up to hit the switch on the lamp.

"Don't even try it," she said with a smile. She walked over and stood by the bed. "What're you reading?"

"Me? Nothing."

She reached under his pillow and pulled out a book that had to weigh five founds. Intrigued, she read the spine. *W. E. B. Dubois: Biography of A Race. 1868–1919.* "What are you doing reading about W. E. B. Dubois?" she asked, blown away. Barrett had a copy of the same title in his library.

The defensive look on his face made her hastily explain, "Please, I'm not fussing at you. I'm not. I think this is so cool."

"Really?"

"Oh yes. Very cool. I don't know any teenagers willing to tackle something like this. This is wonderful."

"You really think so?"

She nodded and handed the book back.

"Where I come from you get laughed at for reading stuff like this."

"Not in this house. So do you like history, or do you like the book because it's a biography?"

"Both. I like history and I like books."

She leaned back and smiled. "You and the colonel have a lot in common."

"What makes you think that?" he asked suspiciously.

"A love of books and history. Books and history are his thing."

"I thought being a hard ass was his thing."

She grinned. "Don't tell him I said this but being a hard ass is his thing. Books are his thing too. Loves to read."

"You're lying."

She raised her hand. "If I'm lying, I'm flying."

She could see him digesting that. "Wait until all of his books are shipped here. You're not going to believe how many he has."

"Think you can ask him if I can borrow some sometimes?"

"I could, but it might mean more to you both if you asked."

"Trying to get us to bond?"

She smiled but didn't reply.

"Is he going to make me start exercising?"

She was confused. "Why do you think that?"

"The way he kept looking at the equipment at the rec center and then looking at me."

Sheila shrugged. "I couldn't tell you. Do you want to start exercising?"

"No."

"Okay."

"I've got asthma. I could die running around," he said, feeling the need to explain.

"True, but do you know who Jackie Joyner Kersey is?"

"From the Olympics? We read about her in school for Black History Month."

"She has asthma too.

Preston stared.

"Yep. So, you don't necessarily have to die, I guess, huh?"

"I guess not."

She left the subject alone. Preston would certainly be leaner if he lost thirty pounds or so, but she wasn't fostering him to force him into doing something. She did plan to make sure he continued to eat healthy foods, though, and for now that would be her focus. "In the future, if you want to stay up late and read, be my guest. I'm going back to bed. Don't be up too late now; you have a date with a paintbrush in the morning."

"I know," he replied glumly.

She walked over to his door but before she could leave, he said, "Mrs. Payne?"

She turned to him.

"Thanks a lot."

"You're welcome. See you at breakfast."

CHAPTER

24

A few days later, Bernadine got a fax from the PI firm looking into Zoey's past. According to the records provided by the Florida Child Agency, Zoey had an aunt, her mother's sister, but the address hadn't been a current one. Bernadine's investigators found her. The next morning, Bernadine was on a plane to Toledo, Ohio.

Bernadine had the hired driver of the black town car slow down so she could see the addresses on the fronts of the pale stone houses. The neighborhood was upscale. Well-maintained lawns and perfectly placed flowers led the eye to three-car garages and rolling driveways. "Here it is. Stop, please."

He stopped the car and she checked her paperwork one more time to make sure the address on it did indeed match the one on the house. The driver came around to open her door. She stepped out and started up the walk. On the other side of the street a woman working in her yard stopped and stared, but Bernadine ignored her as she pressed the bell and waited for someone to come to the door.

It was opened by a middle-aged woman with frizzy brown hair pulled back into a tail. She was dressed in standard soccer mom sweats. Brown. Her surprise at finding Bernadine on her porch was quite plain. She pulled herself together though, stammering, "May I, *uh*, help you?"

Bernadine smiled to set her at ease. "Hi. I'm Bernadine Brown. I'm looking for Yvette Raymond Caseman?"

"Why?"

"I'd like to speak with her about her niece Zoey."

Even larger surprise. The woman shot a quick panicked look down at the idling limo as if trying to see if someone, presumably Zoey was inside.

"She isn't with me," Bernadine offered quietly.

The woman visibly relaxed, which didn't endear her to Bernadine at all.

Yvette asked, "Are you one of my sister's friends?"

"No. I'm a social worker. Your niece is one of my cases."

"Oh. What do you want with me?"

"To ask you a few questions, if you don't mind?"

"What about?"

Bernadine had hoped to have this conversation inside and sitting down, but that didn't seem to be what the aunt wanted, so she asked, "Do you have any idea why she doesn't speak?"

"No."

When she didn't elaborate or ask more, Bernadine sighed inside and plowed ahead. "What about her musical training?"

"What musical training?"

"Her piano playing? Did she take lessons?"

"I wouldn't know. My sister played, though. Maybe she taught her. She won a scholarship to Juilliard after high school. My parents didn't want her to go so far away, but she was determined. Bonnie always got her way; always."

Bernadine let the sibling snipe pass. "Zoey plays as if she were classically trained."

"Bonnie played like that from around age four. No lessons—no training, just played. Everybody *oohed* and *ahhed* over that, of course, calling her a genius. When she got the Juilliard scholarship, you'd've thought she was Christ on a bicycle the way people fell all over her."

"I take it you two didn't get along?"

"No. She was spoiled, selfish, and manipulative."

"Are your parents still living?"

"No. I'm the only one left—outside of my kids."

"And, Zoey," Bernadine reminded her quietly. "May I ask why you didn't take her in after your sister's death?"

"My sister died a crackhead. When the social workers said Zoey might be brain damaged because of the drugs, my husband and I decided we couldn't do it. We have three beautiful, healthy children, we didn't want them exposed to that."

"I see. Well, she's in foster care and doing pretty good so far."

"Glad to hear it. Anything else?"

Bernadine reached into her purse and drew out a business card. "If you'd like to visit her or get in touch, just give me a call."

She gave the card a dismissive glance. "Sure."

Bernadine knew the aunt wanted her off the porch yesterday, but she had one more request. "You wouldn't happen to have a picture of Bonnie I could take back to your niece."

"Yeah. Hold on."

She came back some minutes later and handed her an envelope. "I have to go now. I'm supposed to be picking up my youngest from kindergarten."

Bernadine didn't keep her. "Thanks for your time."

The door was closed before Bernadine could turn around.

While the driver took Bernadine back to the airport, she slid the small photo out of the envelope. It was a high school picture, and the smiling face staring up at her could've easily been Zoey's own, the two favored each other so much. Looking closer, Bernadine now understood Zoey's obsession with all things green—it was the color of her mother's eyes.

Bernadine presented Zoey with the picture when she returned home. As the little girl studied her mother's face, the tears that coursed down her cheeks broke the heart of every adult in the room. She slowly traced a finger over the image, the memories obviously filling her while Bernadine and the Garlands looked on silently. Zoey turned sad eyes to Bernadine and held them there.

Bernadine whispered, "I thought you might like to have it. It was given to me by a lady who knew your mom."

Zoey stared at the picture again.

Finally, Roni said to her, "Honey, I think there might be

a frame around here we can put it in. Come on; let's see if we can find one."

After they were gone, Bernadine told Reg about the trip to Toledo and her visit with Zoey's aunt. When she finished, she added, "I don't think Zoey's going to get much support from her. She couldn't wait for me to leave."

"That's too bad."

Bernadine agreed.

"So, do you think her mother taught her to play?"

"Who knows. Truthfully we don't know a whole lot more than we did before, except that the mother was a pianist."

"And Zoey has a picture of her."

"Yes. That made the trip worth it."

They talked a bit longer, then she left to go home and rest.

Crystal met her at the door. "Did you find out anything?"

"Not much. How are you?"

"Doing good."

Bernadine was dead on her feet. The only thing she wanted to do was hit the shower, the kitchen, and the bed, but she knew it was her duty to spend some time with the teen, so she kicked off her heels and took a seat on the couch.

"Now, tell me about Zoey."

So, she did.

"Her auntie sounds rude."

"Yeah. Good word."

"Glad you got Zoey the picture, though. You hear anything on my mom, yet?"

Bernadine shook her head. "Nothing so far."

"Wish they'd hurry up."

"We'll find her. Don't worry. Now, I'm going to take a shower, then I'll be in my room chilling."

"Okay."

Bernadine headed for her bedroom. She was glad to be home.

Early that next morning, she knocked on Crystal's bedroom door. Breakfast was ready, but it wasn't like Crystal not to come downstairs on time.

When the second knock went unanswered, Bernadine quietly turned the knob and peeked in. Shock filled her eyes as she saw the girl lying in the middle of the floor snoring softly. Confused, she walked over only to see something equally as surprising. Lying on the floor beside her slumbering foster child were sheets of white paper covered with drawings. Bernadine knelt, and careful not to awaken her hip-hop Sleeping Beauty, she scanned the artwork. The girl had a talent. There was a drawing of Zoey sitting in a huge chair and surrounded by demonic-looking beings. Another one that could only be Amari and Preston lay next to it. She'd drawn Amari driving a cool-looking car and leaning out of the window grinning. Horns had been added to his head, which made Bernadine smile. Preston was in the backseat leaning out of his window and holding a fat hamburger complete with bun, lettuce, and drips on his hand. Bernadine was amazed.

Picking up the rest, she walked over to one of the chairs in the room and scanned through them. There were ten in all, and all were outstanding. "Crystal. Wake up," she called looking at a drawing of Devon in a choir robe surrounded by a bunch of ornate crosses. "Time to get up."

The teen finally opened her eyes, gave a sleepy groan, and was about to turn over when she saw Bernadine sitting in the chair. "Hey," she said with a crooked smile.

"Why are you sleeping on the floor, honey?"

Crystal sat up and rubbed at her eyes. "Never had a room this nice. Don't want to mess it up."

Bernadine wished this fostering business had come with an instruction manual. She had no idea what to say to that, so she hoped the right words would come out. "You've been sleeping on the floor all this time?"

Crystal was fully awake by then. In reply she shrugged her thin shoulders. "Yeah. It's so beautiful. It's like something out of a magazine or that show *Cribs*. I don't want to mess it up."

"But it's your room, baby."

"I know but—"

"Crystal, I'm going to need you to not sleep on the floor."

"But, Ms. Bernadine—"

"No, baby. I know all this high-class stuff is new. It was new for me once upon a time too. I grew up on the east side of Detroit sharing a little room with my two sisters."

"You did?"

Bernadine nodded, "Yep, and my parents didn't have the money to buy fancy stuff like this, but I learned over the years that it's okay to like nice things. I've been poor and I've been rich, and this is way better."

Crystal smiled.

"This is our world, Crystal. Yours and mine, and this is how we're going to be rolling. With nice stuff, beautiful rooms. When I take you to Milan next year for Fashion Week, are you planning on sleeping on the floor of the five-star hotel we're going to be staying in?"

Crystal was staring as if Bernadine had just grown another head or two. "Milan," she croaked. "Milan? Italy?"

Bernadine was impressed that she knew Milan was in Italy. "Yes, and Paris and Cairo and Senegal. I love to travel, and I'm planning on taking you with me when you're not in school and," she held up the drawings, "these are very good."

"I've been drawing since I was little. I don't usually let people see them."

"When we go to Hays today, we'll get art supplies. Brushes, paints, easels. Whatever you need or think you need, we're getting. You have a gift, Crys, and I want you to start nurturing it. Who knows, you may wind up going to art school in New York or Madrid or some other cool place."

Crystal dropped her head, and when she lifted it again there were tears standing in her eyes. "God."

Bernadine smiled. "And you said God hasn't been hearing you. Wrong!"

Crystal smiled.

Bernadine got to her feet. "So get up and get dressed. We have some shopping to do."

"Yes, ma'am."

After Bernadine left, Crystal shook her head in absolute amazement, then got up to get ready.

By the end of the day, Crystal had a bedroom filled with art supplies, and they were as precious and as wonderful to her as the little diamond sparklers in her ears. Until Ms. Bernadine came into her life no one had ever encouraged her in anything before, let alone tell her she was gifted. When Crystal finally decided to go to sleep that night, she crawled into her beautiful bed, content.

The female clerk at the County Agriculture Office sighed when Riley Curry came through the door. Every day for the past ten days he'd come in to ask the same question.

"'Morning, Ms. Clark."

"'Morning, Mr. Curry. How are you, today?"

"Be better if I could see Cletus."

"I'm sorry, but there's been no word on the paperwork."

"When do you think it'll get here?"

She shook her head as she did every morning. "I don't know. The hearing officers are pretty busy. They'll get it to us as soon as they can."

"Are they taking good care of him?"

"I'm sure they are. Is there anything else I can help you with today?"

"No, ma'am. I'll be back tomorrow."

"I'll be here."

When he left, she sighed.

Driving back, Riley was sad. He couldn't imagine what

Cletus might be going through. He'd never been away from home this long before and probably thought Riley had abandoned him. Riley understood why they had to hold the hearing. Cletus had killed Prell, but he'd been protecting Riley, so he saw it as self-defense. He told the police about Prell hitting Cletus with the club, and they'd written down his version of the incident. If they put him to sleep, Riley didn't know what he'd do.

Then there was the matter of Genevieve. He had no more idea what to do about her than he did Cletus. They no longer had a home. She was staying with Marie and didn't seem to be of a mind to change that anytime soon. Seeing her at the recreation center, he'd expected her to have more to say, but the hurt in her eyes had spoken volumes. The life of Riley Curry, former mayor of Henry Adams, was officially in the toilet, and he had no idea how to fix that either.

CHAPTER

25

As summer began to wane, Henry Adams's new residents were all settled in. The unpacking had been finished, items that had been shipped, like all the colonel's books, finally arrived, and all the boxes stored.

During the last week of August, the children began school with Marie Jefferson in charge, and Trent was thankful that the 9:00 to 3:00 classroom gave him a break from the ten thousand questions Amari seemed to wake up with daily. He and Preston finally finished painting the Jefferson fence, and since then there'd been no more Stupid Boy Tricks. Trent was encouraged by that. So far, no cars, trucks, or tractors had come up missing, and he was encouraged by that as well.

He'd mentioned to Marie that Amari was behind in his reading, and she promised to handle it as tactfully as she could. Education was paramount, especially for a child with his background, and Trent volunteered to help in any way he could to get the boy up to speed.

Trent's other dilemma was Lily Fontaine. He had fallen for her again, hook, line, and sinker. They'd not gone on a second date because now that the town Web site was up, she was spending her time fielding all the requests for info on Henry Adams coming in from all over the world, or so it seemed. Although he was in love with her, he had enough sense not to let her know, but in truth, he'd begun falling for her again the day she drove into the garage with that smoke-belching rental car.

It was surprising mainly because it wasn't anything he'd planned or that she'd encouraged; his attraction to her was just there, and every day, every time he saw her he slid farther down the slope.

"So when did you resurrect this old dinosaur?" Malachi asked.

The two of them were in the garage looking at an old banged-up and busted-up Chrysler New Yorker. It used to be Trent's high school car. "Been trying to get to it for a few years now."

"Liar," Malachi said with a grin and took a swig of his cola. "I was drinking back then, but even I remember this car. Used to be mine before I gave it to you when you were sixteen."

Trent pretended not to hear and concentrated on removing the passenger-side door. He'd totaled it in a spring ice storm right after graduation. Since then it had been sitting under sheets of plastic and tarps to keep the weather out.

Old man Dancer, Rocky's father and the previous owner of the garage, had promised to help Trent restore it when the time came, but he died six years ago. "I may have a buyer for it when I'm done."

"You are no more going to sell it than I'm going to marry Tyra."

Trent finally got the rusted door off and eased it to the floor.

"Does Lily know you're working on it?"

"Don't see why she should."

Malachi shook his head. "Denial is not a river in Africa, boy."

Trent chuckled. "I know, Dad."

"Doesn't sound like it to me. When are you going to tell her how you feel?"

"When are you going to tell Bernadine how you feel?"

"Already have, but she's in denial too."

"Not like you to go after a woman over forty, or even fifty for that matter."

"Things change, but in your case, sometimes they don't."

Trent knew he shouldn't ask, but he did, "What do you mean?"

"Means you're still in love with Lily Fontaine."

"Not necessarily," Trent lied.

"Pitiful. You're working on the car you took her to the prom in, and both of your ex-wives looked just like her."

"No they didn't."

"Yeah, they did. Maybe not exactly, but overall they resembled her a lot."

Trent wanted to remind Malachi that he'd been drinking back then too, but he kept that to himself. "Like I said, I think I may have a buyer for this when I'm done."

Malachi shook his head. "Whatever you say."

A moment later, Amari came strolling in. With his backpack on and his jeans and blue polo he looked like the normal everyday eleven-year-old coming home from school.

"Hey, Trent. Hey OG."

Malachi grinned. "Hey, kid."

Trent asked, "How was school?"

"Ms. Marie is trippin', but it was all right. Gave me a bunch of homework that I can't read, so I'll need your help. I can do the math, though."

"Got your back. If it's any consolation, she used to wear me out too."

"It's not," he cracked. Amari looked over the car as Trent started in on removing the other door. "You taking this to the dump?"

"Nope. Going to restore it. Maybe sell it." He waited for Malachi to throw in his two cents but thankfully he didn't.

"Can I help?"

"Sure. After the math homework."

"Why does there always have to be a catch?"

"It's the way life works."

Amari walked around the old black car. "You sure you don't want to take this to the dump? Looks dead." He stuck his head inside and checked out the panel. "No computer?"

"Nope. No computers back then. At least not the high-tech ones on cars today."

"Zoey could steal this."

Malachi and Trent shared a look. Trent said, "You steal this after I fix it, and I feed you to a combine."

"Can you hot-wire a combine?"

"Go in the office and get your homework started."

"I was just asking."

"Homework."

Malachi stood up. "Come on, boy. I'll buy you a soda and you can get on your job."

Amari shot Trent a grin and followed Malachi inside.

"Mrs. Curry was my reading tutor today."

"Really?" Malachi said, coming in with another Pepsi for him and a can of Dr Pepper for Amari. "How'd it go?"

"Fine, but she seemed real sad. Did you know her husband's big fat pig killed somebody?"

Malachi took a sip. "Yep. Officially, it was pretty tragic."

"How come none of us kids knew about it?"

"Grown folks' business, but it was on the news too."

"I don't watch the news."

"Noticed that."

"Well, I think we should have been told. I can take it. I grew up in the murder capital of the world, but murder by hog? That's wack."

"Is that all you learned from Genevieve today?" The seniors were taking turns tutoring Amari in reading.

"No, she just seemed so sad. Did they really tear down her house?"

"Yeah. She was supposed to be tutoring you, not using you as Dear Abby."

"Who's that?"

Malachi waved him off. "Never mind."

Amari kept talking as if Mal hadn't said a word. "I think she just needed somebody to talk to. Been trying to think of something nice I can do for her. Make her feel better, you know?"

He did and it made him feel good. Beneath all that rock-hard city swagger was a kid with a heart. "Sounds like a good idea, but right now, math. And get started before Trent comes in and starts fussing at us both."

Crystal dumped her backpack on the chair in her room. She was not a big fan of school. She was also getting tired of not hearing anything back about her mom. It had been weeks now since the search began. She was sure Ms. Bernadine was getting tired of her asking about it all day every day, but what else was she supposed to do? It hadn't taken real long to find Zoey's aunt.

She sighed with frustration and made up her mind that if she didn't hear something back by next week, she'd go back to searching herself.

At school the next day, she went over and sat with Amari and Preston outside at lunch.

Amari looked suspicious. "What do you want?"

"Need to talk to you. I'm thinking about taking off."

"And go where?" Preston asked, concerned.

"New Orleans, to find my mom."

"Isn't Ms. Bernadine paying somebody to look for her?"

"Yeah, but they're taking too long."

Preston said, "You should just wait."

"I'm tired of waiting."

"Okay," Amari said, "but why are you telling us?"

"Might need your help."

"Why?"

"Because I'll have to get to the highway and I can't drive."

"Call a cab," Preston said.

"Don't be stupid. What am I going to look like calling a cab so I can run away?"

"If you're running away, you're going to look stupid either way."

"Shut up!" she snapped.

Amari took a bite of the big fat burger the senior ladies had made them for lunch. "Preston does have a point. Why not stay? Ms. Bernadine's got to be the best foster mother you ever had."

"I know that, but this is my *real* mother I'm talking about. My flesh and blood."

Preston wanted to remind her that they were talking about a flesh-and-blood crackhead, but he decided to keep that to himself.

Amari asked, "So when do you want to do this?"

"Next week some time."

"You'll have to get somebody else. I promised myself I wouldn't steal anymore cars. I don't want to mess this up and get sent back. I kind of like it here."

"Are you crazy? We're in Green Acres, there's nothing

to do, no place to go. They don't even have a damn Mickey D's."

Amari looked at her. "No, they don't, but the people here are the closest I'm ever going to get to being in a real family. Shit, I may even learn to read. I'm not messing this up."

She huffed out a breath and leaned back against the table. "You're just scared."

"Right."

"You are. You're just scared of getting caught."

"Yep. So you and your bad weave have a good time *walking* to 183."

"Kiss my ass, Amari," she said, and stalked off.

As she disappeared back inside the rec center, Preston asked, "You think she's really going to take off?"

"Probably."

"You're not going to help her, are you?"

He shrugged and drained the last of his drink. "Don't know."

"Amari?"

"It's her family, man. You and me, we don't remember our mamas. She does. Makes a difference."

"You're going to get caught."

"Maybe, maybe not. Way I figure it, I can probably get her to the highway and get myself back without anybody knowing I was gone if the planning's right."

Preston shook his head. "This is so not going to work."

"Cheer up, maybe she'll hear something or change her mind and we won't have to worry about it."

"We don't have to worry about it now."

"Yeah, we do."

"Why?"

"Because as cracked out as Crystal is, she's part of our family. Remember the candles we lit?"

"I don't think this is what that meant."

"It did to me. When one of us needs something, we step up."

"I thought you just said you don't want to mess this up?"

"I don't, which is why if and when the time comes we need to have a bulletproof plan."

Preston scrubbed his hands over his eyes. "Okay, but we definitely need to keep this on the down low. If Ms. Bernadine finds out or God help us, Tamar, they're going to line us up, give us a blindfold and a last cigarette, and have the colonel shoot us at dawn."

Bernadine sat at the dinner table and watched the silently eating Crystal. She wasn't sure how to deal with the moody and withdrawn young woman she'd turned into over the past few weeks. Granted the girl had always been a little edgy, but now she was spending most of her after-school time up in her room and never had more than a few words to say. She hadn't been disrespectful, so far, but Bernadine wondered if the honeymoon period the foster parenting DVDs had described was coming to an end. "You've been awfully quiet the last few days. Something going on you want to talk about?"

"No."

"If you're sick, we can have Dr. Garland take a look at you."

"I'm fine."

"Sure?"

"Positive." She finished the rest of the food on her plate and then pushed back her chair. "I'll load the dishes and go finish my homework."

"Okay." Bernadine watched her leave the room.

After Crystal went upstairs to work on homework, Bernadine went next door to talk with Lily about what might be going on with Crystal.

Inside however, she found Lily seated at the kitchen table, her hands laced around a cup of tea. There were tears in her eyes.

"What's wrong?" Bernadine asked with concern.

"Just got faxed a report on Zoey. Here—read this. I called the Garlands. They're on their way."

Bernadine took what appeared to be a copy of a police report. As she read, her shaking hand went to her mouth. "My Lord," she whispered. "Rats?"

The Garlands came in.

Roni saw their faces and asked, "What's the matter? We brought Devon back with us, Lily. He and Zoey are out on the porch swing."

Roni and Reg read the report and tears welled up in both their eyes. "Oh no," Roni whispered, "oh, my poor little baby girl."

Reg asked, "Where'd this come from?"

"Miami-Dade Police," Lily said. "Apparently, that initial report of where and how they found Zoey after her mother died never made it into any of the subsequent reports. Fell through the cracks, I guess. All anyone knew except the two officers who found her and dropped her off at the ER was that she was homeless and her mother was dead. She went straight into the state child protection system afterward."

Lily added, "I just got off the phone with one of the officers. She said there were so many rats fighting over Zoey her whole little body was covered." Lily began to cry. "She said she and her partner wouldn't have even known there was a child under the mound of rats if they hadn't heard her screaming."

Roni sank into a chair and put her head in her hands. "I'm going to be sick." She got up and ran to the nearest bathroom. Her husband hurried after her.

Bernadine wiped at her eyes. "So how badly was she bitten?"

"Not very, miraculously. The policewoman said the rats had turned on each other by the time they arrived—trying to keep each other from getting the prize, I guess. Zoey did have to have a series of rabies shots. She was in the hospital for quite some time."

"Lord have mercy," Bernadine said with a sorrowful shake of her head, "and she went through that all alone."

"Yeah."

Roni came back in the room. "I'm sorry."

"Don't be," Bernadine reassured her. "It's awful."

Lily then repeated the information about the rabies shots, and all Reg could do was sigh. "Had that been me with those rats, I'd be on heavy Thorazine to this day, maybe for the rest of my life."

"Tell me about it," Bernadine responded.

Roni said, "At least we now know the story. That helps. It hurts my heart real bad, but it helps. I understand a little better."

They all did.

Bernadine added. "Lily and I have been trying to find a therapist who'll come out maybe once or twice a month to help our kids. If you know anyone, let me know. We need to get Zoey and the rest of them started."

"I have a few names. Let me make some calls and I'll get back," Reg said.

"Okay."

Roni's sadness was reflected in her eyes. "We're going to head home. We'll see you later." Before she left though, she took a moment to give Bernadine a strong hug, and then Lily, "Thanks for all you do."

"You take care, now," Bernadine told her.

The Garlands nodded and departed.

When Bernadine returned home she went up and knocked on Crystal's door.

"Come in."

Crystal took one look at Bernadine's face and asked, "Did something happen to my mom?"

"No, baby. It's about Zoey."

"Oh," she said with impatient disinterest. "Now what?"

Bernadine cocked her head at her, "What's wrong with you?"

"I'm tired of hearing about the little White girl's problems. Every time I turn around, it's Zoey this, Zoey that. I'm waiting for you to find *my* mom, dammit!"

Bernadine pulled in a deep breath in order to keep her temper in check. "Is that what all this moodiness and one-word answers have been about for the past few days? You think I'm not looking for your mother?"

She remained sullenly silent.

"And if Zoey is nothing more than just a little *White* girl, why are you so nice to her all the time?"

Crystal couldn't hold Bernadine's accusatory stare for long, so she looked away.

"I have people looking for your mother all over this country, Miss Thang. Technically, you aren't even supposed to have contact with her until you're eighteen, but I'm willing to try and get around that—for you."

The guilt filling Crystal burned her from the top of her weave down to the soles of the cute new boots she was wearing.

Bernadine's voice was ice-cold. "My people are going to keep looking for your mother, but you won't have to worry about me telling you anything else about the little white girl and her problems. You made it real clear that you don't care, so good night, Crystal. I'll see you in the morning."

She walked out. Bernadine wanted to slam the door so bad but didn't because she was supposed to be the adult. When she got to her room she sat on the bed and wiped away the angry tears filling her eyes. She knew this was going to be hard, but not this hard, this fast.

Crystal was in her room crying. She couldn't believe what she'd said about Zoey because she did care. Everything was all so mixed up and so messed up inside of her, she thought that maybe it would be better if she did leave.

She'd never seen Ms. Bernadine so mad. Every word she said made Crystal feel like the ungrateful little witch she'd been acting like lately, but she couldn't seem to help it. Sometimes it was like she was the only person in the world that mattered and the next minute she was fine. Maybe it was because of the new environment and being out here in Green Acres. Maybe she was losing her mind, but whatever the reason, she'd hurt Ms. Bernadine's feelings and she'd hurt them bad, and she didn't think a simple apology would fix that.

Roni sat at the piano looking at the keys. Reg was across the room watching, silently. When she glanced over at him, his eyes were serious. He knew what she was attempting to do and in a way why. Then Zoey came into the room. She had on her green Shrek nightgown. Seeing Roni seated at the keys, she walked over to Reg and stood by his side.

Roni looked to her and said, "Zo, Mama Roni used to sing and play the piano, but one night, something really awful happened and I stopped because I got scared. Now, I have you and you had something terrible happen to you one night too. I really want to help you not be scared anymore, but I can't help you until I stop being scared, myself, so . . ."

She began to play. The first selection seemed to spring from her fingers without thought. It was one of her favorites, a suite of hymns by Duke Ellington that she'd often played in the past to uplift herself. She played them slow and beautifully just like the great Duke composed them, and she felt the tears begin to flow. She switched next to

gospel, then slid into the familiar old-school hymns of the
A.M.E church, letting the rising notes fill the house and
soothe the hurt she'd carried inside for so long. Her fingers
moved over the keys with the God-given gift born in her
just as it had been in Zoey, and she played on.

Quiet as a ghost, Zoey left Reg's side and walked over to
the piano. She climbed up on the bench.

When Roni quietly ended what she'd been playing, Zoey
began the familiar cords of "Amazing Grace." Roni joined
in, but after the first few notes, Zoey stopped. Zoey started
the hymn again, and just as Roni began, Zoey stopped
once more. Roni looked to her husband for an answer. He
shrugged. Zoey began again, but this time loudly and with
force. Her fingers were spread wide as she pounded the
keys. And then Roni got it. She placed a hand over Zoey's
to stop her, then said quietly, "Start again."

This time when the notes began, the multi-award-
winning recording artist Roni Moore opened her tear-filled
throat and sang emotionally, "Amazing Grace, how sweet
the sound, to save a wretch like me . . . I once was lost, but
now am found, was blind, but now I see . . ."

CHAPTER
26

The air was pretty tense in the Bernadine and Crystal house after Crystal's award-winning performance. Bernadine was so mad, she wanted to shake the teen until her weave fell out, but she kept it together. She didn't scream, shout, or otherwise act out, but underneath she was seething.

Lily summed it up best when the ladies were having lunch that day at the Paynes. "Teenagers are crazy. Insane. From the time Davis was fourteen until his senior year in high school, I prayed every day, 'Lord, let me make it through another day without killing him. Amen.'"

The ladies laughed. Reg and Barrett were at the rec center gym. The kids were in school, so the women had gotten together to share some Girls' Time.

Lily said, "You all think I'm playing. And you have male children too? Wait until they start becoming allergic to soap and think a bottle of cologne will make folks overlook the fact that they haven't washed in days."

Bernadine chuckled, "So how're Preston and the colonel getting along, Sheila?"

She shrugged over her coffee cup, "Still circling each other like two guys in a Kung Fu movie, but so far, there's been no blood. They share a love for books and history, and that's got them both freaked out. I'm sitting back enjoying the show."

Roni said, "I have good news. Called my producer this morning. I'm going back into the studio."

They cheered and raised their cups and hugged her and cheered some more.

"And," she added, "I'm looking at building a recording studio here so I don't have to be away while we work on the new CD. Once word gets out on how state-of-the-art it's gonna be, we'll rent it out, make the town a little bit of money. Put Henry Adams on the music map."

"Wow," Bernadine said. "I like that."

While the others listened to Roni talk about the upcoming CD project, Bernadine's mind slipped back to Crystal and the darkness she sensed on the horizon. If her mother's whereabouts weren't discovered soon, the girl was going to run. Bernadine knew that as sure as she knew God was good.

Sitting in the classroom, Crystal was supposed to be working on a history lesson, but instead she was trying to figure out how and when to leave Henry Adams. Although she liked Ms. Bernadine a lot, even more than a lot, she needed to get out of Dodge. She thought about her pretty room back at the house and decided that all the bling and glitz wasn't her style, anyway. The lifestyles of the rich and famous was for White people and big-money Black people like Ms. Bernadine and Oprah, not for ghetto-raised girls like herself.

But some kind of way she was going to have to convince Amari to take her out to the highway, first. She planned to hitchhike south from there. She didn't want him getting into trouble on account of her, but she had to go. The people Ms. Bernadine hired weren't ever going to call back, so it was up to her to handle her business alone.

There was a mile-long walking track behind the rec center, and Lily used it as often as she could. She'd just finished her first quarter of a mile when she spotted Trent behind her on the track jogging in her direction. Back in the day when they were on the high school track team and he'd run up on her slow like he was doing now, her heart would do flips at the sight of him in his warm-ups and cleats. Sort of the same way it was doing now.

"You trying to make a brother chase you to Topeka," he asked when he caught up.

She kept up her pace. "You chasing me?"

He stopped. "Yeah. I think I am."

She stopped. Speechless for a moment, she studied his face. "As in chasing me, chasing me?"

He nodded. "Unless you have a problem with it."

She had to shake her mind loose so she could make her mouth open and say, "No. *Uh*, no."

"You sure? You look a little rattled."

"Well, yeah. I wasn't expecting this, I guess."

"I wasn't either, to tell you the truth. Decided to stop fighting it, though."

"You've been fighting it?"

"Since the day you first drove into the garage."

"You acted like you wanted to shoot me."

"I did, or at least that's what I told myself."

She looked off into the distance and thought about what might have been had it not been for her. "Can we take it slow?"

"Slow as you want."

The hurt she'd caused him still nagged at her, though. "I'm sorry," she offered softly, one more time. And she was.

"Let's call it a remix. A lot of people never get a second chance." He smiled down at her. "I don't have a track medal this time."

"It's okay," she said remembering. The last time they'd done this, he'd given her one of his track medals on a chain. He'd placed it around her neck and she'd worn it proudly to let everybody know she was his lady. "I don't need one."

"Sure?"

"Positive."

"How about we do dinner together this evening at my place? I've got some steaks in the freezer I've been wanting to grill. Devon's invited too, of course."

"Sounds good. Should I bring anything?"

"Nope. Everything is on the house."

She nodded, smiling.

"See you tonight."

"See you tonight."

He jogged off and you could have knocked Lily over with a feather, but she wanted to jump up and down and yell to the world about just how happy she was.

The dinner was fun. He grilled, she sat and let him wait on her.

Amari and Devon watched them both from the seats at the outdoor table. "Did you know anything about this?" Amari asked Devon.

"About what?"

"Ms. Lily and Trent."

"What about them?"

Amari shook his head, "Never mind. I forgot you're only eight." But he kind of liked the idea of the two of them getting together.

At the end of the evening dusk was settling, and Trent realized how big of a turn his life had made; first Amari and now Lily, his Lily. Watching her as she and Devon got ready to go home, he could finally acknowledge how much he'd missed her, her smile, her being near. For some reason they'd been given a second chance. He agreed with her about taking it slow because he wanted to savor every moment the future had in store.

"Devon and I are going to take off." Lily now understood why she'd been so hesitant about committing to Winston. She'd been waiting for this—Trent to come back into her life.

"How about I walk with you?"

"I'd like that."

Amari and Devon were staring up at the two adults as if the encounter was being played out on a movie screen.

Without taking his eyes from Lily's, Trent said, "Amari, I'll be back in a minute."

"Okay but curfew's at ten, remember."

Trent chuckled. "Go on in the house."

Amari grinned. "Bye, Ms. Lily. See you in the morning, Creflo."

"Bye, Amari," Lily replied, tickled by his antics.

With Devon walking between them they crossed the street to her house. They both knew that this short time together hadn't been enough, so when she reached the porch, she said, "Come on in."

She sent Devon up to his room to take his shower, and she and Trent went out back to the deck. He took a seat on one of the chaise longues and she walked to the railing and looked up at the sky. The stars were out.

"I remember the very first time I saw you," he told her quietly.

Amused by that, she turned his way. "Do you?"

"Yep. Track practice. Sophomore year. Didn't know who you were then, but thought you were cute. You had on a gray tee and your shorts. Had those nice track girl legs going on."

"Well, I don't remember the first time I saw you."

"Wound a brother would you."

"Telling you the truth. I knew of you, of course, all the girls did, but to me you were just this big-time four-sport jock with a swelled head."

"You're a hard woman, Lily Fontaine."

"You were cute, though."

"Finally, a bone."

In the silence that followed, the memories ebbed and flowed like tributaries of time. "I remember the first time you took me out, though."

He remembered too. "Where we'd go?"

"Dairy Queen. You came to pick me up in Black Beauty—that New Yorker your father gave you. Whatever happened to it?"

"Totaled it in an ice storm a few years after we graduated." He didn't tell her about the restoration. He wanted it to be a surprise.

"That's too bad. We had some good times in that car."

"Yeah, we did."

"Nice backseat too, as I remember."

"Thought we were supposed to be taking this slow."

She shrugged. "Just remembering."

"*Uh-huh.*"

He got up and walked to where she stood. As their eyes met and their feelings entwined they were both filled with the wonder and realization of what this all meant. He reached out and slowly traced her mouth. The intensity put a sweet shake in her knees and she closed her eyes.

The kiss was gentle; searing. He eased her close and she came willingly as he wrapped her in his arms and she wrapped him in hers.

Wearing his Spiderman pajamas, Devon came downstairs to let Ms. Lily know he was done with his shower. Through the glass door that led out to the deck, he could see her kissing Mr. Trent and his eyes widened, then he put his hand to his mouth and giggled. Now he understood what Amari had meant. Still smiling, he left them alone and went back upstairs to his room.

After Trent's departure, Lily floated upstairs to tuck in Devon. The sight of him lying in bed looking so sweet and content always tugged at her heart. She came over and sat on the edge of his bed. "Finished up your Bible reading for the night?"

"Yep."

Devon now had variety in his answers. Every response was no longer, yes or no ma'am. She attributed that to him being around the other children, especially Amari. It was a joy to watch him become less wooden and more lifelike.

"Do you think Ms. Bernadine is ever going to let me be pastor?"

"I don't know, baby. She's got so much on her mind right now, she's probably forgotten, but I'll ask her again for you."

He nodded.

She eyed the old flowered pillowcase he was lying on. It was the same one that had held his entire world when he got on the jet with them in Birmingham. It had been old then, and now, after so many washings had become even more threadbare and thin. "We need to figure out what to do about your grandmama's pillowcase, baby. If you keep sleeping on it, it's going to waste away." She knew it was the only thing he had left of her besides his memories. "We could maybe have Ms. Agnes turn it into a quilt, or maybe get a frame for it and hang it on your wall."

He turned slightly and stroked his hand over the faded cotton. "Okay."

She touched his head.

"Is Mr. Trent going to be your boyfriend?"

Now that was an eight-year-old's question. "I think he might be. Is that okay with you?"

"Yes. I like him. Amari too."

"Even when he calls you Creflo."

He nodded. "He's filled with the devil sometimes, but God still loves him and I do too."

That wasn't the eight-year-old. She leaned down and gave him a hug, "God loves you a lot too. Just like I do."

She gave him a quick peck on his smooth little forehead. "Good night, Devon. Sleep well."

After dousing his lights, she slipped quietly out of his room.

Bernadine spent the morning out on her deck on the phone tying up some loose ends, one of which involved the matter of Devon's land. Her lawyers had contacted the courts in his former hometown just in time to keep the 110 acres previously owned by his grandmother from going into foreclosure for unpaid property taxes. Bernadine's check had canceled the court's actions, and now the land was being held for the boy in her name. She'd transfer everything to him when he reached eighteen.

Next, she made a call to the investigators looking into the case of Crystal's mother, but still no results. The lack of progress was as frustrating to her as it was to Crystal, only because the girl wouldn't be able to move on with her life until some type of closure was found. Praying something positive would happen soon, she scanned the rest of the day's to-do list.

" 'Morning."

Hearing the voice, she looked out to see Malachi standing in the yard. "Just passed Lily on her way to the track, and she said you were working back here. You want to take a break?"

Surprised by how nice it felt to see him, she said, "Sure, come on. Want some coffee?"

"I'll take a cup, sure."

She gathered up some of the papers she had spread out on the table and put them in a pile. "Have a seat. I'll get your coffee."

She returned carrying a silver tray topped with a steaming mug and a dainty silver sugar bowl and matching creamer.

"I don't know many women who have silver trays."

"Stop it," she said, laughing.

He doctored up his coffee with the sugar and cream then sipped contentedly while watching her. "So what's been going on in the high-powered world of Ms. B. E. Brown?"

"Not much. I heard about the tiger you got for Zoey. That was sweet."

"Like I told the Garlands, I know what it's like to be alone in the dark. Maybe it will help."

She knew he was talking about his bout with alcoholism. "I just wish I could find something to help Crystal."

"Still nothing on her mama?"

"No. Crystal insists she's in New Orleans, but my people have looked everywhere. Nothing."

"If she's a crackhead, you may never find her."

"I know, but it means so much to Crys that I do. I'm pretty sure she's going to run away and try to look for her on her own, and I'm scared to death."

"Sometimes you can't keep folks from doing what they think they need to. Especially somebody as headstrong as she is. If she takes off, we find her and bring her back. Simple as that."

"I hope so."

He eyed her over his cup and noticed the weariness in her posture and the tiredness in her eyes that neither her fancy clothes nor expensive makeup could hide. "You're carrying a lot on those shoulders of yours making sure everybody gets the love they need, but what about you? Who's rubbing your shoulders at night when you finally get home? Who's fixing you dinner and reminding you not to work so damn hard all day every day?"

She met his eyes across the table.

"We all need balance, Bernadine. Took me a long time to figure that out, but it's one of the best things I ever learned."

"I'm fine."

"No, you're not."

"So you're an authority on me now?"

He shook his head. "Here we go. Draw down, girl, would you. Just trying to get you to slow your roll some before you run over yourself."

"I'm fine." With all the stuff she had on her plate, his advice was the last thing she needed.

"Okay, I was just trying to look out for a friend." He stood, drained his coffee, and left the deck.

Stung by guilt, she called his name, but he kept walking until he disappeared. She dropped her head and felt like crap.

CHAPTER
27

Thursday night at the rec center was Movie Night. Tamar and her friends ran the concessions, offering popcorn, baked goods, and other small treats. Anybody who wanted to come was welcome. Admission was free.

On screen tonight was the digitally animated film *The Incredibles* for the kids, and the second feature, for the adults, was *Stormy Weather*, featuring the lovely Miss Lena Horne.

As everyone found their seats, Bernadine saw Malachi enter accompanied by a short, well-dressed middle-aged woman she didn't know. They both had popcorn as if they were on a date, and when he looked over and spotted Bernadine he gave her a cool nod before turning his attention back to his companion.

Bernadine slumped in her seat and focused on eating her popcorn. Was she jealous? She didn't want to admit it, but yeah, she was, just a little. Was she planning on dealing with her feelings? No.

Lily and Trent came to sit nearby, and she was happy to

have their company. They looked so happy now that they'd finally reconnected after so many years apart, she couldn't help but be happy for them.

Amari walked down to tell Trent, "Preston and I are going to watch the movie for awhile, then go shoot some hoop in the gym."

"Okay, but let me know if you decide to head home before the show's over."

"Gotcha."

Once Amari was back in his seat he looked over to Crystal on his right and to Preston on his left and said, "We're on."

Riley Curry had had enough of state regulators and their red tape. He was going to get Cletus out of jail and he was doing it tonight. Because this was the plains of Kansas and not someplace like Los Angeles or Detroit, there were no all-night guards, which he planned to take full advantage of.

When he reached the grounds, he backed his old white truck up to the area where the holding pens and barns were, then cut his lights. In the silence, he walked up to the gates. Using a pair of old bolt cutters, he made a hole in the chain-link fence big enough for Cletus to be able to pass through without difficulty. The cutting made his healing collarbone smart a bit, but he ignored it and then stepped through.

Putting the bolt cutters under his arm, he clicked on his flashlight and looked around. He had no way of knowing if his hog was inside one of the barns or in the pens out back, so he moved deeper onto the property to see what he could find.

It didn't take him long. Cletus was in one of the pens and was lying down asleep. "Cletus," he called out in a hoarse excited whisper. Riley was so happy to see him. "Wake up, big boy. Cletus!"

He tested the edge of the wired enclosure warily, hoping it wasn't electrified to give him a shock, but nothing happened so he used the bolt cutter on the hanging padlock and pushed open the gates.

One of the big lights mounted on a nearby barn lit the scene well enough for the now-awakened hog to recognize Riley for who he was, or at least that's how it seemed because the pig trotted over and Riley hugged him around his massive neck. There was little time for celebration, however, since he didn't want to risk discovery, so a few moments later, Riley and the hog hurried to the truck. Cletus climbed the ramp into the bed, Riley slammed the tailgate shut, and they were off. Riley had no idea where they were going, but he'd figure that out later. Cletus was rescued. It was the only thing that mattered.

Just as the action in *The Incredibles* began to heat up, Amari, Crystal, and Preston slipped outside. While Preston and Crystal kept watch, Amari took a quick look around the vehicles in the nearby parking lot for a suitable target.

Since he didn't have a lot of time, he decided Malachi's would have to do. Unlike some of the others, Malachi's red truck was old, there was no alarm system, clubs on the steering wheel, or any other visible deterrents to slow down a thief. He quickly got inside, took a minute to work his way into the steering column, found the wires he needed by touch alone and started that baby up.

His accomplices squeezed in beside him on the front seat, Crystal in the middle. They quietly closed the truck's doors and rolled away. The way Amari figured it would take fifteen minutes tops to get Crystal to the highway and another fifteen to get back. The thirty-minute window might be tight, but they were under way now, and it was too late to turn back.

"I appreciate this, Amari."

"Just be careful who you hitchhike with, okay?"

"I will, don't worry. I'll call you soon as I get there."

Preston asked, "You really think you can find her?"

"Yeah, I do."

They rolled past Tamar's house and then by the Jeffersons' and the fence they spent the summer whitewashing. Amari was driving as fast and as safely as the dirt roads allowed because he wanted to bring the truck back in one piece.

"Time?" he called out.

Preston lifted his wrist and peered at his watch. "We've been gone seven minutes."

"Okay." The wooden blocks for the gas and brake that he'd made last week in the carpentry class Mr. Dobbs ran at school seemed to be working well. They were crude versions of the ones he'd had in Detroit, but he just needed them to stay in place until this was over. He was admittedly stressed but he couldn't deny how good it felt to be behind the wheel again. Malachi's truck was no Escalade, but it moved.

When they saw the signs leading to Highway 183 South, the teenage occupants cheered. Almost there.

"Any particular place you want to be dropped?" Amari asked, keeping his eyes on the road ahead and on his mirrors. There'd been no traffic so far, but the ramp to the highway was just ahead and the big lights lining the major north-south corridor could be seen. The last thing he needed was a run-in with the po-pos.

Crystal looked around as they merged onto the highway. "Up there, underneath that big light."

It was about a quarter of a mile ahead. Even though Amari's blocks allowed him to reach the pedals, he was still short and he could just see over the wheel. When they came off the ramp, he merged ahead of a semi that moved over to let him on, and when Amari looked up the trucker was looking right down on him. "Shit!"

"What?" Preston called out in alarm.

"Look back and see if that trucker's on his radio?"

"Why?"

"Just do it!"

Crystal and Preston both turned.

Crystal cried out, "Yeah, he is."

He cursed again, "He's probably calling the police."

The air in the truck was tense. Amari took the truck up to eighty. He could feel the body rattling but he ignored it, focusing instead on getting to the lighted spot where Crystal wanted to be dropped off. Eyes glued to his mirrors because he could smell the police nearby, he said to her, "Crystal, you're going to have to get out quick. Okay."

She readied herself and said in a shaky voice, "Okay."

Preston was praying silently, "Please don't let us get caught," over and over again.

Just as Amari eased the truck to the shoulder and began to relax, he spotted a county sheriff's cruiser ahead sitting with its lights out.

"Dammit!" he yelled and floored the truck back onto the highway and past the cruiser, which of course gunned out onto the road and gave chase.

Preston had never been in trouble with the police in his life, except for the fire, but that didn't count. He was so scared he wanted to cry. "Drive, Amari!" he screamed. "Drive!"

He didn't have to tell him twice. They could hear the sirens now, and when they looked back they could see the blue light on the top of the police car spinning wildly. Amari scanned the road ahead for a turnaround or a ramp or anything else that would enable him to shake the car on his ass, but there was nothing. Back home in Detroit he could have used the interconnecting expressways or a nearby neighborhood to lose himself in, but this was Kansas, so he floored it and kept going.

When Malachi's phone buzzed in his pocket, he took it out and peered at the lit-up caller ID in the darkened movie theater. Wondering what Sheriff Will Dalton wanted with him, he excused himself from his date and stepped outside to take the call.

Afterward, he went back inside to alert the people the sheriff would be needing to see.

In the backseat of the cop car, Amari was understandably glum. The sheriff had been nice enough not to throw the three of them in jail, but the family reunion he was driving them to wasn't going to be pretty.

Needless to say, he was right. There was a lot of yelling, Crystal crying, and privileges taken away: like the video game center, which just about killed Preston, and no more of Tamar's homemade ice cream, which personally devastated Amari, but it was the disappointment on the faces of all the adults that hurt the most, especially Ms. Bernadine's.

Malachi didn't press charges, but he did want to press Amari into a small pancake. "You're going to owe me for the rest of your life for this stunt, young gun," he pointed out as he walked with Trent and Amari back to the house. His lady friend had driven herself back to Hays.

"I know."

"Got a bunch of barns around here that need mucking out. Planning to put your name on the pitchforks as the beginning down payment."

"Look, I'm sorry. I know I screwed up, but I was just trying to help Crystal."

"We understand that," Trent told him.

"Are you going to send me back?"

Malachi looked over at his son. This was entirely Trent's call. He knew what his son was going to say, but Amari needed to hear it from him.

"No, Amari."

"You sure? I'm a big boy, I can take the truth."

Trent stopped and said coolly, "The truth is, you steal any more cars, and people will be asking, 'Whatever happened to that boy Amari that used to steal cars?' And the answer will be, 'His daddy killed him, remember? Funeral was years ago.'"

Amari met his eyes.

"Don't ever put this town on front street with the police again. You hear me?"

"Yes," he said softly.

After a moment of silence they resumed the walk, and Amari looked up at Trent, "Can I ask you something?"

"What?"

"You just called yourself my dad. Is that who we are, father and son?"

"Would you rather be father and daughter?"

For the first time since being brought back by Sheriff Dalton, Amari allowed himself a smile.

Trent looked down at this boy who would probably make his life way more interesting than it needed to be before he went off to college said, "Yeah, Amari. Father and son. Which makes Tamar your great-grandmother and the old guy next to you your grandpa."

"I prefer OG," Malachi said with a sniff.

Trent cracked, "Stands for Old Geezer, right?"

"Do you hear the hate?" Malachi asked his grandson.

Amari grinned and they walked on. He now had a dad, a granddad, and a house with his own room. For a reformed car thief, Amari thought life was pretty good.

Preston was sitting up in his room waiting for Round Two. As if getting blasted by the adults at the rec center hadn't been bad enough, now he was going to have to endure an additional round of torture at the hands of the marines. He'd told Amari from the beginning the plan was bogus, but no, he wanted to help Crystal.

Looking back on the incident, he had to admit he'd been more scared than he'd ever been in his life. If the truck hadn't run out of gas at the end of the chase, no telling what might have happened. Amari managed to get the truck out of traffic and onto the shoulder. When they got out of the truck, Amari and Crystal immediately raised their hands above their heads, knelt on the pavement, then laid down flat, arms and legs spread-eagled, as if they'd had run-ins with the cops all the time. He of course had been standing up so scared and frozen by the big beams from the cop car that he couldn't move. Only after the sheriff advanced with his gun drawn and barked, "Get on the ground, son!" did he join his friends facedown in the gravel and dirt on the side of the highway. He never wanted to experience anything like this ever again.

The knock on his door broke into his thoughts. Seated in the chair at his desk, he looked toward the door. He took in a deep breath, steeled himself, and called quietly, "Come in."

It was the Paynes. He'd expected only the colonel. He was glad Mrs. Payne had come too. Her husband was less likely to commit murder with her looking on.

Barrett asked, "How are you? Quite the night."

"Yeah. I was terrified."

Barrett studied him for a moment. "Didn't expect you to admit that."

"I don't see why not. I've never been in trouble with the police before, except for setting that house fire. But I had to then! She wouldn't give me an inhaler and the doctor said I might die if I had another bad attack. Anyway, I told Amari it was a stupid plan from the beginning."

He saw the adults pass a look between them but didn't know them well enough to decipher the meaning.

"But you went along."

"Yeah. There I was lying facedown in the dirt. Amari and Crystal acted like it was no big deal."

Mrs. Payne stated the obvious. "You children were lucky you weren't killed in that high-speed chase."

He looked down at his lap. "I know. Guess you'll be sending me back, *huh*?"

Barrett asked, "That's up to you. Do you want to go back to Milwaukee?"

Preston looked into each of their faces. "No, ma'am and sir, I don't."

"Good, because we'd like you to stay and grow and mature and do all the things a young man with your great potential is capable of."

Preston's mouth dropped. He turned wide eyes to Mrs. Payne, who responded with a smile and said, "Since there isn't going to be a bloodbath, I'll let you two men talk alone."

Once she was gone, Barrett said, "Surprised by what I just said?"

"Yeah. I—I didn't think you liked me very much."

"I do. I like that you enjoy books and history and that

you're great at video games, but I don't know much else about you."

"I don't know much about you either, except that you like books and history, and about your father."

"And that I'm a hard ass."

Preston wasn't sure if he was supposed to smile or not. "Yeah, that too."

Barrett grabbed an empty chair and sat, "Time for you and me to get acquainted." He stuck out his hand, "Name's Barrett Montgomery Payne."

Preston took hold of his large strong hand. "Preston Christopher Mays. Nice to meet you."

"Same here. So, Preston, tell me about yourself."

Bernadine and Crystal entered the silent house. Bernadine understood why Crystal had done what she had, but all of the awful terrible things that might have happened had Sheriff Dalton not been in the right place at the right time made her want a stiff drink. She was just about to tell the teary-eyed Crystal to go on up to her room and that they'd talk in the morning when she saw a note on the table.

Picking it up, she read the wording and then slowly set it back down. "Crystal, that's from Lily. The investigators found your mom. She's in prison in Illinois."

CHAPTER
28

Genevieve, Marie, and Agnes were having breakfast at Tamar's the following morning, when a report came on the local television news that Cletus had escaped. Genevieve's hands flew to her mouth.

"Riley did always want that hog on TV," Tamar pointed out. "Guess he's getting his wish, twice now. Once for killing Prell and now for busting out of the pen."

Agnes smiled. "Hush so we can hear."

The camera showed the pen where Riley had been locked up, then panned to the big hole in the fence.

The young female reporter said, "As far as authorities can tell no one has ever kidnapped, or shall we say pig napped, a suspect from the Department of Agriculture's pens before, and a warrant has been issued for the hog's apprehension."

"Lord," Tamar breathed.

"Police believe the hog's owner, Mr. Riley Curry, for-

mer mayor of Henry Adams, may be the person responsible
for freeing the murdering animal."

A picture of a smiling Riley wearing his black pinstripe
suit with the rose on the lapel, flashed up on the screen.

The reporter finished up by saying, "If you know of Mr.
Curry's whereabouts, please call the sheriff's office."

Tamar picked up the remote and was about to click it off
when the anchor said, "And last night, there was a reported
carjacking. Three teens also from Henry Adams were alleg-
edly involved. We're trying to get more information on this
story and will bring you more details at six."

"Dammit," Tamar whispered, and clicked it off.

Bernadine and Lily were outside on Bernadine's deck,
and Bernadine was on the phone. After seeing that morning's news report on the so-called carjacking, Bernadine
had put in a hasty call to her lawyers to contact the authorities and find out what the heck was going on. They'd just
called back.

"What do you mean I have to go to a hearing?"

She listened to her lawyer, and what he had to say did
not make her day. "But Malachi isn't going to press charges,
and there was no child endangerment."

She looked up at Lily, who was now eyeing her with
mild alarm.

Bernadine's lips tightened. "Okay. When's the hearing
and where?" She repeated the time and date so Lily could
write it down. "September twenty-ninth, nine a.m., county
courthouse. Okay. What about Crystal? How soon can we
get in to see her mother?"

She listened, then replied, "Okay. Stay on it and let me know as soon as possible."

She closed the phone. "Well, looks like someone dropped a dime to a judge last night about the joyride, and we've all been summoned to appear."

"Why?"

"It seems that this same judge is concerned that I'm running a loose ship and he wants to talk about it."

"Damn."

"No kidding. The legal beagles said the clerk was real snippy and said if the judge didn't like what he heard, they'd start proceedings to shut down the program and ship the kids back."

"Over my dead body!"

"Mine too. Dammit! If Crystal had just waited another two hours."

"I know."

Bernadine sighed. "Okay. We can deal with this."

Lily searched her face. "This is real serious, Bernadine."

"No, kidding."

Later, she called all the parents and the elders together at the center and told them what was going on.

Roni jumped to her feet, "Hell, no! They are not taking my child."

Barrett said, "It was little more than a prank. Nobody was hurt."

Bernadine agreed. "The county sees it differently, I suppose."

Sheriff Dalton entered the room. "Malachi called me.

I've come to offer my apologies. I've got an overzealous deputy who just happens to be the boyfriend of that little girl reporter. He went home, told her about what occurred on his shift, which he admitted he does every night, and she started making calls."

Malachi said, "Is he still alive?"

"Just barely. Gave him the speech about police confidentiality, then gave him a week off without pay. Again, real sorry."

He turned to Bernadine. "I want to apologize to you personally, Ms. Brown. You've been good for us up here in this part of the county. My brother-in-law worked on your buildings, and anytime that lazy bum can get hired and I don't have to feed him, I'm pleased."

She smiled, "Thanks, Sheriff."

"No problem. If you need me to testify at the hearing, just let me know. Gotta go. You folks take it easy."

He left.

Bernadine looked out at the worried and angry faces. "I don't think we should tell the kids anything at this point, but they will have to be at the hearing, so how about we tell them when we get closer to the date? They've had enough worry in their lives."

Everyone agreed.

Three days later, Bernadine and Crystal were on the jet with Katie flying to Illinois.

"Do you think she'll be glad to see me?" Crystal asked.

"I would think so."

The two were still tiptoeing around each other, but Bernadine hoped this trip would help their relationship by resolving some of Crystal's issues and allowing them to begin moving forward.

"Ms. Bernadine, thank you for all you've done. I know I haven't been acting real grateful lately."

"You have a lot of stuff you're dealing with in life, Crys. Let's hope this visit with your mom will help fix some of that."

When they got to the airport, there was a car waiting to take them straight to the facility where Crystal's mom, Nikki, was being held.

As they rolled through the prison gates and onto the grounds, the place was more modern than the old nineteenth-century-looking brick and stone building Bernadine had been expecting.

Crystal looked out at all the cars in the lot and the herd of people moving toward the entrance. "Must be visiting day."

Bernadine agreed. Most of the visitors were women, many of them older, most of them walking with or carrying children. She shook her head sadly. She had no idea how many prisoners the place housed, but judging by the numbers of visitors, she assumed a lot.

Inside, they were passed through security. Their purses were checked and their bodies wanded for weapons and other prohibited items. Crystal looked grim. Bernadine wasn't feeling real cheery herself. Prison wasn't a place for cheer.

The female guard took them down a few long hallways that appeared to hold offices of some sort and then into a small room. She gestured for them to take seats in the two plastic chairs set up by a small blue table in the room's center.

She told them, "They'll bring her in in a moment. I ask that you not touch the prisoner in any way or make any sudden moves. Privacy with visitors is not allowed, so there'll be guards here at all times. Any questions?"

They shook their heads.

"Okay." The guard took out a walkie-talkie, spoke into it for a moment, and then a door at the back of the room opened.

Nikki Jackson was shackled at her ankles and wrists by a long connecting silver chain. Her hair was hidden beneath a black stocking cap. She was wearing a faded blue shirt and matching loose pants. In another setting the clothing might have passed for hospital scrubs, but this was a prison and the clothing was her uniform.

She was painfully thin, so much so that she looked as if she could've easily slipped the chains that hobbled her movements as she shuffled into the room wearing prison-issued slides. When she saw Bernadine and Crystal, she stopped and studied their faces. It was plain she had no idea who her visitors were.

Crystal went to stand up, but Bernadine placed a gentle hold on her arm. The guard said no sudden movements. Crystal sat but her eyes never left her mother.

"Do I know y'all?" Nikki asked curiously, hobbling closer to the table and continuing to look into their faces. She sat, and the guard who'd been her escort took up a position at the door.

"It's me, Crystal."

Nikki looked into Crystal's face. "Crystal who?"

Crystal looked so crushed, Bernadine's heart broke.

"Your daughter," Crystal replied quietly.

Nikki looked hard at the face staring back at her and then the smile that suddenly widened her face showed the missing teeth, a result of the years of crack abuse. "Baby girl," Nikki whispered with recognition and affection. "What are you doing here?"

"We came to see you."

Nikki turned her attention to Bernadine, who introduced herself. "I'm Bernadine, Crystal's foster mother."

"You don't look like any foster mother I've ever seen," she said, taking in the expensive suit and the jewelry. "You look like you doing pretty good for yourself."

Bernadine showed a small smile.

She turned back to Crystal. "How'd you find me?"

Crystal looked more relaxed. "Bernadine hired some investigators."

Nikki flicked a look Bernadine's way, "Really?"

"She's been real nice to me."

"Glad to hear it. So, what do you want? You looking for your daddy? What?"

"No. I—I've been worried about you and wanted to see if you were okay."

She shrugged. "I'm locked up and going to be locked up for the rest of my life. I ain't got no money or nothing if that's what you came to find out."

"I'm not looking for money. I just wanted to find you."

"Well, you did. Anything else?"

Bernadine could see the hurt fill Crys's eyes.

Nikki did as well. "What's the matter?"

"I thought maybe you'd be glad to see me."

"I am glad to see you, and I'm glad for you to see where I'm at because I don't want you following in my footsteps and wind up in a place like this shit hole." She turned then to Bernadine. "She a good girl?"

Bernadine nodded.

"Then Crystal, I want you to cut that blond shit out of your head, take off all that ho-looking makeup, and be like that lady sitting next to you. You don't want to be around anything close to the life I been livin'. You hear me, girl?"

Crystal nodded.

"Stay away from those fast boys and those blunts and concentrate on getting an education. Go to college."

Nikki asked Bernadine, "Does she listen to you?"

"Most times."

Nikki leaned in. "Start listening, Crystal. All the time. I didn't. People couldn't tell me nothing 'cos I thought I knew every damn thing already, but I didn't know shit. And don't come back here and see me again."

Crystal looked struck. "Why not?"

"'Cause I'm dying. Doctors here give me three months, tops. HIV."

Crystal's eyes filled with tears.

Nikki shook her head. "Don't cry. It's another one of those things where I didn't listen." She directed another question at Bernadine, "She going to be with you a long time?"

"For the rest of her life if I have a say."

"Good."

The guard by the door said, "Two minutes."

Nikki nodded. "Crystal, I have to go back. You are going to be okay."

"I don't want you to die."

"I know, but we all do, sooner or later."

She took a last look at Crystal's tear-stained face and said, "You be good for Bernadine now, and do something with your life."

"I promise."

She nodded. "Guard."

The guard by the door moved to her side and without a backward glance Nikki Jackson walked out of her daughter's life. On the other side of the door, where her daughter couldn't see, she got halfway down the hall, fell brokenly to her knees, and wept.

Riley and Cletus crossed the state line into Texas. Riley was not only tired of driving he was also hungry. Deciding he had to stop, he pulled into the parking lot of one of the fast food franchises and cruised around it for a moment, looking for police cars. Seeing none, he parked. After taking one last glance around, he got out.

Inside, he ordered burgers for himself and Cletus, then quickly walked back outside. He stopped at the sight of a very large red-haired woman standing by the bed talking to Cletus. When Cletus raised his snout to welcome Riley back with his burgers, the woman turned and gave Riley a big ol' Texas smile.

"Is this your hog?"

"*Uh*, yes ma'am," he wasn't sure if he should be friendly or not.

She reached out and scratched Cletus behind the ears. "He's gorgeous." She went into baby talk, "Yes, you are, aren't you, big boy, Aren't you?"

Riley grinned.

"Name's Eustasia Pennymaker."

He juggled the bags so he could shake her hand. "I'm Riley."

"How you do, Riley? You don't sound like you're from around here."

"*Uh*, no. *Uh*—we're from outside Las Vegas."

"Welcome to Texas.'

"Thanks." He moved by her to get to the bed and took the burgers out of the bag. As he fed Cletus, she asked, "You here visiting or on business?"

"We're just traveling. Got up one morning and decided we wanted to see the country. Never been to Texas before."

"Well, I got a few hogs myself."

"Do you?"

"Yep. Smartest animals on the planet, if I do say so myself."

Riley smiled, "I tell folks that all the time."

"Unless they got hogs of their own they don't much believe you, do they?"

"No, they don't."

She turned her eyes on Cletus again, "He's a fine specimen. What's he weigh, six, seven hundred pounds?"

"Closer to six."

"Well I have a female named Chocolate that would absolutely adore him. Where y'all headed?"

Riley fed Cletus the third quarter-pounder with cheese. "Figured I'd find me a motel close by."

"Nope. You're staying with me."

"I am?"

"Yep. You married?"

"*Uh*, no. I'm not."

"Even better, while Chocolate's entertaining big boy here, I might want you in my straw tonight," she cooed slyly and then laughed. "I got plenty of room. Two hundred acres."

Riley was staring.

"You game?"

It took him a moment to recover, he was still stuck on being in the straw. He managed to stammer. "Sure. Why not?"

"Okay. Let me go in and grab a diet Coke and a couple fish sandwiches and you can follow me back to my place."

And in a few minutes they were on their way.

CHAPTER
29

It rained the day of the hearing, and for Bernadine the bad weather wasn't a good sign. They'd driven the short distance to the county courthouse in a caravan, and the lawyers were scheduled to meet them there. The kids looked scared, the parents did too, but no one was more scared than Bernadine. If this hearing didn't go their way, many lives and hearts would be shattered.

Inside they were all whisked away to a courtroom to wait for the judge. The lawyers arrived. Bernadine had hired one of the best defense trial lawyer teams in the country. The lady in charge was named Andrea Scott. A representative of Scott's firm had also handled Bernadine's divorce. Andrea took a moment to meet all the kids and their parents and to assure them things would be okay, then she and her people set up to get ready.

The judge entered and they all rose to their feet. His

name was O'Hara but it might as well have been O'Hell the way he treated them. It was apparent from his first question that his mind was already made up. "Which one is Brown?" he snarled.

Bernadine stood. He reminded her of an evil little elf from a fairy tale. He was short, bald, crotchety, and looked old enough to have been the late Morton's Prell's daddy.

"Give me one good reason why I shouldn't send these juveniles back to where they came from?"

Surprised by the venom in his voice it took her a moment to respond. "They're not bad kids, Your Honor. They just used poor judgment."

"Carjacking is a bit more serious than poor judgment."

Andrea Scott interjected, "Your Honor, a carjacking involves a weapon and—"

"Did I ask you to speak?"

"No, sir, but—"

"Then quiet down until I do."

Andrea's jaw tightened but she stayed silent.

"Now," he looked through the papers in front of him. "Which one is Emery?"

"That's Amari, Your Honor."

"Don't correct me."

Amari looked down at his shoes.

"You got a pretty extensive record here, young man."

"Yes, sir."

"Six arrests for stolen cars in the past year. Reason?"

"I want to be a NASCAR driver, sir."

The judge eyed him with surprise.

Trent did too. It never occurred to him or anyone else

that Amari might have a reason for stealing the cars that he had.

"NASCAR, huh? How're you going to do that if you're in jail, because that's where it looks like you're heading."

"Not anymore sir, Ms. Bernadine and my foster—"

"That's enough. Take your seat."

Bernadine shared a look with Andrea.

"Where's Malachi July?" He pronounced it *Maleekee*. "Where do you people get these names?"

Malachi stood. "It's from the Bible, sir."

"Really? Why didn't you press charges when they swiped your truck?"

"They're kids and one is being fostered by my son."

"Son. Stand."

Trent got to his feet.

"Which of the juveniles is yours?"

"Amari, sir."

He looked over at Amari again, and said to Malachi, "You're not doing him a favor by coddling him. Kansas state prisons are full of kids coddled by folks like you two. Take your seats."

The July men were seething but they sat.

"Preston Mays. Stand up."

Preston stood.

"Where's his foster parents?"

The Paynes stood. Barrett had on his full dress uniform.

"Name?" he asked Barrett.

"Col. Barrett Montgomery Payne. United States Marine Corps. Retired."

"This your boy?"

"Yes, sir."

"I'd expect more from a boy being raised by a marine. All three of you, sit."

Bernadine took a look around at her people. Devon was holding Lily's hand and had a look of terror on his face. Zoey was sitting in Roni's lap, and Mama Roni looked like she was about to jump up and kick somebody's ass. Beside her, Reg appeared quietly furious.

"Crystal Chambers."

She stood. O'Hara took one look at the gold weave and asked coldly, "And who do you belong to?"

"Ms. Bernadine."

He eyed her, then Bernadine, and said, "Take a seat."

Crystal pleaded "Your Honor, this is all my—"

"Sit. Down. Now!"

Fire shooting out of her eyes, she viewed him for a long moment, then sat.

He stared around for a moment. When his eyes settled on Zoey seated in Roni's lap he asked, "And you are?"

Roni and Reg stood. "Mr. and Mrs. Garland, Your Honor."

"And the child?"

"Our foster daughter, Zoey Raymond."

O'Hara looked down at his papers then glanced at Zoey cringing by Roni's side. "Sit."

He gave the faces in the courtroom one last look over. "Come back in an hour. I'll render my decision then."

Andrea Scott protested, "Your Honor. I'd like to present my case."

"Not necessary, counselor. I've heard all I need to hear. One hour." He banged the gavel, picked up his files, and swept from the courtroom.

Bernadine looked over at the bailiff, who offered a chagrined shrug of his shoulders.

Bernadine turned to her people. "You all take the kids out in the hall. I want to talk to Ms. Scott."

Their anger equaled her own.

Roni snapped, "He can rule any way he wants. I'll take Zoey back to New York and tie his Rumpelstiltskinlooking behind up in courts for years. He is not taking my child!"

Crystal asked, "Is he going to send us away?"

"Not if I can help it. You all go on out in the hall."

She saw Lily talking softly to Devon, and Barrett was on the phone. Bernadine hoped he was calling in reinforcements and that they'd come armed. When she met Malachi's eyes he shook his head angrily as he and Trent and Amari headed toward the doors.

Once Bernadine was alone with Andrea and her team she said, "This is outrageous."

"Tell me about it, but you'd be surprised how many judges there are just like him from sea to shining sea."

She leaned against the table and said frankly. "We can get this cleared up on appeal, but while we wait for a spot on the docket, the kids are probably going to be placed on hold with the Child Welfare Office, and there's no telling where they may wind up."

"Oh hell, no. Not while I'm breathing."

"Oh hell yes, unless you have a trump card that'll blow

Rumpelstiltskin out of the water, we're cooked for this round."

Bernadine had no card, all she had was a direct line to the Big Sister up above, and so she prayed.

The one hour dragged into two before the hearing finally reconvened. Everyone was on pins and needles as they waited for O'Hara to enter the courtroom. Bernadine prayed.

Two seconds later, her prayers were answered.

As O'Hara entered the room, he had venom in his eyes, but as stepped up to take his seat, he tripped over the hem of his voluminous black robe, then uttered a sharp cry of surprise as he stumbled and fell behind the bench and disappeared. A loud *thump* followed, then came a moan, and finally silence.

Bernadine was to say later that it looked like something out of a bad Chevy Chase routine.

Judge O'Hara was out cold when the EMTs carried him from the courtroom on a stretcher. Needless to say, another judge had to be called in.

Judge Amy Davis came in about thirty minutes later.

She looked out at the people in the courtroom. "Can I have everyone identify themselves, please, so I'll know who's who, and then we can get started."

Once that was accomplished, she addressed Andrea. "Now, tell me what happened."

Andrea did, and as she spoke, the judge took notes.

"So, in reality there was no carjacking?"

"No, Your Honor."

"Amari, Preston, and Crystal, will you step up here, please."

When they reached the bench she stared sternly and asked, "Are you planning any repeat performances or has all this trouble you've caused everyone been enough for one lifetime?"

"Enough," they responded contritely.

"I hope so. You have been given a unique opportunity to have a great future, especially if everything I've been reading about Ms. Brown on the Internet for the past few minutes is true."

She looked out at Bernadine. "I saw the CNN piece. You're doing good work."

"Thank you."

She turned her attention back to the Three Musketeers and said sternly and with force, "Do not. I repeat. Do not show your cute little faces in my courtroom ever again, or you will be praying for O'Hara to return. Got it?"

They nodded.

"Step back and go sit with your parents."

She turned her eyes to Bernadine. "As for you, Ms. Brown, I know how dumb teenagers can be. I have three at home. That being said, I again applaud you for your work and your commitment to these children. Not many folks would do what you're trying to do. However, if I don't mete out some kind of penalty, my unconscious colleague is going to return and make life a living hell for both of us, so this is what we're going to do. I'm going to place your program on court-ordered probation for the next calendar year under my jurisdiction. If at the end of the probationary period there are no more stupid teen tricks, you'll be free and clear of the order. Does that work for you?"

"Works for me."

"Amari, Crystal, and Preston?"

"Yes, Your Honor."

"Good. Works for me too." She brought down her gavel. "Court dismissed."

After her departure cheers filled the courtroom. There were hugs, happy tears, and lots of relief.

As they rolled away, Bernadine looked up to the now sunny heavens and whispered softly, with all the joy she had in her heart, "Thank you for this blessing. Thank you so very, very much."

After the caravan returned to Henry Adams, they threw a huge party at the rec center, and because the next day was Saturday, it went late into the night. There were toasts and dancing and more hugs than you could shake a stick at.

Bernadine was ecstatic. Sure there were still some loose ends: like would Crystal let go of her bad weave, would Zoey ever speak, would Lily and Trent get married now that they'd found each other again, and where in the world were Riley and Cletus, but she couldn't worry about any of that now. All she wanted to do was revel in the happy realization that her dreams of hope had come true. She had all the blessing she needed and she didn't need anything more.

FROM

**BEVERLY
JENKINS**

AND

AVON A

Dear Readers,

My fictional town of Henry Adams, Kansas, made its debut in 1994 as the setting for my first published novel, *Night Song*. The story takes place in 1882 and is centered around the town's school teacher, Cara Lee Henson, and the love she finds with Sgt. Chase Jefferson, a Tenth Cavalry Buffalo soldier. It also highlights the little known history of the Great Exodus of 1879 and the thousands of Black people who migrated west after the fall of Reconstruction. The newspapers of the time dubbed the Exodus "Kansas Fever" because it was the destination many of the Dusters chose.

The most famous town of course was Nicodemus, founded in 1877 in the Great Solomon Valley in Graham County, Kansas. During the 1880s Nicodemus flourished. There was a sizeable population, a newspaper, churches, and many successful businesses, but when the train spur promised by the Missouri Pacific never materialized the area began its decline. By the end of WWII Nicodemus was all but dead. However, the hopes and dreams of the founders continued to live on in the few descendants that remained, and on November 12, 1996, an act of Congress placed Nicodemus on the National Register of Historical Sites, thus making it an official unit of the National Parks Service. More recently, the population has risen and an annual reunion is held to honor the past. I like to place my stories where Black folks really walked and it was out of historic townships like Nicodemus that my fictional town Henry Adams came to be.

Although the town of Henry Adams is a product of my imagination, the man for whom it is named was very much real. Born into slavery, he served three years with the United States Colored Troops (USCT) and was twenty-two when the war ended. His first act as a free man was to see if he could travel across Louisiana without a pass. The journey didn't go well. He was accosted, beaten, and shown that he was no more free than he'd been before the war, so he took it upon himself to investigate conditions elsewhere in the South.

With the help of other Black vets and the members of local vigilance societies Adams sent five hundred men into the fields with orders to infiltrate plantations and farms and report back with their findings. He personally spent fourteen years in places like Louisiana, Texas, and Arkansas compiling evidence, organizing laborers and showing rural freedman how to exercise their newly won rights. His notes were later given to Congress during the hearings convened surrounding the Exodus. Historian Dorothy A. Sterling calls Adams a one man investigating committee. I call him remarkable and as I noted in my novel, *Winds of the Storm*, which features Adams's shadowy investigative network, a full historical treatment of his accomplishments to the race and to American history is long overdue.

Now, to *Bring on the Blessings*, or BOB as it was

called during its creation. Like Bernadine's quest, BOB grew out of an article featured in the July 7, 2002, issue of *Parade* magazine. It was titled "A Place Called Hope," and written by Lou Ann Walker. Hope Meadows, the town's true name, was founded by University of Illinois sociology professor Brenda Krause Eheart. Her dream was to establish a viable intergenerational community of foster parents, children, and seniors complete with all the values and love of the small town she grew up in. After a long and frustrating road of phone calls and faxes, she ultimately convinced the U.S. Government to let her use an abandoned Air Force base in Rantoul, Illinois, as the site. Because of her field of study, Eheart knew first hand of the struggles faced by foster children and the dire future faced by those who never leave the system.

I cut my teeth as a writer of historical romance. Many of my novels are set in nineteenth-century small towns. For years my agent has been after me to pen a small town kind of novel, and for just as many years I never gave it serious consideration because I was content writing award-winning historical romance and contemporary romantic suspense, but when I read the Walker article, the story was so moving that just like Bernadine I put the magazine away with the idea of maybe doing something along its lines in the future. That future came to be during the summer of 2007. My agent was in contract negotiations with my editor at Avon and suggested it might be time for that small town book. I'd like to say I was gung-ho ready. I wasn't, but she convinced me to step out of my comfort zone and to give it a try.

As the story began to form in my head, I knew Bernadine with her Oprah-like money would be the engine and that I wanted to create my own fictional version of Hope Meadows. There would be foster children of course, and elders, and the town would have the old school values that were so prevalent when I grew up in the '50s and '60s, but where to place the story? During my writing career I have created two fictional nineteenth-century towns: Grayson Grove, Michigan and Henry Adams, Kansas. I toyed with the Michigan town for a while, but as more characters came to the table with the surname July, I settled on Henry Adams. During that initial phase I also knew the town would sell itself on eBay. The precedent for that is Bridgeville, California. The residents sold the town on eBay in 2002 for seven hundred thousand dollars. The BBC Internet report on the sale was something else I cut out and saved with the idea of using the quirky detail sometime somewhere.

Zoey was the first of the foster children to appear to me. Her physical description is based on a little girl named Elizabeth who attends my church. The first time I saw Elizabeth I knew I had to put her in a book, so she became Zoey, even though her life doesn't mirror Zoey's in any way. Amari came next, followed by Devon and Preston. Preston's opening scene with the foster parent refusing to buy him an inhaler came out of a similar story told to me by a family social worker, only that real child was a three-year-old toddler. I thought I had all of the kids formed and accounted for, but then Crystal showed up hitchhiking on that rainy night in Dallas, so she was added to the cast of characters as well.

My editor asked me what I wanted readers to take away from this story. My first hope is that you enjoyed meeting Bernadine and the residents of Henry Adams. My second is that the story moves at least one person to look into fostering or adoption. There are thousands of children waiting for loving homes in states all over this nation. A disproportionate number of them are African American, and the hardest to place are sibling groups, children with special needs, and teens. If you don't wish to foster or adopt as my late husband and I did, there are myriad organizations working for children that could use your help. How about your local Boys and Girls Club, the Y, the Salvation Army, or the youth program where you worship? Can you volunteer or mentor? As Bernadine said, we all have gifts we can share with a child. When you touch a child you can change a life so please consider sharing yours.

If you would like the back story on the original residents of Henry Adams please see my novels, *Night Song* and *Something Like Love*. For the back story on Colonel Payne's ancestor Deputy Marshal Dixon Wildhorse and the fascinating bittersweet history of the Black Seminoles, please see my novel, *Topaz*. For more information on the Great Exodus of 1879, Henry Adams the man, and other historical underpinnings that led to the creation of BOB, please see the sources below.

Burton, Arthur T. *Black, Red and Deadly*. Austin, Texas: Eakin Press, 1991.

Foner, Eric. *Reconstruction: America's Unfinished Revolution, 1863–1877*. New York: Harper and Row, 1988.

Katz, William Loren. *The Black West*. Garden City, New York: Anchor Books, 1973.

Littlefield, Daniel Jr. and Lonnie E. Underhill, "Negro Marshals in the Indian Territory." *Journal of Negro History*. 56 (April 1971).

Mooney, Charles. "Bass Reeves, Black Deputy U.S. Marshal." *Real West* (July 1976).

Painter, Nell Irvin. *Exodusters: Black Migration to Kansas After Reconstruction*. Lawrence, Kansas: University Press of Kansas, 1986.

Sterling, Dorothy A. *The Trouble They Seen: Black People Tell the Story of Reconstruction*. New York: Doubleday, 1976.

Thybony, Scott. "The Black Seminole: A Tradition of Courage." *Smithsonian*, vol. 22, no. 5 (August 1991).

Well, I guess that's it. Hope you enjoyed the story. Until next time, be blessed.

B

Beverly Jenkins has received numerous awards, including three Waldenbooks Bestsellers Awards, two Career Achievement Awards from *Romantic Times* magazine, and a Golden Pen Award from the Black Writer's Guild. In 1999, Ms. Jenkins was voted one of the Top Fifty Favorite African-American Writers of the Twentieth Century by AABLC, the nation's largest online African-American book club. To read more about Beverly visit her website at www.beverlyjenkins.net.

Beverly Jenkins

BOOKS BY BEVERLY JENKINS

BRING ON THE BLESSINGS

ISBN 978-0-06-168840-9 (paperback)

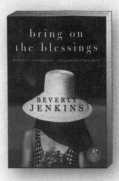

"*Bring on the Blessings* is a tasty reading confection that you'll savor long after the story ends."

—Angela Benson, *Essence* bestselling author of *Up Pops the Devil* and *The Amen Sisters*

A SECOND HELPING
A Blessings Novel

ISBN 978-0-06-154781-2 (paperback)

"A story like none other, and done in a way that only Beverly Jenkins can do. Simply superb!"

— Brenda Jackson, *New York Times* bestselling author

SOMETHING OLD, SOMETHING NEW
A Blessings Novel

ISBN 978-0-06-199079-3 (paperback)

"There is beauty in Jenkins' storytelling that should be the standard by which to judge fiction writing. . . . Brava Ms. Jenkins, you have done it again and left us wanting more."

—*Romantic Times* Top Pick

A WISH AND A PRAYER
A Blessings Novel

ISBN 978-0-06-199080-9 (paperback)

Anyone worried that life in a small town could get boring certainly hasn't lived in Henry Adams. With a pig on trial, the town's foster children still trying to find their place, and new love blossoming, there is plenty to occupy our favorite residents.

Visit www.BeverlyJenkins.net to connect with Bev!

Available wherever books are sold, or call 1-800-331-3761 to order.